About the Author

Jane Peart, award-winning novelist and short story writer, grew up in North Carolina and was educated in New England. Although she now lives in northern California, her heart has remained in her native South—its people, its history, and its traditions. With more than 20 novels and 250 short stories to her credit, Jane likes to emphasize in her writing the timeless and recurring themes of family, traditional values, and a sense of place.

Ten years in the writing, the *Brides of Montclair* series is a historical, family saga of enduring beauty. In each new book, another generation comes into its own at the beautiful Montclair estate, near Williamsburg, Virginia. These compelling, dramatic stories reaffirm the importance of committed love, loyalty, courage, strength of character, and abiding faith in times of triumph and tragedy, sorrow and joy.

Gallant Bride

Book Six
of the Brides of Montclair series

JANE PEART

Zondervan Books
Zondervan Publishing House
Grand Rapids, Michigan

GALLANT BRIDE
Copyright © 1988, 1990 by Jane Peart

Zondervan Books is an imprint of
The Zondervan Publishing House
1415 Lake Drive, S.E.
Grand Rapids, Michigan 49506

Library of Congress Cataloging-in-Publication Data:

Peart, Jane.
　　Gallant bride / Jane Peart.
　　　　p. cm. —(Brides of Montclair series : #6)
　　ISBN 0-310-67001-2 (paperback)
　　I. Title. II. Series: Peart, Jane. Brides of Montclair series :
　bk. 6.
　PS3566.E238G3　1990
　813'.54—dc20   90–12705
                                                          CIP

Edited by Anne Severance
Designed by Kim Koning

Printed in the United States of America

90 91 92 93 94 95 / LP / 10 9 8 7 6 5 4 3 2 1

For my daughters,
whose love and support
have enriched both my personal and professional life

chapter
1
Lucas Valley, California—1868

WHO COULD that be? Blythe asked herself, setting down the water bucket she was carrying from the well up to the weathered frame ranch house. Shaking back her long, auburn hair, she shaded her eyes against the late afternoon sun as a rickety buckboard pulled by two pack mules came through the ranch gate.

At fifteen Blythe had lived most of her life in Lucas Valley and knew nearly everyone in the small, northern California community. But she did not recognize this scraggly bearded stranger. She stood watching his approach a minute longer, then picking up her calico skirt, ran with coltish grace toward the house to the porch steps, calling "Pa! Pa! Come see!"

Immediately a tall man opened the front door and stepped out, looking in the direction of her pointed finger.

"Wonder who it is, Pa?" she whispered.

"We'll find out directly, child," Jedediah Dorman said quietly, moving to the edge of the porch as the wagon drew to a shaky stop in front. The driver pushed his battered brown felt hat back on his forehead, wiped his brow with a red bandana, then turned a dust-coated face toward them.

"Howdy." Jed's greeting was friendly but cautious.

"Howdy," the man replied, his eyes traveling the lean height of the rancher, taking in his blue denim shirt, faded but freshly ironed, the good leather boots, the man's direct gaze, his honest, kindly face. Then they moved on to the girl at his side, who was staring at him with the wide velvety-brown eyes of a doe. Not more than a child, he guessed, but tall and glowing with health. Yep. He reckoned he'd come to the right place.

"Name's Ben Mulligan. Jes' come down from the hills. Been prospectin' for the last year. Passed a mine site thet looked to be deserted, so I thought I'd take a look 'round and found—" He jerked his thumb toward the back of the wagon. "—a pretty sick feller. Must've been minin' with a partner, but no one else was about—only this man, a-burnin' with fever, out of his head. I couldn't leave nobody in that state—to die alone. And I figgered he was close to doin' jest that."

Blythe moved closer to her father, slipping her hand through his arm. She shivered. She'd never seen a dying person before.

"Anyhow," the man went on, "this here is the first place we come to. I'm lookin' to leave this feller with folks who kin take keer of him. I'm on my way to git new supplies, register my claim, head back to my mine. Mebbe I shouldn't uv moved him, but, like I say, didn't feel I could rightly leave him."

The prospector halted, waiting for Jed to say something.

Jed nodded. "Mighty good of you, mister."

"Figgered it was the least I could do." He shrugged and spat a long, thin stream of brown tobacco juice onto the dusty path. "But I cain't take him no farther. He's pretty far gone. See what you think." With that he looped the reins around the wooden brake, jumped down from the driver's seat, and walked to the back of the wagon to let down the panel.

Jed patted Blythe's hand reassuringly. Then, moving quickly and lightly for such a big man, he joined the other. Blythe followed close behind.

On the floor of the buckboard, wrapped in a filthy blanket, huddled a man of indeterminate age. His hair was a mass of tangles, his face covered with a dark stubble of beard. Even as they looked on, he stirred restlessly, mumbling incoherently. Hard chills ravaged his body.

Jed put out one large hand and touched the man's forehead, then drew it back in surprise. "You're right. The poor fellow's on fire with fever," he said. "Help me get him into the house. We'll see what we can do."

"I'm much obliged to ye. Now, if ye'll lift his shoulders, I'll git his legs."

Together, the two men wrestled the inert form from his resting place. But as they began tugging at the stricken miner, he thrashed about, flinging his arms as if to ward off some unseen attacker.

"No, you'll not take me alive!" he shouted in a hoarse voice. "To the last man, we'll hold on!"

"Easy there. We mean you no harm." Jed's voice was soft and soothing. "No one is going to take you."

The man was too weak to struggle further. He slumped against them as they continued to ease his body forward. At last they swung him free of the buckboard and moved toward the house.

Blythe sprang to action, running ahead to hold the door open.

"Go turn down the quilt on my bed, there's a good girl," Jed directed once they were inside. "Then draw some more water."

She did as she was told, both frightened and strangely excited by this unusual turn of events. By the time she returned to the house with the water, the man was settled in her father's bed.

She poured a dipperful of the spring water into a basin beside the bed and watched as her pa wrung out a clean cloth and bathed the sick man's face and brow.

The bedraggled prospector stood at the foot of the bed. "Then ye'll be takin' 'im on?"

Jed did not look up. "I hardly think we can do less than you. Yes, we'll take him . . . until he's well enough to travel. He must have folks somewhere who'll be worrying—" With that, he turned to Blythe, saying, "Blythe, offer our friend here a cup of coffee."

"Well, thanky, I'd take kindly to that, ma'am. Then I best be on my way. Want to make the nearest town with an assayer's office 'fore sundown."

"You'd be welcome to stay for supper," Blythe offered, leading the way into the kitchen.

"I'm thankin' ye, ma'am, but now I know this feller's in good hands, I can rest easy." He twisted his dented hat in gnarled hands and followed her into the kitchen.

Blythe went to the stove, took off the blue enameled coffeepot, then poured out a steaming mugful and handed it to the prospector.

"Nice place you have here." He sipped the hot brew gingerly as he peered around the big front room. "Been so long in the wilderness, I'd purt' nigh forgot what a real home looks like."

Blythe's gaze followed his as it swept the area, from the shiny black stove with its polished trim and the starched curtains at the windows to Pa's big rocker by the low bookcase where his leather-bound volumes of Dickens were proudly displayed. A round table in the middle of the room had been freshly set with a blue and white checked tablecloth, centered with a small pitcher containing golden wild poppies and purple lupin. Blythe had arranged them herself only this afternoon.

"This don't look like most of the ranch houses I've seed out here," he observed. "Looks more like a farmhouse back East."

"My Pa's from Kentucky," Blythe informed him. "Some of our furniture did come from back East. Pa says lots of folks who crossed the prairie in covered wagons brought all their worldly goods with them. Then, when they needed money to buy livestock or for a grubstake, they had to sell off some things—even prized possessions. Pa's got a right good eye for quality," she said with some pride. "Besides, he likes to help people out."

"He's a good man, your pa." The old man nodded.

As if the sparse furnishings had gained new value through her visitor's compliments, Blythe's eyes touched and lingered lovingly on her favorite pieces—the mellow pine hutch that held the set of Blue Willow china, the mahogany drop-leaf table, and the little curved loveseat.

"Well, I'll be movin' on," he said taking a last gulp of coffee and setting down the mug. "I'll jes' water the horses, iffen ye don't mind, then I'll be shovin' off."

Coming to the doorway, Jed said, "I know this man—whoever he is—will be grateful when he hears how you went out of your way to help him."

"No more'n anybody'd do—"

Jed shook his head. "Not necessarily. The world would be a better place if what you say were true. But I was a miner myself for a good many years, saw a lot of things—cruel, inhuman things—. No, I'm afraid there are not many Good Samaritans around."

"You mined in these parts?" The prospector perked up his ears.

"Not far from here. Up in Truckee and Grass Valley, Jacksonville," Jed replied. "But that was a long time ago. I'm a homesteader now. A rancher." He smiled. "I'll see you out. Blythe, stay there by the bed for a few minutes while I help our friend on his way."

The two men walked out into the gathering dusk, and Blythe crept into the bedroom and over to the bed and looked at the dark-haired stranger, sleeping fitfully. How handsome he was, even though he was so sick. Thick hair tumbled about a high forehead, and heavy lashes fanned out over the sunken cheeks. The nose was well-shaped—and the mouth beneath the beard looked gentle.

Who was he? What had brought him here?

The man moaned, and Blythe, remembering what Pa had done, soaked a cloth in the tepid water, wrung it dry and gently sponged his forehead. His lips were dry and cracked. When he tried to moisten them with his parched tongue, Blythe took the tip of the cloth and pressed it over his mouth. He moved his head back and forth on the pillow, then sighed. His eyelids fluttered slightly, but he did not open his eyes.

She bent to catch a murmured word, but she couldn't make it out. A name?

She wet the cloth again, folded it, and laid it over his brow. As she did so, his hand went up and closed over hers for a moment before it dropped limply to his side.

When Pa walked back into the room, he examined the sleeping man. "I think we can leave him now," he said in a low voice. "He's resting. We'll have our supper, then I'll sit out the night with him. In the morning I'll ride into town and bring Doc Sanderson out to have a look at him."

Blythe tiptoed to the kitchen. She took the chicken out of the oven where it had been baking and cast a critical look at it. It was a little too brown, but that couldn't be helped. The potatoes were roasted crisply, just the way Pa liked them, and there was apple cobbler for dessert.

She thought of the handsome stranger in the next room as she dished up the vegetables and carried them to the table.

Her father was there ahead of her, his sleeves rolled up and his sandy hair, threaded with silver, slicked back from an encounter with the kitchen pump. He reached for Blythe's hand and they bowed their heads while he asked a blessing.

"Dear heavenly Father, we thank Thee for this food Thou hast provided for us, and for the hands that prepared it. We ask Thy blessing of healing and health on the stranger Thou hast brought to our door. In the name of Christ Jesus, we pray. Amen."

"Amen," Blythe echoed and passed the bowl of potatoes. "Did that prospector tell you anything more, Pa? Did he find anything—any gold—at the mine site?"

Jed shook his head. "Said there was nothing, only a few tins of food and some panning equipment, but no gold nor any evidence that there had been any."

"But do you think he was telling the truth?" she persisted. "He seemed in an awful hurry to get to the assayer's office. Could he have taken something that didn't belong to him?"

"Seemed honest enough to me, Blythe. Matter of fact, he gave me a happersack he found in the lean-to. He thinks it might belong to the poor fellow in there." Jed jerked his head toward the bedroom. "I didn't look inside, but the old codger said he found a book or two and some personal papers that might be needed if the man . . . well—"

"You mean . . . if he dies?" Blythe's eyes grew wide.

Her father acknowledged the truth with a brief shrug. "He's pretty sick, and we don't know how long he was lying there alone before Mulligan found him."

They ate in silence for a few minutes, though Blythe tasted nothing. "Mr. Mulligan said something about a partner," she said at last. "I wonder if the partner stole whatever had been found and got away."

Her father nodded solemnly, savoring the last of his cobbler. "Could be. Partnerships are tricky." He paused. "Out here, gold and greed often team up, and when gold fever strikes—it can ruin a life. Turn men into animals."

"Do you think something like that happened? To *him*?"

"Maybe." Pa pushed back from the table, his gaze shifting to the darkening sky through the open kitchen window. "If he gets well, I reckon he'll tell us. If not . . . then I guess we'll never know."

chapter 2

IT WAS Blythe who was sitting beside the stranger's bed the morning after his fever broke. Pa had gone out to feed the livestock, do the milking, and turn the horses out to pasture.

Sitting there, half day-dreaming, she was alerted by a sound from the bed and tiptoed over in time to see the lashes flicker open for the first time. His eyes, a clear blue, were puzzled as they darted about, checking his surroundings.

Frightened, Blythe stepped back as his gaze settled on her.

"Who are you? Where am I?"

"I'm—I'm Blythe. Blythe Dorman. And you're in Lucas Valley . . . in our home . . . Pa's and mine . . . on our ranch."

His dark brows met in a frown. "But how did I get here?"

"Someone—a Mr. Mulligan—brought you. He found you at your mine site. You were very sick . . . almost dying, I think," she stammered, wishing Pa would come in. She cast a desperate look out the window toward the corral and, with relief, saw Jed's rangy figure striding back to the house. "Pa will explain everything."

"So, you're awake, are you?" Jed spoke from the bedroom door. "Welcome back to the land of the living! We thought you were a goner for a while."

The stranger gave a wan smile. "I guess I have you to thank," he said feebly.

"I'd say your thanks should go first to the good Lord, then to the old prospector who brought you down off the mountain. And Blythe here had a hand in the nursing."

"Well then, thanks to . . . all of you."

"How do you feel?" Jed pulled up one of the straight chairs and straddled it, leaning forward, his hands clasped over the back.

"Weak as a newborn calf." The man shook his head as if still bewildered.

"You've been out of your head for a spell. But gradually things will right themselves, and you'll be able to recollect what happened."

"How long have I been here?"

"A good ten days ago, a man named Mulligan showed up here You were in the rear of his buckboard." Jed looked over at Blythe as if for confirmation, and she nodded. "You were mighty sick. Looked like you'd had a fever for some time before the old fella found you."

"And how did he happen upon my camp?"

"Told me he'd been mining in the high country on his own claim and was coming out on his way to get new supplies, and," he mused, "he seemed to be in a hurry to get to the assayer's office. Seems like he'd run into a storm, one of those fierce ones that sometimes roar in out of the northwest this time of year—icy rain, wind, snow. He stopped to take shelter in what he took to be a deserted mine shack. Then he found you, out of your head with fever. Said he did what little he could for you there, but when the storm was over, didn't feel right leaving you behind. So he bundled you up and brought you to the first ranch house on the trail. That's how you ended up here."

"Well, it sounds as if my luck hasn't completely run out." The man attempted another smile and put out his hand toward Jed. "I am most grateful, sir."

His voice was deep, warm, exciting, with a soft quality Blythe had never heard in a man before.

"I'm Malcolm Montrose," he said.

Jed grasped his hand in a hearty clasp. "Jedediah Dorman, and my daughter, Blythe."

The stranger turned his head and smiled at Blythe, and she felt her heart literally turn over. Color rushed into her cheeks, and she lowered her eyes shyly.

Addressing Jed once again, Malcolm asked, "This man . . . the . . . prospector . . . he didn't bring anything else out, did he?"

"Yes, a canvas knapsack. I'll get it." Jed rose, took a few steps to the corner of the room, and retrieved the bundle.

"And this was all?" Malcolm persisted, his fingers fumbling with the buckles.

"That's all. I suppose your cooking gear and mining paraphernalia are still at your campsite."

"None of that matters. I was going to leave most of that stuff when I walked out—leave it for the next fool looking for the pot of gold at the end of the rainbow!" He shrugged and started pulling out the contents of the knapsack.

"Maybe Blythe and I best leave you alone to sort through your things in private," Jed suggested.

"No need. There's nothing much here—a log I started to keep, a few letters, books—" He was strewing things haphazardly on the counterpane.

Blythe noticed a book with a strange title, *The Idylls of the King*, and a New Testament. She looked over at Pa, wondering if he had seen them, too. She knew he would be glad for the chance to talk with an educated man.

Having emptied the satchel of its contents, Malcolm leaned back against the pillows, looking pale and drained. "Well, he got it," he announced.

"What's that?"

"The gold."

"Gold! But he said—" Jed pounded a clenched fist into his open palm. "I should have known! Why, even Blythe—" He was furious, more at himself than at the scoundrel who had gotten away, she knew. "Mulligan seemed edgy, itching to go—"

"Nearly half a year's hard digging. All gone. What a waste—" Malcolm's voice trailed off in despair. "Last May, my partner and I divided up our findings thus far. He'd had enough of that cruel life . . . wanted to get back to his wife, his family . . . but I decided to stay. . . . Needed more gold. . . . But . . . it was for nothing."

The room was heavy with the silence that followed his words.

Then Jed cleared his throat. "Well, man, you got out with your life, remember that. It's a wonder old Mulligan didn't slit your throat before he made off with the gold. Don't forget to count some of your blessings."

Malcolm closed his eyes wearily and gave a short laugh. Blythe thought she had never heard anything so mirthless and devoid of joy. "You're right, of course. I'm alive . . . for whatever that's worth."

"Now, that's enough for now. You still haven't got your strength back full. Blythe, isn't there some stew simmering in the pot? How about dishing up a little for Mr. Montrose."

In the days that followed, Blythe's interest in their strange "guest" grew rapidly. Who was he and where did he come from? It was such a mystery. He was totally unlike anyone Blythe had ever known. Certainly, he was different from the miners and ranchers of Lucas Valley.

She thought he was as handsome as any prince pictured in the fairy-tale books Pa had ordered by mail for her when she was a little girl. During his illness Pa had cut the man's beard, and clean-shaven, he was even more handsome. His dark hair swept back from a high forehead in deep waves; even though his face was thin, his features were noble.

His manner was reserved, respectful toward Jed, gentle toward Blythe, and he was so appreciative of everything that was done for him, but he seemed sad much of the time, and Blythe delighted in doing little things to make him happy, see him smile.

He was all she had ever imagined in a romantic hero, the kind who rode on a white steed straight out of a storybook to rescue a fair maiden. In her imagination, she was the maiden, Malcolm the brave knight.

When he was at last able to move about, sitting for short periods in a rocker on the front porch, she saw that he was very tall—even taller than Pa. Though he was still painfully thin, the breadth of his shoulders bespoke a once magnificent physique, and his rare smiles revealed fine white teeth.

One day he asked if he might read one of the Dickens books from the shelf, and she had happily selected *David Copperfield*.

"How did you happen to come by these books, Blythe?" he asked, paging through the volume.

"Papa sent away to a bookseller's in New York. Since I can't get into the school in town in wintertime, he wanted me to have them to keep up with the town students," she reported. "I use them to copy my letters, practice my penmanship by writing out whole chapters, and, of course, improve my reading skills." Then she added shyly, "*David Copperfield* is my favorite. Except it is so sad. I hated it when Dora died . . . she was so sweet and lovely."

Malcolm's eyes clouded for a second. Then, looking down at the book in his hand, he said, almost to himself, "Dickens writes about life,

Blythe. And in life some of the sweetest, some of the loveliest things . . . die."

The mood of melancholy passed, and Malcolm flashed his wonderful smile. "Thank you, Blythe," he said. "I shall enjoy reading this again."

He went back into the bedroom and closed the door, leaving her dazzled and dreamy.

chapter

3

On an early fall afternoon in late spring, Blythe, riding her mare Milly home from school, took a shortcut through the grove of aspens on the other side of the creek that ran through the Dorman property.

She enjoyed school because soon the long winter's snows would prevent her regular attendance. Often the schoolmarm let her help the younger children with their sums and reading. Blythe loved children, had often longed for brothers and sisters. It had been lonely growing up alone on an isolated ranch. Lonely, that is, until Malcolm had come.

This winter promised to be different even if they were snowbound. If Malcolm stayed, that *would* make a difference. He and Pa got along well; in the long evenings they played checkers or discussed books. Pa was a great reader. Sometimes Malcolm read aloud in his deep, rich voice with its soft accent. Blythe loved those times best, listening to Malcolm read, often from his favorite Tennyson book, *The Idylls of the King*.

At the edge of the creek, obeying an irresistible impulse, Blythe slid off the horse and let her drink. Then she stripped off her stockings and shoes, bunched up her skirt, and tucked it into her waistband. She stuffed her shoes and stockings into her saddlebag and waded into the creek, wrinkling her nose with pleasure as the cool water swished around her ankles and feet.

Reaching the bank on the other side, she scrambled out and looked up. To her surprise she saw Malcolm sitting under a tree, leaning against the trunk, a half-open book in his lap. He was grinning at her.

Mortified to be caught with her skirts above her knees, she let them fall, and to cover her embarrassment, she asked, "What are you reading?"

He held up the book so she could see the title.

"*Idylls of the King*—again?"

"I never get tired of it—it's one of my favorites."

"Oh, mine, too!" she quickly agreed. "I love hearing all those wonderful stories of bravery and honor. I wish people still did things like that, believed like that."

"Some do—" Malcolm smiled sadly.

Blythe sat down on the grass beside him and wiggled her toes in the cool grass.

"Was that fun? Wading?" Malcolm asked.

"Oh, yes!" she confessed, laughing.

"My brothers and I used to do the same thing the first days of summer—often losing a shoe or stockings in the attempt."

"How many brothers have you?"

"Two. That is, I *had* two."

Blythe, busily putting on her shoes and stockings, failed to see the shadow that crossed Malcolm's face.

"That must have been nice . . . growing up in a family, I mean," she hurried on. "I have always longed for brothers and sisters. But Pa declared he would never remarry after my mother died, and so—"

"I can understand that," he said quietly.

Concentrating on lacing her shoes, she did not look up. "Tell me about your family, Malcolm, about your home. Pa says he knows only that you come from Virginia. Do you know I have never been out of California? As a matter of fact, I've never been anywhere but Sacramento and Lucas Valley."

"You're still young, Blythe. You've your whole life ahead of you to travel, to see the world."

"Yes, I know," she sighed. "Pa says when I'm sixteen or maybe eighteen, we will go first to San Francisco, then—" she laughed gaily, "—who knows? Maybe to Europe or Egypt or the Holy Land."

"How old are you, Blythe?"

"Fifteen."

Malcolm looked at her with a certain wistfulness.

"Have you ever been to Europe, Malcolm?"

"Yes, twice. Once when I was a little older than you and then later—" He stopped abruptly. Wincing, he rubbed his forehead.

Blythe saw it at once. "Malcolm, are you in pain?" she asked anxiously.

"Memories, Blythe. Sometimes memories can be painful."

"Yes, I suppose they can. Pa has those kinds, too. About Mama." Blythe cast about for a way of distracting him from his sad thoughts. "You haven't told me about Virginia, Malcolm. Is it like California?"

"Not really. It's very different, in fact. Not such wide, open spaces, so few people." He shifted his position beneath the tree and put his book aside. "My home is called Montclair," he began. "It's named after the wife of my ancestor who came to America from Scotland years and years ago. Since her name was Claire, and our family name was Montrose, the two were combined.

"My family has lived there for generations. It's a beautiful house, Blythe, whitewashed brick—the brick was made right there on the plantation. There are green shutters on all the windows, and those on the first floor are like great doors opening onto the long, front porch.

"Inside, all the rooms are large, with high ceilings, and there are crystal chandeliers and a curved staircase that winds up and around with a banistered balcony that circles the lower entrance."

"It sounds like a palace!" Blythe murmured in an awed voice.

Malcolm looked at her sharply as if jolted back from a trance. "Yes . . . yes, I guess it does, though we children never saw it like that. It was just our home, where we grew up. But then later, when it all changed—" Again, his voice took on a somber tone. "Maybe we did live like a kind of royalty, but we didn't know it . . . not until it was too late."

A silence fell that Blythe hesitated to break. Malcolm seemed deep in thought.

"There were acres and acres of meadowlands where our horses grazed—" he continued at last, now speaking slowly, as if seeing the scene unfold before him. "And on the hillsides, sheep. My father was known to stable the best horses in the whole of Mayfield County. There was a huge barn and a coach house, where our carriages were kept—a barouche, a phaeton, a Victoria—all with upholstery imported from Italy and splendid wood and brass fittings."

"Oh, Malcolm!" Blythe was entranced.

"There are lovely gardens and a velvety green lawn that sweeps down in terraces toward the river. The James River flows by at the end of the plantation. In the early days, ships bringing supplies and furniture from

21

France and England docked there. But after awhile, most of our goods were made right on the grounds by our own people."

"Your own people?"

"Yes, the black people. Our servants." He frowned. "Slaves." He spoke the word as if it left a bitter taste in his mouth.

"Slaves?" echoed Blythe.

"Yes, we owned slaves, I'm sorry to say, though it was the custom and much accepted then. Necessary, really. Anyway, that's all over now. The War finished it." He rose and paced restlessly with his hands behind him. "It was wrong, of course," he admitted. "But that was another lesson learned the hard way. War is a harsh teacher."

After a long while, Blythe dared a question. "Do you find our life here . . . strange?"

"No, not strange exactly. Isolated, I'd say. Montclair, too, is in the country, but there is always company, people coming and going, parties, balls, dancing . . . at least, there used to be—"

"There are parties in Lucas Valley sometimes, Malcolm. Socials. Church suppers. Maybe when you're better, we could go to town—"

Malcolm laughed shortly. "I don't think so, Blythe. I've lost my taste for that kind of thing, I'm afraid. Besides, I don't expect to be here much longer."

"Oh, don't say that, Malcolm!" Blythe scrambled to her feet and put a restraining hand on his arm.

"I can't impose on your father's hospitality forever," Malcolm said mildly.

"But . . . Pa wants you to stay, Malcolm. I know he does. And with winter coming on, you can't go back to your camp." She rambled on, seeking to persuade him. "You could stay here . . . with us. There are lots of things you could do to help Pa around the ranch."

A distant look came into Malcolm's eyes. "I suppose I have no real place to go—"

"Well, then there's no hurry to leave, is there?"

He smiled. "Well, I'll talk to your father, Blythe. I'm getting stronger every day. Maybe I could hire on as a ranch hand. Yes . . . why not?"

The wind began to rise, and Malcolm shivered and struggled to his feet. "It's chilly. We'd best be getting back to the house, Blythe. One thing I don't need is another bout of pneumonia."

Blythe whistled for her horse. The mare raised her head and shook her mane, but took her time fording the stream to the other side. To entice her, Blythe plucked a crabapple from the pocket of her pinafore and held it out.

She looped her lead around her wrist and led her mare, munching contentedly on the apple, up the hill toward the house. Neither she nor Malcolm spoke again until they reached the corral.

"I'll settle Milly for the night," Blythe said. "And—and do please think about what I have said. . . . Pa needs you . . . and he'd be so disappointed if you should leave—"

By the time winter gripped the Valley, Malcolm had become a part of the Dorman household. Though he moved out to living quarters Jed fixed for him in the loft of the barn—complete with pot-bellied stove, shelves and a comfortable bunk—he took all his meals with Jed and Blythe. She found herself dreaming up delicious new dishes to tempt his appetite and began to spend almost as much time before the mirror as in the kitchen—doing the best she could to tame her mane of auburn hair and pinch some color into her cheeks before each mealtime. There was little she could do about her wardrobe, though. She was fast outgrowing her daytime calicos. Well, she'd just have to wait until spring and see Mrs. Coppley, a distant neighbor who sometimes did some sewing for her.

She was pleased that Malcolm and her Pa had forged an easy companionship. During the long winter evenings, both men settled into a comfortable routine—reading by lamplight, playing checkers, or merely reminiscing about their mining days. Jed had many stories to share about the hectic "gold-rush days," but outside that one golden afternoon, when he had told her about Montclair, Malcolm had rarely spoken about the life he lived before coming to California.

When Malcolm was fully restored to health, he worked long hours, mending fences weakened by winter snowbanks, helping with the foaling, taking care of the livestock, and riding out to round up strays that had escaped through broken places in the corral. He was fast becoming Pa's right hand, and the bond between them grew stronger throughout the winter months.

But for Blythe, who had learned to depend upon his company that winter, the long days of summer threatened to steal away the tenuous relationship she had established with Malcolm. Perhaps he thought of her, not as the ripening woman she was becoming, but as the fanciful child who dreamed of princes and fairy-tale palaces.

chapter
4

ALMOST WITHOUT their knowledge, by the next spring Malcolm had become part of life at the Dorman ranch. He was an indispensable help to Jed. He knew horses and took over that part of the daily work. He liked working in the big vegetable garden as well. Here he often worked alongside Blythe, who basked in his company.

He had gained weight and muscle from the ranch work, and his skin was bronzed from the sun. With his dark hair and extraordinarily blue eyes, he looked more than ever like the storybook prince of Blythe's daydreams.

She plied him with questions, trying to ferret out the mystery of his background, weaving it in with her own fantasies. She had already dreamed a fairy tale of her own about Malcolm, that one day when she was grown up—eighteen, maybe—he would fall in love with her. Then they would marry and live here on the ranch with Pa happily ever after.

One day, forgetting this vision was only in her own imagination, she asked him how many years older than she he was.

"Too many," he replied shortly.

"My Pa was years older than my mother, and they got along beautifully, never had a cross word, he said." She babbled on, unaware of Malcolm's sudden discomfort.

"Don't talk foolishly, Blythe, or think silly things." Then he stood up abruptly and walked away, leaving her alone in the garden.

Abashed, Blythe promised herself never to speak to Malcolm like that again.

Most of the time things went along pleasantly and smoothly between them, and life at the ranch moved tranquilly until the accident.

Jed and Malcolm were reshingling the roof of the house, shoring up places that the last winter's heavy snows had weakened. Jed was on the top rung of a ladder and stretched his arm to pick up a shingle from a stack just beyond his reach. The movement caused the ladder to totter, and as Jed tried to right himself, the ladder toppled over backwards, throwing him to the ground and crashing down on top of him.

Blythe and Malcolm had helped him into the house, but within an hour he was rigid with pain, his face clammy with the sweat that beaded on it, biting on his lip to keep from crying out.

Malcolm rode into town for Doc Sanderson. The diagnosis was three ribs broken and a badly injured spine. Even with that, Jed might have recovered, except that pleurisy set in and Jed remained confined to his bed.

Blythe did not realize how seriously ill her father was until one bleak late-October day.

It was mid-morning when Doc Sanderson's buggy drove up the rutted road and through the gate. Blythe busied herself in the kitchen making coffee while the doctor looked in on Jed. When he came out, he accepted the cup of steaming liquid she offered without a word.

"You got any kinfolks, Blythe?" he asked at last.

"No, sir." She shook her head, feeling a kind of cold knot twisting in her stomach.

"You mean to say your Pa has no other family? No one at all?" Doc Sanderson fixed her with a penetrating gaze. Then he asked abruptly, "How old are you now, Blythe? From the look of you, I'd say you were near a grown woman."

"I'm nearly seventeen, sir."

"Any beaux? Any young man come a'courtin' yet?"

Blythe blushed, shook her head. "No, sir. Pa said that when I was eighteen, we'd go down to San Francisco, get a nice hotel suite, and stay awhile. He plans on asking a banker he knows there to introduce me to some suitable young gentlemen. Pa doesn't want me to marry a miner or even a rancher, he says. He's going to take me to Europe, too . . . maybe next summer—"

Blythe realized she was rattling on foolishly, but the expression on the doctor's face frightened her, and she stopped, mid-sentence.

Doc Sanderson tugged his scraggly mustache, scowled, and cleared his throat. "Well, Blythe, I'm afraid your Pa ain't goin' to get any better—not by next summer, that's for sure. As a matter of fact, he's gettin' worse every day. He may live awhile yet, but he can't last much longer, and that's the plain truth." He sighed heavily, ran a hand through his sparse hair. "Now, you're a sensible girl, so you'd best be makin' plans for . . . after. You can't live out here by yourself so far from ever'body and ever'thing." He looked up at the ceiling while Blythe waited, her heart thudding. "So I was wonderin' if you'd like to have me make some inquiries around town, see if there ain't some family that would be willin' to take you in. What I'm tryin' to say is, there's two families I'm thinkin' of could use a good, strong hand, and thataway, you'd have a place, a home, until such time—" His voice trailed off, and he shrugged helplessly.

Shocked by the way the doctor was talking, Blythe drew herself to her full height and looked him directly in the eye. When she spoke, her voice was firm and confident. "Thank you, sir, that's mighty kind of you. But I feel sure my Pa has provided for me so that I wouldn't have to work as a hired girl. This place would go for a fair price if I decided to sell it. But I don't think I'm going to have to make any plans for myself. I think I'll just talk to Pa and ask him what he wants me to do . . . if he isn't better by spring."

"He'll be dead by spring, girl. That's what I've been tryin' to tell you." Doc Sanderson shook his head, and turned away. Stunned, Blythe heard the sound of his booted feet striking the wooden floor on his way out the door, then the sound of buggy wheels clattering down the dusty road toward town.

She had held herself stiffly during their conversation, unwilling to believe the doctor's words. It was true that she and Pa had only each other. If he died . . . then she would, indeed, be all alone in the world.

At that moment, the front door opened, and Malcolm came came in, a questioning look on his face.

"I saw the doctor leave—"

"Oh, Malcolm!" Blythe cried, her voice breaking.

"What is it? Is your father worse?" He took a few steps toward her.

"Doc Sanderson says—" At the look of compassion on Malcolm's face, the tears that had threatened earlier spilled over. He opened his arms, and Blythe gladly sought the comfort of his embrace. She felt his hand on her hair, cradling her head against his strong chest, the roughness of his wool jacket against her cheek. "Oh, Malcolm, I'm so afraid. Doc says Pa's dying! What will I do? I'll be alone—"

"I'm here, Blythe. Hush, now, hush. Everything will be all right," Malcolm murmured tenderly as she clung to him.

On the day of Jed's funeral, Malcolm was at her side on the long walk down the hill from the little cemetery behind the church, where they had buried her father. The other mourners kept a discreet distance between themselves and the grieving young woman as Malcolm explained to Blythe that she would be staying with the Coppleys instead of going back to the ranch house.

"But why?" she asked, puzzled.

"Because, Blythe, now that your Pa's gone, it just wouldn't be proper for the two of us to continue to stay at the ranch together. It'll take me a little time to make the arrangements, but then we'll be leaving—"

"Leaving? I don't understand."

His voice was very gentle, very patient. "It's this way, Blythe. Your Pa and I had several long talks before he died. You know how fond I was of him—he saved my life really—and I think . . . I *know* he thought well of me. I had planned to leave last summer, go back to Virginia, then your Pa had his accident. Well, I couldn't leave. Not after all he'd done for me—taking me in when I was sick, broke . . . you understand." Malcolm paused, lifted his chin and gazed over Blythe's head to the horizon, where the sun was beginning its slow descent, firing the hills with gold and casting long purple shadows along the floor of the valley.

"Well, what it comes down to is this, Blythe. Your father's main concern was you—what would happen to you if he died. It was all he worried about those last days. He wanted to be sure you would be well cared for. He wanted us . . . no, he *meant* for us to be married."

"Married?" Blythe was incredulous. Tripping over a loose rock, she nearly stumbled and Malcolm's hand shot out to steady her. *"We— us—married? Married to each other?"*

Malcolm did not meet her astonished look. "It's what your father wanted. He told me he had great hopes for you, that you should one day go back East, where he felt you'd have certain . . . cultural advantages not possible in such a remote place as Lucas Valley. Oh, of course," he hurried on, seeing her frown, "this was a fine place to bring up a young child, but he always intended something more for you,

28

something better . . . when you came of age. When his health broke, he didn't know how to bring it about until—" Malcolm paused, then his voice took on a determined tone. "After we're married, I'll take you back to Virginia, to my family home in Mayfield. It belongs to me now. You'll learn to love Montclair as I do. It would please your father, Blythe, and I gave him my solemn word as a gentleman that I'd take care of you."

Blythe could hardly believe his words. Had Malcolm told Pa he loved her, actually asked for her hand in marriage? She was too shocked to question him, and yet there was something troubling about the proposal.

"I'll need three weeks or more to get things settled here," he went on, not sensing her uneasiness. "The ranch and livestock will be put up for sale as your father instructed. Then I'll make our travel arrangements. We'll book passage on a ship leaving San Francisco for New Orleans, take the train to Atlanta and on to Richmond, then home to Mayfield and Montclair. After those details are worked out, we can set a date for the wedding.

"In the meantime, you'll stay with the Coppleys. It's all settled. With no child of their own, they're looking forward to your visit." A slight smile tugged at the corners of his chiseled mouth, and he touched her arm lightly. "You're not to worry about anything, Blythe. I'll take care of everything."

Bewildered by these sudden changes, Blythe went along with Malcolm's request. Since Mrs. Coppley was the town seamstress, Blythe knew her from years past, and she found the couple to be as warm in their welcome as Malcolm had promised.

Still, there were nights when she wept for her father, and others when she lay awake in sleepless apprehension of the new direction her life was taking. But, in spite of the swinging pendulum of her emotions, she began to feel the old joy in living again—that buoyant spirit that had never failed her. Running like a swift-moving stream in the deepest part of her heart surged a thrilling anticipation at the thought of her future with Malcolm Montrose.

chapter

5

You DON'T think it's too soon, do you?" Blythe asked anxiously one day at breakfast, about two weeks after she had come to live in the Coppley household. "I mean, having the wedding so soon after burying Pa?"

Mrs. Coppley replied firmly. "Now just put that nonsense right out of your head, child. Folks out here don't take no 'count of things like proper timin'. A woman alone in these parts is in a sorry state, and Mr. Montrose is too much the gentleman to be askin' anything your Pa hadn't settled with him aforehand. Why, lands, I'd say it's a downright miracle, him comin' along when he did. What in the world would you do if not marry him?" she demanded, setting the coffeepot down with a bang.

"It just seems . . . wrong somehow . . . feeling happy when Pa's been gone such a short time."

"Your Pa loved you, Blythe. Never saw a man so set on his youngun as he was on you. He'd want you to be happy, safe. He thought highly of Mr. Montrose. I wouldn't wonder if he knows all about it up yonder and is rejoicin'."

So with this comforting reassurance, Blythe put aside all lingering doubts and began making her plans for the wedding, now only three weeks away.

She pored over the mail-order books showing the latest in wedding finery, turning back more than once to a sketch of a gown that, to her mind, surpassed all the others.

"Don't think it's a mite . . . well . . . too fancy?" Mrs. Coppley asked, tapping her teeth with the tip of her pen.

"Oh, no, I love it!" exclaimed Blythe. "I've never had anything so pretty—all ruffles and flounces and lace. It's perfect!"

"Well, if you say so. After all, a girl gits married only onct, and her weddin' dress ought to be just the way she wants it." She wrote up the order.

Blythe saw little of Malcolm during this hectic time, for he was arranging for their departure and handling the multitude of details connected with her Pa's estate. Though the ranch had not been sold, Malcolm had hired a lawyer to see to the final closing, and he assured her that the livestock, wagon, and horses had brought a goodly sum— enough to cover all their travel expenses.

Since they would be leaving by stage for San Francisco right after the ceremony, Blythe was to pack her trunk and carry with her only one smaller carpet bag containing her new white cambric nightgown, challis dressing gown, and the cotton camisoles, pantaloons, and petticoats she had made under Mrs. Coppley's supervision.

When she assessed her wardrobe, taking note of the few dresses she had, Mrs. Coppley set her mind at ease. "Surely you'll have time for shoppin' in San Francisco, or maybe when you git to New Orleans. Mr. Montrose will be wantin' better for his new bride than this old seamstress can whip up. He'll be sure to take you to some of them fine stores in those cities!" Her eyes twinkled. "After all, you'll be on your honeymoon!"

Honeymoon. Blythe let the unfamiliar word roll on her tongue as she said it to herself over and over.

"Yes, my girl," Mrs. Coppley nodded sagely, "you're on the brink of a great adventure!"

As Blythe packed the trunk that would be placed on the stagecoach, then loaded aboard the ship they would be sailing to the southeast through the isthmus of Panama, then on to New Orleans, she realized that when she next unlocked it, she would be in her new home, Malcolm's family home—Montclair.

The last things Blythe put into the trunk were some of her mother Carmella's belongings. Before she folded them carefully and placed them on top, Blythe spread them out on the bed. As a child, she had often asked her father to show them to her, and he had obliged on two or three occasions. But, as she grew older and noticed how sad it made him, she had stopped asking.

Tonight, however, was different. She had never felt closer to her mother than at this moment as she sat stroking the Spanish shawl—black silk with red and white roses embroidered in satin.

Pa had told her the whole romantic story of their courtship and brief, unlikely marriage—a "49er" and a gypsy from Seville. He had met her when her traveling dance troupe was touring the gold towns of northern California. He loved her on first sight and followed the troupe, paying her court, much to the displeasure of the leader, who valued his talented protegé as a drawing card. He had been furious to learn of their wish to marry. But when Pa offered gold for her hand, he readily agreed. Then, when Blythe was only two, her mother had succumbed to a lingering lung infection and left the grieving widower with a tiny daughter to bring up alone.

When she was five, Pa had taken her to Sacramento and placed her in the care of the nuns at a convent school before returning to the mines.

Her memories of St. Felicidad were vague impressions rather than distinct images—remembered scenes, sights, smells that evoked feelings. There were shadowy arches, where slanted sunshine threw patterns on the rough stucco walls; a red tile roof shining above the eucalyptus trees; brilliant splashes of color in the flowers that grew in the mosaic tiled courtyard; the play of water from the fountain merging with the sound of the organ music flowing through the chapel window; the gentle voice of a nun in her halo of starched white bending over Blythe as she corrected her needlework; the texture of coarse gray linen as the sleeve of her robe brushed Blythe's cheek

In less than three years, Jed struck a rich vein, bought the ranch property in Lucas Valley, and came to fetch Blythe home to live with him. It had seemed strange to leave the sheltered environment of St. Felicidad to take up ranch life. Yet, in a very short time, she was completely at home there.

Now she was making another change, starting a new life in an entirely different part of the country. If it were not for the fact that she adored Malcolm, the thought would be terrifying.

But she wouldn't be alone. She would be with Malcolm—safe, cared for, happy—and that would make all the difference. She might be starting a new life, but with Malcolm as her husband, what did she have to fear?

The night before the wedding, Blythe found herself in a state of nerves. But Mrs. Coppley's practical manner allowed no foolishness.

"Now, my girl, there's plenty to do, so stop acting like a jittery butterfly and let's get started."

They pulled the tarred-wood tub into the center of the kitchen floor, and filled it alternately with kettles full of water heated to a boil on the stove and pails of cold well water brought in earlier. Then Mrs. Coppley leaned over the tub and scrubbed Blythe until her skin glowed pink. Then she washed her hair. Scalp tingling, and wrapped in a warm blanket, Blythe sat in front of the stove while Mrs. Coppley brushed her hair into gleaming silken streamers.

"And you must wear it up tomorrow, my girl," she said firmly. "A married lady you'll be then."

"But will it fit under my new bonnet?" Blythe asked, glancing anxiously at the polished straw with its blue ribbons and roses.

"It will and it must," declared Mrs. Coppley.

Winter comes early to the Sierra foothills, and on the morning of her wedding, when Blythe woke up and looked out the window, she saw snow on the peaks of the distant hills glistening in the sunshine.

She was breathless with excitement as she got ready. Her brand-new dress was stiff, and Mrs. Coppley laced her so tightly into the unaccustomed corset that Blythe felt she could hardly draw a breath. But the mirror assured her that the fitted basque was becoming and fashionable and showed off her newly accented curves.

Her bonnet was perfection, even though it was anchored onto her coiled hair by two wickedly sharp hat pins. Assured by Mrs. Coppley that she looked "fine and fittin'," Blythe set out for her wedding, heart high with hope.

The small frame church was packed. Lucas Valley people welcomed any event that broke the dreary monotony of their lives, Blythe knew. Still, with such a fine turnout, she felt a pang of guilt that she and her Pa had never formally joined the church. Their attendance had been irregular, to say the least. Winters, they were snowed in for months at a time. In spring and summer, something always needed to be done on the ranch to prevent Jed's hitching up the wagon for a trip into town that would require the better part of the day. And, to tell the truth, on some summer Sundays, the weather was so sweet and fine that they often chose to spend the time fishing and picnicking down by the creek.

"Humph!" Mrs. Coppley had snorted once when she was fitting Blythe for some sturdy dresses that would do for her style of living on the ranch. "You ought to be havin' a nice Sunday-go-to-meetin' dress. That's what comes of not havin' a woman in the home!" she pronounced emphatically. "A 'refinin' influence' as Pastor Burke keeps exhortin' us. That's what we womenfolk out here in the West are called to be."

But Blythe had not grown up without any knowledge of the Scriptures. Her Pa cherished the old Bible that had belonged to his mother, and every evening after they finished supper, he read aloud a chapter or one of the Psalms.

Still, Blythe was surprised to see the number of church folk who had come to celebrate the union of two who were not fellow members, and now turned smiling faces in her direction as she started down the aisle on Mr. Coppley's arm, and she smiled back in gratitude.

Malcolm stood at the front, his face composed, his expression grave. As she came forward, he offered his arm and she turned to meet him, eyes shining, mouth softly curved, body tensed with excitement.

If there was anything the Reverend Clarence Burke liked better than delivering a eulogy at a funeral, it was conducting a wedding ceremony. This he did with a flourish and flair that could have earned him a pulpit in some big city church. At least, so the ladies in Lucas Valley often said at their Sewing Circle. Today was no exception, and his deep, well articulated words resounded in the tiny wood structure as he began.

After he had asked each in turn to respond to the promises of love and honor, he offered a benediction of grace on their union: "I pray that your love will endure long; that you will be patient and kind to one another, never envious nor jealous, never acting in unbecoming ways. That you would never insist on your own rights, but bear all patiently, ready to believe the best in all circumstances. Remember, love never faileth, and God will never forsake those who obey his commandments."

As Blythe listened, tears came unbidden to her eyes. With Malcolm, it should not be too difficult to abide by these precepts. She hoped only that she would be a wife worthy of him.

"Now, Mr. Montrose, you may kiss *Mrs*. Montrose," Reverend Burke suggested, his cherubic face wreathed in smiles.

Blythe lifted her face hopefully, and Malcolm bent down and brushed her lips lightly. It was, she realized, their first kiss.

chapter
6

BLYTHE PERCHED on her trunk in the midst of the turmoil on the San Francisco dock. Her eyes were wide with excitement, her cheeks flushed, her heart pumping wildly as she watched the noisy confusion around her.

Never before had she heard such a jumble of voices and languages, breathed in an atmosphere of such assorted sounds, smells, and sights. Swarthy stevedores loading cargo filled the air with foreign-sounding words that Blythe was sure would burn her ears if she knew their meaning. Chinese men, with saffron skin and flying queues, wearing cotton smocks and straw sandals, carried trunks and large boxes that looked much too heavy for their skinny backs. Carriages of every description crowded down the hilly street to the wharf, bringing men, women and children dressed for travel—all prospective passengers for the same ship Blythe and Malcolm were waiting to board.

Anyone without Blythe's youthful sense of adventure might have been overwhelmed by now, for their whole trip from Lucas Valley had been a series of mishaps. But so far, she had met each one with the resilience and resourcefulness of a seasoned traveler. A few hours out of Lucas Valley the stagecoach, hurtling down a narrow mountain road, had broken an axle and lost a wheel, nearly toppling down a steep gorge and dumping the passengers to almost certain death. Fortunately, no one suffered anything more serious than a few cuts and bruises.

After the driver assessed the damage, all the men bent their efforts to repair the axle and reset the wheel, but it was useless. At last, the driver unhitched one of the horses and rode to the next station for help. The passengers had camped on the hillside under a makeshift lean-to and, bundled in their own cloaks, spent a damp, uncomfortable night.

Blythe had to stifle almost hysterical laughter when she realized she was spending her wedding night huddled on a hillside next to the only other woman passenger!

By the time the driver returned with the new wheel, it was midday, and darkness was creeping on before the stagecoach was fit to move again. The passengers piled back in and continued the bumpy ride to the Junction where they were fed a slap-dash meal, then herded back into the stagecoach to continue the journey. With the trials of travel, the camaraderie among the passengers began to diminish, and they rode in gloomy silence the rest of the way. Malcolm had given up his seat inside to ride on top with the driver, so that the stout older woman could have more room. She had complained pitiably of her rheumatism and what the accident had done to her joints.

Blythe didn't mind. She had been so proud of Malcolm, the only one who had shown himself to be a gracious gentleman in spite of all the tribulations of the journey. She curled up in one corner, rolled her cape up into a pillow, and was soon sound asleep.

She had been awakened with a jerk when the stagecoach came to a jolting halt. Someone was shaking her. There were moans and groans as the other passengers stretched stiff muscles and gathered themselves and their belongings together.

Malcolm was at the door to hand her down. He looked troubled. "We're at an inn, still quite a distance from San Francisco," he told her. "With all these delays, we'll be lucky to make the city by our sailing date."

The inn was old and musty, and the only accommodations were communal dormitories—one for the men and another for women. But Blythe was too tired to care. She followed her elderly traveling companion up the steep stairway and, with her cape still wrapped around her, shared a creaky, lumpy bed.

After a hasty breakfast of bitter coffee and hunks of stale bread, they boarded the stage again. When they arrived in San Francisco, Malcolm had immediately hired a hack to take them straight to the dock.

There he had set Blythe down with the trunks and boxes and instructed her not to move while he went to see about the tickets for their passage.

All that Blythe had experienced so far had given her a heightened awareness of what it was like to be fully alive. It seemed to prove Mrs. Coppley's prophecy that she was in for high adventure, and she reveled in the panorama unfolding before her. In fact, so caught up was she in the drama of the fascinating scenes that she did not see Malcolm, pushing his way through the crowd, until he was almost upon her.

"Sorry to have left you so long," he said, "but it is a madhouse here. And there has been a mix-up about our passage. Oh, we're still going," he reassured her, "but it seems they have overbooked, and we will have separate cabins, each of us having to double up with other passengers. Well, there's nothing to be done about it. We're lucky they didn't sell our space when we were a day late checking in—"

Not waiting for her reaction, Malcolm turned, collared a passing Chinaman, and managed to convey his need for someone to carry Blythe's trunk while he shouldered his own belongings. Then, grabbing Blythe's upper arm, he began maneuvering a path through the crush of people toward the gangplank.

A ship's officer glanced at the tickets Malcolm thrust at him, then pointed them vaguely to the right. Still gripping Blythe's arm firmly, Malcolm forged ahead, down a narrow passageway crammed with other passengers trying to find their quarters. At last, he stopped in front of a closed door and rapped loudly.

It was opened in a minute by a pale, pretty woman looking a little disheveled. She was holding a child of about two in her arms.

Courteously, Malcolm introduced himself and explained their predicament.

"Of course, I understand," she said and gave Blythe a tentative smile, then added, "I'm Mrs. Arnold Thompson," Then she stepped aside so that Malcolm could enter and allow the Chinaman to shove Blythe's trunk underneath one of three tiny bunks.

"Sorry for the intrusion," Blythe said shyly.

"Oh, it will be nice to have company," the other woman said sincerely. "I hope you like children. A few minutes ago, one woman refused to share this cabin. Made quite a fuss, she did. Said she couldn't abide the thought of spending two months in such close confines with a 'squawling brat'! Imagine! My Daisy's no brat, but a sweet, well-behaved baby."

"I'm sure she is." Blythe smiled at the golden-haired child who smiled back and held out a dimpled hand to her.

"Well, I see you'll do nicely here." Malcolm looked relieved. "I'd better go see about my own quarters. I'll be back later." He nodded to Mrs. Thompson. "Thank you, ma'am. I know you'll find my wife a congenial companion."

When he left, Blythe surveyed the small space in which she was to spend the next eight weeks.

"Do call me Amelia," insisted Mrs. Thompson, laughing at the look of dismay on Blythe's face. "In these close quarters, we'll soon become well acquainted, so we might as well start out on a first-name basis."

"I suppose you're right, so you must call me Blythe." She smiled, her disappointment in not being with Malcolm dissipating somewhat in the warmth of this new friendship.

"I'm on my way to join my husband," the young woman confessed happily. "Arnie is an Army officer stationed in Louisiana. We'd been together only a short time when he got his orders, so though we've been married three years, we've barely seen each other at all. You see, during the War, men who posted out West were not brought back to fight in the South. So poor Arnie had to stay in the dreary Northwest, at Fort Humboldt. But a good Army wife never complains when her husband's future is at stake," she explained, "so I haven't minded too much spending six weeks here in San Francisco until I was able to book passage back."

Amelia finally paused for breath. "Your husband is very handsome," she declared. "Such a distinguished-looking gentleman. . . . How long have you been married?"

Blythe counted the days on her fingers.

"Oh, my! Then you're practically still on your honeymoon! But how wonderful to spend it in New Orleans after this awful trip. Your husband seems a sophisticated, cultured man of the world, so I'm sure he'll take you to the best of restaurants and perhaps the theater when you arrive." She frowned in a pretense of petulance. "I almost envy you, for I shall have to set up housekeeping in Army headquarters right away. And you should see some of the places we Army wives have to make into a home!"

Even at twenty and for all her worldly experience, Amelia did not seem much older than Blythe, so it was easy, in the forced intimacy of their cabin, to become friends. A good thing, Blythe thought, for there were as many vicissitudes to this sea journey as there had been on the overland trip.

The first befell them very soon after the ship pulled out of the harbor and crossed the bay. Amelia became miserably seasick, and Blythe found herself both nurse to her new friend and nursemaid to little Daisy.

Because of the crowded conditions on the ship, she was able to get only minimal help with changes of linen, fresh water, and other necessities required to alleviate poor Amelia's condition. Malcolm proved to be of some help, coming around each day to check on Blythe and to see if there was anything he could do for her or her cabinmate.

Other than that, however, Blythe saw little of Malcolm. He told her the occupants of his own cramped quarters were pleasant enough, and he had found some gentlemen who enjoyed whiling away the long, boring days at sea with card games.

This rather surprised Blythe. She had never thought him the type to play cards. When he jokingly remarked that he had already won enough to make up for the money spent on their trip, she had been even more shocked. Games of chance were linked in her mind with the saloons and gambling establishments at the other end of Main Street in Lucas Valley—the section of town where "decent people" never set foot.

Pa had always looked down on the men he knew who gambled away all their hard-earned money, and often quoted the maxim: "Gambling is the Devil's own way of leading men straight to perdition."

But when, in a burst of confidence, she had voiced her concern to Amelia, the young woman merely shrugged. "Oh, think nothing of it. Your husband is just bored and restless. Card-playing is a harmless diversion that will end with the journey," she said with an air of authority. "My Arnie told me that the men at Fort Humboldt nearly perished from boredom. It turned out the Indians weren't hostile at all, so the men spent many nights at cards. Believe me, there could be worse pastimes."

"But I never dreamed Malcolm would be the gambling kind," Blythe persisted.

"How long have you known him?"

"Over a year."

"Men are a marvelous mystery," Amelia remarked philosophically. "No matter how well you think you know them, they constantly surprise you."

Blythe reluctantly conceded that her friend's superiority of age and years of marriage gave her more wisdom in such matters. Gradually, she dismissed her nagging fret over Malcolm's new interest. She would have felt a little abandoned indeed had it not been for Amelia's lively companionship, and the long days at sea were happy enough.

Never having had a sister or even a best friend, Blythe delighted in getting to know Amelia. Because her cabinmate's sunny disposition and optimistic outlook were much like her own, they laughed away many of the trivial problems and inconveniences of the journey. Indeed, they even used some of them as subjects for merriment, giggling together like school girls.

Amelia had been reared in a family of sisters and knew many feminine secrets that Blythe had not yet discovered. One of them was the enhancing use of beauty.

"You have such glorious hair," Amelia complimented her. "Let me show you some more becoming ways to wear it," she suggested, loosening the braided coil that Blythe had attempted to maintain since the day Mrs. Coppley had wound it for her.

As Amelia brushed and swirled the luxuriant tresses, Blythe remembered a filigreed tortoise-shell Spanish comb that had belonged to her mother, and fetched it from her portmanteau.

"Perfect!" Amelia exclaimed. "See? You can wear it above the figure-eight roll at the nape of your neck." And she proceeded to show Blythe how to secure the comb.

"Your husband should be proud as a peacock with such a pretty bride!"

Blythe hoped Malcolm would notice her new hairstyle when he came to the cabin for their daily walk along the ship's deck. This he never failed to do even though she sensed it might be an interruption from the congenial company of his fellow card players. But that day Malcolm had seemed distracted, and they had taken their promenade silently.

When he left her again at the cabin door, he apologized, explaining that he had been dealt a bad hand in that day's game.

"That's to be expected," he shrugged. "Lady Luck is fickle. She's bound to change with the next deal."

Even though Malcolm passed it off lightly, it troubled Blythe that Malcolm should spend time that they could be together with strangers. She missed his companionship, longed for when they could become closer, get to know each other intimately, have the *real* "honeymoon" Amelia teased her about.

In the weeks the two had spent together, Blythe felt she had never been as close to anyone as to Amelia, had never known another human being as well. She began to wonder how she would manage to part with someone who had become such a dear friend.

They had talked about so many things—their childhoods, their families—Amelia declared the romance of Blythe's parents was the most romantic story she had ever heard. They also shared their hopes, dreams, secrets they had never told anyone else. Blythe learned the details of Amelia's long and ardent courtship with Arnold, one of West Point's finest, and was dismayed by the comparison to her own courtship with Malcolm. Why, he had kissed her only once . . . and that, on her wedding day!

Blythe was tempted to ask Amelia for answers to some of her vague questions about married life. She knew only that there was more to be known. A flustered Mrs. Coppley had made a few stumbling attempts at explanation of what she termed "a husband's rights," but Blythe had not the slightest notion of what she meant. But, somehow, Blythe could not bring herself to approach Amelia on this subject, and so let the opportunity pass.

At length, the long and eventful journey came to an end. The ship docked in New Orleans, and the two young women who had become so close, finally had to bid each other affectionate and tearful good-byes.

Malcolm came for Blythe, helped her gather her belongings, motioning to a black man he'd hired to carry her trunk. Together, the four of them—Amelia, Blythe, and Malcolm carrying Daisy—made their way for the last time through the narrow passageway, out on deck, and down the gangplank.

They were halfway down the ramp when, out of the throng of people on the dock, a deep, male voice shouted, "Amelia! Over here! Darling!"

Blythe saw him at the same instant Amelia did—a big, broad-chested man, resplendent in a dark blue uniform shining with braid. He shoved his way forward, waving his wide-brimmed blue Army hat.

Amelia clutched Blythe's arm. "It's Arnie! Arnie, we're coming! Oh, Arnie!"

Rushing ahead of Blythe and Malcolm, she flew into his arms as he swept her off her feet and into a long embrace. When he finally set her down, Amelia, straightening her tipped bonnet, turned around and beckoned Blythe and Malcolm.

"Arnie, I want you to meet Blythe, my dear friend. We were bunked together because the ship was overcrowded and she was such a dear, and such a help with Daisy. Oh, Arnie, see how Daisy has grown?" Amelia reached for the baby Malcolm was still holding. "And this is Blythe's husband, Mr. Montrose."

Captain Thompson, smiling broadly, tore his eyes away from his little daughter to thrust out his hand toward Malcolm. "Very pleased to meet you, sir."

To Blythe's astonishment, Malcolm made no move to shake the captain's outstretched hand. Instead, she saw the grim set of his mouth, the telltale flexing of the muscle in his jaw, felt his fingers press into her arm.

"Come, Blythe, our carriage is waiting."

As he tried to lead her away, Blythe resisted, seeing the startled expression on Captain Thompson's face, Amelia's hurt and bewildered one. "Malcolm!"

He dropped her arm and walked away, leaving her behind.

"I'm sorry, I don't know—" Blythe stammered. Then, giving Amelia a quick hug, she kissed Daisy and, flushed with embarrassment, hurried after Malcolm.

She had to move quickly to catch up to his long stride. He waited for her stiffly beside the rented carriage and handed her in without a word. Giving the driver the name of a hotel, he got in beside her. As the carriage lurched forward, he stared straight ahead.

Blythe's voice was shaking with indignation as she demanded, "How could you, Malcolm? How could you be so rude to Amelia and her husband?"

Malcolm turned to her with flashing eyes. "You didn't really expect me to take the hand of a *Union* Army soldier in *friendship*? Shake the hand that may have pulled the trigger that shot my brothers, friends, killed and wounded men in my Company?"

Struck by the violence in his words, Blythe drew back. *Where was the quiet, soft-spoken, gentle man she had come to know and love?* she asked herself as she looked into the face of a stranger.

chapter
7

AFTER MALCOLM'S outburst, Blythe retreated into silence, but she was very upset. It was so unlike Malcolm to have behaved in such a boorish manner toward the Thompsons, to have spoken to her so harshly. She tried to make excuses for him. Perhaps it was because he had been taken prisoner during the War and confined in a Yankee prison under brutal conditions that had wrecked his health and embittered him. Maybe the sight of Captain Thompson in the hated blue uniform had brought back all Malcolm's terrible memories.

She had to forgive him, to understand. She hoped Amelia was not too hurt. They had exchanged addresses. As soon as she was settled at Montclair, she would write her friend and try to make amends.

From the dock, they drove through the crowded streets jammed with carriages, the sidewalks teeming with people, the air humming with noise and pungent with the exotic smells of coffee and spices and the heady sweetness of flowers.

At length, they drew up in front of a magnificent domed structure, iron-lace galleries and Ionic columns ornamenting its façade. A uniformed doorman, his tunic sporting gold epaulettes and two rows of shining buttons, opened the carriage door and assisted Blythe out. She gazed about her in round-eyed wonder as Malcolm, his hand supporting her, led her up the steps and into the lobby.

From the shimmering crystal of chandeliers to the marble floors and sweeping staircase, it was ultimate elegance. Speechless, Blythe waited while Malcolm signed the registry. At the desk clerk's signal, a porter stepped forward to carry their luggage up the circular stairway and along a plush carpeted hallway to their suite.

Blythe could scarcely believe her eyes as she stepped across the threshold. Crimson velvet draperies fringed with gold hung over filmy lace curtains at the windows. The tiebacks were clumps of bronzed grape leaves with bunches of white glass grapes spilling down as if they grew there. The room into which they were ushered was furnished with gracefully arranged gilded chairs cushioned in crimson. A round table with curved legs held a crystal vase of red roses. Through an arched doorway, there was another room where an ornately carved bed rose in a splendor of gold satin canopy and coverings.

As soon as Malcolm had tipped the porter and closed the door behind him, Blythe spun around, clasping her hands together like a child. "Oh, Malcolm! It's like a dream! I've never seen anything like it!"

"That is fairly obvious," Malcolm observed dryly.

Wounded, Blythe looked quickly into Malcolm's face and saw something she'd never noticed before. Irritation, annoyance . . . contempt?

A new and uncomfortable thought occurred to Blythe. What did she—a girl from a frontier town, brought up without refinement or culture—know of Malcolm's world? More disturbing, still, was Malcolm's silent appraisal. He appeared to be making a fresh assessment of her—and not entirely liking what he saw, if that ridge between his dark brows was any evidence. At that moment, the gap between them seemed an unbridgeable chasm.

"Due to all the delays, we haven't much time," he said. "We were a week later than scheduled getting to New Orleans, and our train tickets to Richmond are for day after tomorrow. But we shall have to do something about your clothes." He frowned.

Blythe gazed mutely at the gray worsted traveling suit, new when she had left Lucas Valley. Of course, the long and arduous journey had taken its toll, but Amelia had helped her freshen it and had contributed clean white linen collar and cuffs for their arrival in New Orleans. Seeing it now, however, through Malcolm's critical eyes, Blythe was ashamed.

"Tomorrow you must buy yourself some suitable clothing. I can't take you to meet my mother in *that*."

Though Malcolm's disapproval wrenched Blythe's heart, she brightened at his suggestion. Amelia had predicted Malcolm would take her on a shopping spree once they got to New Orleans, where the shops and stores were reputed to be the finest anywhere outside Paris, France itself.

"Oh, Malcolm, what fun!"

"Well, perhaps, ladies consider shopping . . . fun," he said with a sardonic smile. "Not I. I couldn't possibly face an afternoon in some ladies' emporium, listening to prattle about fabrics and styles."

"Surely you don't mean for me to go alone?"

Again she saw that frown, that look of annoyance she had begun to dread.

"My dear Blythe," he said with suppressed impatience, "you are a married lady now, and it is not unusual for married ladies to shop alone. For directions to an appropriate salon, you have only to consult the concierge downstairs. She is employed for the sole purpose of providing such information to hotel guests. It's really quite simple."

Blythe swallowed back another plea for him to accompany her. She did, however, venture one last question. "But what about tonight? I have nothing to wear to dinner."

"Dinner? I'm afraid we've already missed the Ladies' Seating. I suggest you ring the maid to bring hot water for a bath, then I shall have a tray sent up to you later. I'm sure a warm bath and early retirement will be welcome after the . . . deprivations . . . of our long journey."

"But, Malcolm—" Blythe protested.

"Yes?"

"What about you? Aren't we to dine together?"

"I plan to take advantage of the bathing and barbering facilities off the lower lobby. After that, I'll have dinner. The Gentlemen's Seating continues until eight, which is much too late for you."

His tone was one of dismissal. Blythe could think of no reply, even though this was not her idea of their first evening together in New Orleans.

By the time she had finished her long bath—luxuriating in the warmth, the fragrant soap, the sponges, the soft towels—the maid opened the door for the waiter to bring in the dinner Malcolm had ordered.

It was a meal fit for a king . . . or a queen, Blythe thought, as she ate hungrily, even in lonely splendor. There was fresh crabmeat, tiny pink shrimp, mounds of rice with a delicious spicy sauce, succulent asparagus with a lemony glaze.

When she finished, she could barely keep her eyes open and, crawling beneath the quilted coverlet, she fell into a deep and dreamless sleep.

Blythe awakened the next morning to the sound of Malcolm's voice in the next room. He was talking to a waiter she could see through the arched doorway.

A moment later, Malcolm appeared and smiled. "So you're awake at last. Come, sleepy-head. I've ordered breakfast."

At least his disposition had improved, Blythe thought, allowing herself a small surge of hope. Perhaps today they would see some of the interesting sights Amelia had told her could be found in New Orleans.

A table, covered with a white damask cloth, was set in the alcove near the windows. A napkin as large as an apron was folded beside the white porcelain plate, with a confusing array of silver on either side. A silver chafing dish held fluffy scrambled eggs, and there were covered platters of crisp bacon, tiny sausages, hot croissants and a mound of creamy butter, thick strawberry preserves, and the darkest, richest, most fragrant coffee Blythe had ever tasted.

After months of the limited menu aboard ship, Blythe ate with appreciation.

"Oh, Malcolm this is wonderful," she sighed when she had satisfied her ravenous appetite. "What are we going to do today?"

"Well, I still have to see about our train reservations, check out our route, buy our tickets. And you, my dear, are going shopping, remember?"

"I still wish you'd come with me, Malcolm."

"There is nothing to be timid about, Blythe. A saleslady in the shop will be more than eager to help you with your purchases. That's her job. *Not* mine," he added emphatically. "Once she sees how much you have to spend, I'm sure she'll have no trouble at all finding just the right things for you." Malcolm took out his wallet and began to count out several large bills, which he placed on the table beside Blythe's plate.

"Goodness, Malcolm, this looks like a lot of money!" On the ranch, Pa had always handled their finances, seen to their needs.

"This isn't Lucas Valley, Blythe," Malcolm reminded her with a lifted eyebrow. "You'll find the price of clothing in New Orleans very different from what you are accustomed to paying. I want you to have something especially fashionable and in good taste when I introduce you to my mother."

He put on his jacket, picked up his hat, and started to the door, then paused there with his hand on the knob. "Don't look so forlorn. For most ladies, shopping is a pleasant pastime." He smiled reassuringly. "I'll be back later this afternoon to see your new things. Now, have a good time."

After he left, Blythe dressed and went down to the lobby to find the concierge. But one look at the impressive woman, elegantly attired in black taffeta, and wearing pince nez and a superior expression, sent Blythe scurrying back to her room.

While she was mustering up the courage to try again, a chambermaid came in, bringing fresh linen and towels, and Blythe seized this opportunity to inquire about the location of a dress shop.

"Some of the ladies I's worked for patronize a place jes' down the block and over two streets. Miss Francine have some mighty pretty dresses and bonnets."

Conquering her temerity and clutching the scrap of paper on which she had written the maid's directions, Blythe soon found herself standing in front of a shop distinguised by a bay window and marked with a sign lettered in gold, *Francine's Fineries*.

Wide-eyed, Blythe opened the door and walked into an ornately furnished interior.

"*Bonjour,* mademoiselle." A handsome, elegantly gowned woman greeted her while inspecting her from head to toe.

"I—I came to buy a gown—" stumbled Blythe, more than a little intimidated. "But, perhaps I'm in the wrong—"

"Not at all, mademoiselle. You have come to one of the finest boutiques in New Orleans. We serve our clientele individually. Here," she said, encompassing the room in a flourishing gesture, "we do not display our fine garments for all the world to see." She bit off each word with an ill-concealed contempt for lesser emporiums.

Blythe felt an urge to giggle, thinking of Horen's General Store in Lucas Valley, where all the merchandise was in plain sight—piled on counters, in shelves, on the floor.

"Now, what can we do for you?"

"A traveling outfit, please," Blythe said shyly.

The winged brows flew up. "Traveling?" The eyes roamed slowly over Blythe's slender figure.

"Yes, would you have something suitable—"

"*Mais, oui,* mademoiselle, of course we have *many.* You have but to choose." At this, she clapped her hands sharply.

Instantly, a thin, sharp-featured young woman appeared. She was dressed all in black and wore a tape measure around her neck.

"*Oui,* madame?"

"Justine, our customer is looking for a traveling costume. Will you conduct her into one of the dressing rooms, *s'il vous plait?*"

"*Oui,* madame. This way, mademoiselle."

Blythe followed obediently.

"Disrobe, mademoiselle, so that I can take your measurements," Justine instructed in a whispery voice once they were closeted behind heavy velvet draperies.

Blythe did as she was told, divesting herself of her jacket, waist, and skirt, down to her cotton camisole and petticoats, then stared in astonishment. The three-sided mirror gave her a view of herself she had never seen before—front, back, both sides, all at once. She felt abysmally out of place—like one of Pa's barn swallows in a gilded cage.

"Have you any preference of color, style?" Madame Francine asked when she joined them, again surveying Blythe, inch by inch.

This was too much for her innate honesty. "Oh, madame, I know nothing of fashion!" she blurted. "This is my husband's idea . . . to have the latest—"

Again the dark brows took flight. "Husband? But you did not say—"

"Oh, he is insistent that I have something new and elegant."

The black eyes narrowed. "And what price range did you have in mind?"

Blythe slipped her small pouch purse off her wrist, pulled open the drawstrings, and brought out the handful of crumpled bills Malcolm had left with her.

"Here, madame." She pressed the bills into the woman's hand. "This is all the money I have. Is it enough for an outfit such as I described?"

Madame looked down at the clump of paper bills and made quick work of counting them. Her expression reminded Blythe fleetingly of an old cat who had just been surprised with a full bowl of fresh cream. The woman and her assistant exchanged a look.

Then Madame Francine pursed her lips and tilted her head to one side in a studied appraisal. "And you are in New Orleans . . . on holiday?"

Under the intense gaze, Blythe blushed. "On our honeymoon, you might say."

"Ah-h-h-h—" This, from Justine.

Even Madame Francine's countenance softened a little, though her black eyes glittered like jet beads.

"And monsieur will be taking you out to dine, of course, to show off his beautiful bride, *n'est ce pas?*"

Blythe smiled happily. "I hope so."

Then the two got to work, Madame issuing orders like a drill sergeant and Justine fluttering around with pins in her mouth as she nipped in darts and adjusted pleats, her fingers flying, her needle moving like magic.

In Blythe's mind, this episode bore little resemblance to the ordeal of fittings in Mrs. Coppley's back room. Those were tedious, something to be endured. "My lands!" the frontier woman would exclaim, exhorting Blythe to stand straight. "Ain't you never goin' to stop growin', child?"

Instead, while Madame Francine and Justine fussed around her, there were clucks of approval and admiration.

"*Magnifique!*"

"*Trés belle!*"

As she turned at their direction, Blythe felt a warm glow of happiness. She so hoped Malcolm would be pleased with the results of this shopping expedition. When they finally had fastened the last button, adjusted the fitted basque to each one's satisfaction, Madame Justine sighed, "*Voilá!* "

"What do you think, madame?" asked Justine, sitting back on her heels at Blythe's feet.

Blythe could hardly believe her eyes when she saw her reflection. Staring back at her from the mirror was a tall, statuesque stranger. The violet silk grenadine jacket had wide satin reveres corded in deep purple satin; the skirt's fluted ruffles were also trimmed with purple cording, caught in loops with braided bows.

"Oh, my!" she gasped. "I hardly recognized myself!"

"And now for the *pièce de resistance!*" declared Madame Francine. "Come along, *ma cherie.*"

Blythe followed her into an adjoining room where she found herself surrounded by the most extravagant assortment of bonnets she had ever imagined.

Seating Blythe at a dressing table before a gilt-edged mirror, Madame

Francine tried on one after the other of the beautiful creations, with Justine looking on in awe.

"What glorious hair you have, madame," Justine whispered.

"The color is *naturelle,* one presumes?" added Madame Francine.

"Yes," replied Blythe, who had entertained some suspicion about Madame's own black tresses.

"But, of course," Madame nodded as if there had never been a doubt.

"Now, this is perfection," she said at last, settling a violet silk bonnet over Blythe's red-gold curls. The confection was lined in shirred lilac chiffon, with a cluster of feathery purple plumes peeping fetchingly over the brim.

"*Enchanté!*" exclaimed Madame and Justine in unison.

Blythe floated back to the hotel on a cloud of happy anticipation. She could not imagine what Malcolm would say when he saw her new outfit, though she expected he would echo the salesladies' lavish compliments.

Blythe had never before been told she was beautiful, and until Madame had pointed out the fact of her unusual coloring—the auburn hair inherited from her father's Kentucky kin and the dark Spanish eyes of her mother—she had not thought it at all *extraordinaire*. This one time, however, she *felt* extraordinary, and longed to hear the confirmation from the lips of the one whose opinion mattered most.

She hurried upstairs to their hotel room, and upon opening the door and seeing Malcolm seated there reading the newspaper, she pirouetted gaily in front of him, awaiting his enthusiastic reaction.

"Great Jehoshaphat! What kind of a getup is that!" he shouted and struck his forehead in dismay.

Blythe stood before him, dumbstruck by the violence of his reaction. "Isn't it all right?"

"*All right*? It's all wrong! Completely. Here, give me that bonnet!" he demanded and, when she handed it to him, he began ripping off the purple plumes.

Blythe watched in horror as he tore off all the trimming, then said curtly, "Now . . . the jacket."

She took off the offending garment slowly, wondering what on earth he planned to do. She gasped when he withdrew a small knife from his pocket. Horrified, she watched as Malcolm methodically cut the threads holding the looped satin cording and lace edging from the lapels and cuffs.

"Oh, Malcolm!" Blythe wailed. "You've ruined it!"

"Ruined it? I've *rescued* it. If we weren't leaving on the train tomorrow, I'd try to remedy this fiasco entirely! But there isn't time. You'll have to finish picking the threads so it will look half-way presentable." He flung the jacket over the footboard of the bed.

Malcolm then proceeded to put on his own waistcoat, adjust his cravat.

"Will we be dining out?" Blythe asked hopefully.

"I think I best order something brought up here for you, since it will take you the better part of the evening to repair that damage." His voice was iced with sarcasm.

"But I thought—aren't we going to see something of New Orleans?" protested Blythe.

Malcolm was already moving toward the door as if the conversation were at an end. "I saw quite enough of New Orleans during the months I spent here before sailing to California. Those were not the best months of my life, I might add, although educational in many ways." He paused in the doorway. "I don't think you'd particularly enjoy it, Blythe. Get a good night's rest. We start a long journey tomorrow."

If he noticed her disappointment, he did not act upon it. Instead, he told her, "I have been invited to a private club here by some friends I met on shipboard. I shall probably be late. Don't wait up."

After Malcolm left, Blythe looked at the ravaged dress, the deplumed bonnet. Was it really so inappropriate? Her face burned with humiliation as she wondered what Madame Francine and Justine had really been thinking. Even now, they must be laughing at her ignorance, her naïveté.

Maybe Malcolm was justified to be so horrified at her selection, but did he have to be so harsh? He was doubtless under some great strain. But what wounded her most deeply was the feeling that the real reason Malcolm had not wanted to take her to dinner was that he was ashamed to be seen with her!

chapter

8

Montclair—1870

BLYTHE WOULD always remember Montclair as she saw it first across what seemed like acres of golden daffodils. Seated in the hack Malcolm had hired at the Mayfield railroad station, she exclaimed, "It's so big. I never dreamed it would be so big!" She turned in amazement to Malcolm, but his closed expression halted any further comment.

He had barely spoken a word since they left the train from Richmond. His face was a mask, except for the tell-tale muscle quivering in his cheek, a sign she had come to recognize as extreme stress. It was the look of pain in his eyes, however, that bewildered her. Why, now, when they were so close to his beloved home, did Malcolm seem so anguished?

She turned away, gazing out the window. On the long trip from New Orleans to Virginia, she had had much time to ponder their relationship, to reflect on the man who was now her husband—the man she thought she knew. Now she realized that her knowledge of Malcolm had been very limited.

He had been unfailingly courteous and considerate in the past hours, but with each mile they traveled, they had moved further and further apart. By the time they reached Richmond, the gulf between them seemed impassable.

Had it begun with the scene with the Thompsons when they had landed at the dock in New Orleans? Or the terrible display of anger in the hotel room? She did not know. All she knew was that Malcolm's stony silence had become almost more than she could endure.

The carriage, obviously as old as it was shabby, swayed precariously and groaned to a stop as they drew up in front of the deep porch with its tall pillars and long, shuttered windows.

Malcolm stepped down, exchanged a few words with the black driver when he paid him, then leaned back inside the carriage and extended his hand to Blythe. "We're here," he said flatly.

Blythe stepped out and looked around her. The place seemed to be deserted, no one about.

She tugged at her jacket, straightened the brim of her bonnet, adjusted the bow under her chin. "Do I look all right?" she asked anxiously.

But Malcolm did not answer. He was staring up at the house, and her eyes followed the direction of his gaze. This was no story-book palace. She could see now that the broad steps leading to the veranda were sagging, the paint peeling from the siding and on the pillars.

Bewildered, Blythe turned to Malcolm, but he just took her by the elbow, and said brusquely, "Come. Let's go in."

He hesitated in front of the wide paneled door, put out one hand to the tarnished brass door handle, then pushed it open and went inside, leaving her to follow.

Tentatively, she walked into the high-ceilinged entrance hall. Her eyes took it all in—the large framed paintings, the parquet floor, the graceful curving stairway, a huge crystal chandelier hanging from a sculptured obelisk. She drew in her breath and held it for a long moment.

Almost immediately, she felt the chilling sensation. There was a strange stillness. No sound of voices, no activity. And even though she whispered, Blythe's words seemed loud. "Isn't anyone here, Malcolm? Didn't you let anyone know we were coming?"

Malcolm frowned. "No. It wasn't necessary. This is *my* home."

He didn't say our *home,* Blythe thought, and a lump thickened her throat.

In a few long strides, he crossed the hall and flung wide the louvered doors opening into a huge room. Blythe slipped up beside him.

"What a beautiful room!" she murmured as she moved with him into the center. *Or it must have been . . . at one time,* she thought, for the brocaded damask draperies, the flowered carpet, the carved mahogany furniture with its tapestried upholstery were all worn thin and stained from years of neglect.

Blythe saw Malcolm's pained expression and realized that he was surely remembering how this house used to be, how he had last seen it. *It's like someone has died,* she mused, *and he's grieving for all the years he can't call back.*

Impulsively, she reached out her hand in a comforting gesture. But he moved away from her touch, walked over to one of the shuttered windows, opened it, and stared out.

Standing uncertainly in the middle of the room, Blythe caught sight of her reflection in the large, gilt-framed mirror hanging above the white marble fireplace. Her beautiful ensemble, now devoid of its trimming, looked plain and ugly to her . . . like this house must appear to Malcolm.

Just then, Malcolm wheeled about. "Someone must be here . . . one of the servants, surely," he said, and he strode past Blythe and out into the long hallway, toward the back of the house. Blythe had to hurry to keep up. At an open door he stopped so abruptly that she bumped into him.

"Garnet!" she heard him say.

The name he had called meant nothing to Blythe, yet there was a tremor in his voice as he spoke it. Curious, she crowded near to look into the room.

A young woman, her arms filled with daffodils, was standing near a table in the middle of the room. At Malcolm's greeting, she dropped the flowers, and a yellow spray of blossoms spilled out of the vase where she had been arranging them.

"Malcolm! Malcolm, is it really you?!" Her cry held a mixture of emotions—shock, disbelief, then exultation. For a moment she stood absolutely still, and Blythe had a chance to get a good look at her.

Dressed in faded calico, the woman was as slender as a wand. Her small face had paled, emphasizing the prominent cheekbones and making the chin appear a bit too square. But her eyes, widened in shock, were magnificent, Blythe thought—the color of deep amber—and her hair, a lovely tawny gold.

"Oh, Malcolm, I can't believe it's true!" She uttered the words in a low moan.

"Yes, Garnet, I've come home," Malcolm said. "You look like you've seen a ghost. But, I can assure you, I'm very much alive." And there was that soft, teasing tone that Blythe loved but had not heard in Malcolm's voice for much too long.

At this, Garnet rushed forward, her arms outstretched. In the next moment, they were embracing. Blythe lowered her eyes, feeling like an intruder.

Finally, Malcolm said quietly, "Garnet, may I present my wife, Blythe. Blythe, my sister-in-law, Garnet Cameron Montrose."

Blythe lifted her head and looked into the other's stunned gaze. Garnet's face had gone chalky-white, even as Blythe felt hot color rise in her own cheeks. The expression on the woman's face, as she struggled for composure and comprehension, was embarrassing to see. She looked as though she had been struck a blow.

The silence seemed to stretch interminably. Blythe became conscious of the loud ticking of a clock keeping pace with her pounding heart. There was a tension here she did not understand but could acutely feel. She put out her hand in greeting, but Garnet evidently did not see it, for her own frail hand fluttered to her throat as if she were choking.

Garnet looked from Malcolm to Blythe and back again. She moistened her lips. "I must prepare your mother, Malcolm. This will be too great a shock for her if you just—" She halted, struggled to go on. "If you'll excuse me." She inclined her head to Blythe, then brushed past her. They could hear the sound of her light footsteps in the echoing silence.

Finally Malcolm turned and, with a kind of helpless gesture, said, "Garnet's my brother Bryson's widow. He was with Mosby. But then you probably don't know anything about the Raiders or about the War—" His eyes fixed upon her for a piercing moment, then he sighed and turned away. "Of course, you were too young . . . too far away—"

Blythe again felt the urge to cry out in protest, to defend herself . . . but against what? Malcolm's upspoken, yet implied, criticism. Could she help it if she had been only a child during the great War that had split the eastern part of the country?

"I'm sorry, Malcolm." Blythe spoke softly. "About your brother, I mean."

He made no reply, but moved distractedly around the small room that formed an alcove off the main dining room. Then he stepped through and walked around the long table, ran his hand along the backs of the graceful chairs, and stopped to finger a glazed blue vase, to pick up a bowl, holding it up so that the sunlight caught the prisms cut deep into the glass and threw dancing rainbows against the wall.

With a kind of inner knowing, Blythe sensed that he was reacquainting himself with the things he had almost forgotten—all the dear, familiar things. All that had gradually become vague images in his mind were springing to life at his touch.

Suddenly Blythe became aware that her mouth was dry, her throat parched. She was terribly thirsty. The train ride from Richmond had been long and tedious, followed by the dusty drive along country roads from the Mayfield station to Montclair. She had had nothing to eat since early morning, and her head had begun to ache with a dull throb.

She was about to ask Malcolm where she might find some water when Garnet reappeared.

"Malcolm, I've broken the news of your homecoming to your mother. Of course, she wants you to come up right away. She is very excited—" She paused, looking at Blythe. "I haven't told her yet about . . . I think perhaps you should tell her yourself."

"Yes, I think you're right. I'll go to her." He started to leave, then remembered Blythe. "Mama is very frail," he explained. "Too much excitement might—"

Blythe nodded, feeling numb.

"Perhaps *you* should come with me, Garnet . . . in case—"

"Of course, Malcolm."

Without another word, the two left the room, leaving Blythe standing there alone to absorb this strange twist in their homecoming.

This was not how she had pictured Montclair. She hadn't been at all prepared for the present reality of it. She had always seen it through Malcolm's eyes, as it was before the War, before his two younger brothers were killed, before the South had lost its long struggle. Not like this.

Suddenly she, too, was overcome by a bone-deep fatigue. She untied her bonnet strings and took off her bonnet. In the rush of the day's activities, some of the hairpins had fallen out of her hair, and she idly plucked the rest before shaking out the thick mane of russet curls. Putting her hand to her scalp, she massaged it gently. It felt good to be free of the confining headpiece, the grip of the pins.

Her thirst grew demanding, and her stomach was queasy. Since it appeared that Malcolm and his sister-in-law would not be returning right away, she set out to find the kitchen for herself.

Cautiously, she walked to the door opposite the one they had entered and pushed it open. It led into a narrow room with built-in cabinets from floor to ceiling on either side. This must be the pantry, she guessed, and the kitchen must be nearby. Instead, she found a door opening onto a back porch and a breezeway with a ramp leading out to a small brick house. She remembered now. Malcolm had told her that, in the South, the kitchen was often separated from the main house because of the heat in summer. This, then, must be where the dishes were kept. A short search produced a glass. Happily, she also found a kitchen pump in the corner and filled the glass with water.

She was drinking thirstily when a deep, masculine voice from behind her said, "Hello!" It startled her, causing her to jump. The glass flew out of her hand and shattered on the floor. She spun around and saw the tall figure of a man standing in the doorway of the outside porch.

"I *am* sorry! I didn't mean to frighten you." His voice had the same slurred softness of a native Virginian as Malcolm's. "I thought you were my sister Garnet."

He took a few steps forward into the room, and Blythe noticed that he walked with a slight limp. There was a distinct family resemblance between this man and Garnet, although his features were strong and masculine, and his wind-tossed hair and mustache held a reddish tint rather than gold. His hazel eyes were curious as he regarded her.

"I beg pardon for walking in on you. I'm so used to coming here . . . as if it were my own house. Sorry, I didn't introduce myself. I'm Rodrick Cameron, *Rod*, Garnet's brother." He paused expectantly, waiting for her response.

"I'm Blythe," she said shyly. "Blythe Dorman . . . I mean, *Montrose*. I'm Malcolm's wife."

She saw the same expression of disbelief that had earlier crossed Garnet's face.

"Malcolm! Malcolm is *here*? He's come home?"

"Yes, today. We just arrived from Richmond . . . or rather, from Mayfield. But we've been on our way from California for weeks . . . months, really—" Her voice trailed off, uncomfortable under his intense scrutiny.

He shook his head as if to clear it. "Does Mrs. Montrose know? Does *Garnet?"*

"Yes, they're both upstairs with Malcolm's mother now."

Rod shook his head again as if he still found it hard to believe. "Well!

I hope she doesn't have a heart attack. What about Mr. Montrose? Has Malcolm seen him yet?"

"No. We've seen no one else."

"Oh, that's right. Garnet said he was away. I forgot." Rod leaned against the wall and turned his broad-brimmed hat over and over in his hands. "Well," he said again, "this is a great surprise."

Then he bent stiffly and began to pick up the shards of glass scattered on the floor. Blythe stooped to help. He dumped them in a basket near the door, then brushing his hands, said, "Maybe you didn't know, but none of us has seen Malcolm in over seven years. In all that time, we had no idea if he were dead or alive. He just . . . disappeared. Oh, we knew he'd gone out West, but there has been no communication . . . no word at all—

"You see," he hesitated a second, then continued, "we all grew up together. I live on the neighboring plantation, Cameron Hall. Malcolm is like a brother . . . we were all so close—"

Again Rod paused, and gave Blythe a long, sympathetic look. "This must be just as hard for you . . . coming here like this. Forgive me if I seem . . . well, you couldn't possibly understand. But it's almost as if my real brother, my twin, Stewart, had come walking back into our lives. Of course, Stew was killed in the War. I don't even know if Malcolm has heard . . . so many . . . so much was lost—"

She nodded, miserably uncertain as to what was expected of her, whether she should offer her condolences. Then he seemed to become aware of her unease and continued in a compassionate tone.

"But you're too young to know about the War, aren't you? We've all grown old here . . . before our time. You look so very young—"

"I'm sixteen—nearly seventeen," Blythe said a little defensively.

"Sixteen!" Rod shook his head and continued staring at her. "And how long have you and Malcolm been married?"

"We were married in December, then we boarded a ship in San Francisco for New Orleans. The voyage took two months, and we've been traveling by stage and train for the past two weeks." She cocked her head, musing aloud. "This is March . . . so I guess we've been married for four months."

Whatever Rod might have said next, Blythe would not know, for just at that moment, Garnet's voice rang out from the doorway. "Rod! Oh, Rod, I'm so glad you've come. Malcolm is here! He's come home!"

She flew past Blythe as if she were invisible and into her brother's arms. He held her for a full moment. "I know, little Sis," he said softly. "I know."

Straightening her slender shoulders, Garnet moved out of his embrace, smoothing her hair. When she turned to face Blythe, her countenance was calm and composed. "Malcolm is with Sara now. I left them alone for a while after giving her an extra dose of laudanum. So much excitement—" A tiny frown puckered her smooth forehead then and she asked Rod, "There's nothing wrong at home, is there? I mean, was there any special reason you came this afternoon?"

"No. No special reason. I just happened to be out for a ride and decided to stop by to see you."

A brief smile touched Garnet's lips. "You must have known, somehow, that I'd need you. Of course, you'll stay for supper? You must. Malcolm will want to see you." Again Garnet glanced at Blythe. "It won't be much—we weren't expecting guests." She gave a short laugh and said with a tinge of bitterness, "We rarely have guests at Montclair these days. Excuse me while I see to dinner."

Left alone at Garnet's departure, Blythe and Rod eyed each other self-consciously. Then he smiled encouragingly. "This all probably seems very strange to you just now. But I'm sure you'll soon feel right at home." After another long pause, he asked, "How . . . where did you and Malcolm meet?"

"In Lucas Valley. I lived there with my Pa. Malcolm was very ill when he came to our ranch. He'd been prospecting in the high country until he took a fever. Another miner found him and brought him down the mountain to our place."

"But I don't understand." There was a puzzled expression on Rod's face. "How did you come to marry?"

"Malcolm stayed on until he was well and afterward, since he didn't have anywhere else to go . . . or so he said . . . Pa hired him to work the ranch. Not long after, there was an accident and . . . well, my Pa died last year and—"

"Please," Rod said, "don't go on if it's too painful."

"Oh, I guess it will always be painful. . . . Anyway, Pa was real fond of Malcolm, and Malcolm of him. . . . So when Pa died, Malcolm asked me to marry him, told me that's what Pa had wanted. So—"

Just then, Garnet, carrying china plates and a snowy tablecloth over her arm, came back into the room. "I'll set the table in the dining room," she explained briskly. "After Malcolm comes down, I'll go up and settle Sara, then we can have supper."

"Where is Mr. Montrose?" Rod asked.

"He went to Savannah to see Aunt Lucie, Sara's sister. There was some problem about their stepmother's will. He should be back by the end of the week."

"He'll be relieved that Malcolm's home to help run the plantation and deal with the workers," Rod remarked thoughtfully.

"What plantation? Most of the fields go unplanted, and there are few workers left who are worth their pay. And with all the government paperwork to be done—" She sighed heavily.

"I know. Horses are less trouble." Rod grinned, and Blythe noticed that his face was boyishly handsome.

"You're lucky!" commented Garnet. "We all should be grateful that Cameron Hall escaped the worst of the burning and looting, though having Yankees quartered there was not the most pleasant thing at the time. Still, it could have been burned to the ground. And Dove's idea for the school . . . now that was an inspiration."

Blythe sensed that Garnet was avoiding engaging her in conversation. The exchange between brother and sister seemed, in a way, designed to cover the awkwardness of her unexpected presence. *They don't know what to think of me, or do with me,* Blythe thought.

"I must fix Sara's tray," Garnet said and turned to slide a silver tray from the cabinet.

Blythe knew that Sara Montrose was an invalid. Malcolm had told her of the terrible injury Sara had suffered when thrown off her horse— an accident he had witnessed, which had remained a vivid childhood memory.

Just then, Malcolm walked into the room and, on seeing Rod, called his name hoarsely. Wordlessly, the two men moved toward each other, stood looking deeply into the other's eyes, then embraced. These two who had been boys together, then comrades in arms in a lost cause, were bound by ties stronger than those forged by blood, by roots so deep they bridged the years that had separated them.

They broke apart at last, arms still locked, each searching the other's face for traces of the experiences they had endured separately since they had last met.

"It's good to see you, Malcolm," Rod said in a voice husky with emotion.

"And you, Rod." Malcolm quickly shook his head. "About Stewart—"

"I know," Rod quickly interjected. "And Lee and Bryce—and all the rest. I know."

Garnet disappeared to deliver Mrs. Montrose's tray, and the men talked quietly together as if there were no one else in the room. Blythe felt invisible, for the two men had entered a world that no longer existed, except in their memory. Worse, it was a world she could never share with Malcolm. She listened, only half hearing their reminiscences, until Garnet reentered the room.

"Your mother wants to see you again," she said to Malcolm. "She's very drowsy, but wants to assure herself that you're really here."

"Of course," he said and left without a backward glance.

Rod, noticing Blythe's discomfort, smiled apologetically. "It still seems like a dream that Malcolm . . . and you . . . are here. But we're forgetting our manners, Garnet. Shouldn't you be showing Blythe where she can freshen up before supper?"

Garnet seemed flustered she had not thought of it herself.

"Oh, I'm sorry. It's just that there's been so much confusion—" She bit her lip. "Come along upstairs. We weren't prepared for . . . but you can use my room."

"I just need to wash up a little. Maybe I could use the kitchen pump," suggested Blythe, trying to be less of an inconvenience.

"The *kitchen*?" echoed Garnet. "Oh, of course not! Come." She moved toward the hall.

Blythe felt her cheeks grow hot. Once again, she had committed some unpardonable breach of etiquette. She was glad Malcolm had not been there to be embarrassed by her gaucheness.

Blythe gave Rod a grateful nod, then followed Garnet up the winding staircase and down a long hall with many doors on either side. Finally, Garnet came to one at the end and opened it, stepping inside.

"There are fresh towels on the washstand . . . whatever you need . . . I think," she said. "When you're ready, just join us downstairs." On her way out the door, she turned and asked, "Do you think you can find your way?"

"Oh, yes!" Blythe assured her with false enthusiasm.

She looked around. Was this Garnet's own room?

It was very grand. The high canopy bed with its tall carved posts and the marble-topped bureau and washstands with their fruit-pull handles gave evidence of an opulent era, though the rug, draperies and bed curtains were faded with age and needed replacing.

She poured water from the rose-patterned porcelain pitcher into the matching bowl on the washstand, then unbuttoned her bodice and hung it on the back of the chair. She took one of the linen cloths hanging on the rack, rinsed and wrung it out, and began to refresh herself. The cool water felt soothing as she cleansed away the grime of the train and the dust from the carriage ride along the country roads.

Finally, she tackled her hair. On the ranch, she had done little more than keep it clean and brushed, much like currying the horses in the barn. Sometimes, when the thick hair hung heavy on her neck, she pulled it back with a scrap of ribbon or plaited it in a single braid that reached to her waist. But it seemed this thing of being a lady required great skill, and she wondered if she would ever learn all that was demanded.

She worried with the mass, arranging it as best she could in some semblance of the elegant figure eight Amelia had taught her. But the strands escaped her fingers and curled in wispy tendrils about her face. In frustration, she left it, hoping the sight of her would not bring another frown to Malcolm's face.

Feeling somewhat more presentable, she ventured into the shadowy hallway. She made her way to the top of the stairs and descended slowly. At the landing, she stopped to study a series of portraits hanging along the wall.

These must be Malcolm's ancestors, since the portraits of the men bore a striking likeness to him — noble features, dark wavy hair, an air of intelligence and fine breeding. And the women, each with a unique beauty—an exquisite brunette, gowned in crimson velvet with gilded lace ruffles; a brown-eyed, rosy-cheeked girl with swirling blond hair; a striking, auburn-tressed young woman in riding habit. But it was at the next portrait that Blythe paused longest, enchanted by the wistful expression.

The woman's gleaming dark hair parted in the middle, hung in clusters of curls on either side of the pale oval of her face, and spilled onto her alabaster neck and shoulders. She was dressed in an apricot satin gown with a wide, off-the-shoulder bertha of lace. A handsome little boy with tousled dark curls leaned on her knee, his alert expression and wide brown eyes much like those of his beautiful mother.

Something about the child tugged at Blythe's heart. Could this be a portrait of Malcolm with his mother, for she knew Sara Montrose was a legendary beauty? But no, Malcolm's eyes were a deep blue. Who then—?

As Blythe stood there, pondering the possible identity of this portrait, she heard a door close, then footsteps coming along the hall above. She saw it was Malcolm and turned toward him eargerly. He seemed distracted and as she spoke, looked at her almost as if were trying to remember who she was.

"Are you going to take me to meet your mother now?"

"Not tonight. She was drifting off when I left her, worn out with all the commotion of our coming." He kept looking at Blythe as if trying to place her in this setting into which he had brought her and where she did not yet belong.

Shyly, Blythe slipped her hand through his arm. "I was just looking at these paintings," she said. "I thought perhaps this one was of your mother and you . . . is it?"

"No," he said shortly. "That's Rose, my wife."

Blythe cast him a sidelong glance. A veil had dropped over his eyes. Why had he said "my wife," as if the lovely woman were still living?

He had never said much about his first wife—only that she had died while he was away, fighting with Confederate General Robert E. Lee, and that they had a little boy who lived with his mother's relatives in Massachusetts, a child he had not seen since he was three years old.

That must be he, the little boy in the portrait with Rose. Jonathan.

Malcolm had retreated again into the past. Blythe felt keenly that cool distancing as they continued on down the steps and into the dining room.

The four places set at one end of the banquet-length table seemed dwarfed by the high-ceilinged room with its massive buffet and tall chairs. Garnet was already seated, looking up briefly at Blythe's entrance. Rod rose and held out a chair for her. Malcolm, still preoccupied, did not stop to assist her, but passed by, seating himself at the head of the table.

Garnet murmured a few words of blessing for the food, then began passing the dishes. "It's not much of a welcome-home feast, Malcolm," she said. "Certainly no fatted calf."

"For the return of the prodigal son?" Malcolm lifted his eyebrows.

"It looks fine to me!" Rod said heartily, and Blythe suspected he was attempting to cover some subtle undercurrent with a forced good cheer.

To Blythe, accustomed to the plain ranch fare, the supper seemed more than adequate; the cold chicken, string beans, rice, cornbread and home-canned peaches, all served on elegant china and in cut-glass bowls, seemed "company" enough for anyone. She was very hungry and enjoyed every bite.

The conversation during the meal was mostly a dialogue between Rod and Malcolm about old friends, things that had happened in Malcolm's absence, comrades in arms, and the vanquished military leaders and politicians of the Confederacy who, after the War, had fled to such far-flung countries as Egypt and South America to escape living under a despised regime. They spoke also of those who had survived, had prospered, or had faded into the oblivion of defeat.

Still hungry, Blythe was reluctant to ask for seconds. When she saw that Garnet had barely touched the food on her plate, Blythe folded her hands in her lap, wondering if perhaps it wasn't ladylike to eat heartily.

At the end of the meal, the men continued talking. Excluded from their discussion and, with no effort on Garnet's part to draw her into a separate conversation, Blythe began to feel the fatigue of the long day.

Finally, Garnet rose to remove the plates. At last! Here was something Blythe could do to make herself useful. "May I help? " she asked eagerly.

But Garnet waved aside the offer. "No bother. Suzie will be here in the morning to clean. I'll just stack the dishes and leave them for her. If you'd like, I can show you to your room. I aired the bed and put clean sheets on earlier."

Blythe got to her feet and stood behind her chair. Should she wait for a pause in the conversation before excusing herself? Or, better still, would Malcolm notice and join her?

But it was Rod who once again spared her further humiliation by rising. "You're leaving us, Blythe?"

"Yes, I'm very tired. So, I'll just say good night." She looked to Malcolm for guidance, but he was lost in some private reverie.

"Well then, it was a pleasure to meet you. I'm sure we'll see each other again." Rod spoke with such warmth and kindness that Blythe felt a rush of pure gratitude.

With that, Malcolm pulled himself wearily to his feet, regarding Blythe with a curious detachment. "I'll be up in awhile. Rod and I have much to talk about after such a long time . . . you understand?"

"Of course." Blythe denied the sting of hurt at Malcolm's indifference. Could he not even have escorted her to their bedroom their first night at Montclair? But here was Garnet with a lighted lamp, standing by the door, waiting.

"Good night then," Blythe murmured and turned quickly away to follow Garnet up the stairs.

After Garnet left, Blythe stood in the middle of the room, feeling lonelier than she had ever felt in her life. She walked over to the window and looked out. A new moon was rising behind the tall trees, and she could just make out the dim outline of the driveway leading from the house.

A sharp twinge of homesickness bit deep, a longing for friendly faces, for a familiar landscape, for home.

"This is your home now," she reminded herself aloud. But in her heart, she could not help asking, *Is it really? Can it ever be?*

There had been no fire laid in the fireplace, and the room felt damp, chill. Shivering, Blythe turned back the crocheted coverlet, the sheets. She undressed, crawled up into the high bed, and pulled the blanket up to her chin, fervently wishing Malcolm would come up and take her in his arms to warm and comfort her.

But Malcolm did not come.

For a long time Blythe lay there, tense and hopeful. Once, she even got out of bed and tiptoed out to the hallway, leaning over the banister. The low murmur of masculine voices could still be heard from the dining room. Then, surprisingly, the melodic ripple of feminine laughter!

Blythe felt the loneliness of an outsider. Those three downstairs had a lifetime of memories binding them in a circle of closeness she could never hope to enter.

Sighing, she crept back to the wide, lonely bed, and finally fell asleep. Sleeping soundly, she never heard the sound of Rod's horse galloping down the drive just before dawn, nor Garnet's tread upon the stairs shortly after. She did not know, until the next morning, that Malcolm had never come to bed. He had flung himself on the sofa in the library and there slept restlessly, his dreams haunted by the ghosts of old griefs and longings.

chapter
9

BLYTHE WAS UP, bathed, and partially dressed when a knock came at the bedroom door. She tied the sash of her wrapper about her waist and, with her hair still tumbling about her shoulders, went to answer.

It was Malcolm. She could read nothing in the expression on his face. He neither explained nor offered an apology for the night before.

"Mama has asked us to have coffee with her," he said without preamble. "She is anxious to meet you."

"Now?" Blythe felt a leap of panic.

"Yes. Well"— his eyes swept over her— "that is, as soon as you're presentable. How long will it take?"

She put a hand to her tousled curls. "Oh, only a few minutes more."

"Then, I'll go down and get the coffee. When I come back, we'll go in together."

He left, and she closed the door behind him.

What to wear was her first frantic thought. For Malcolm's sake, Mrs. Montrose's first impression of her must be a favorable one, Blythe realized.

As she inspected her meager wardrobe, she knew at once that the disastrous outfit she had bought for this occasion was the worse for long wear, besides its ruinous altering at Malcolm's hands. Her wedding ensemble, with its ruffles and flounces, would doubtless be all wrong, too.

The only other possibility was the black bombazine Mrs. Coppley had hurriedly remodeled for her father's funeral. It was plain and severe, with just a tiny rim of white ruching edging the high neck and long sleeves. In the early spring of Virginia, it seemed much too heavy and hot, but Blythe had no other choice.

Her hands shook nervously as she did up her hair, striving for the same look that Amelia had achieved with such ease. But the natural waves resisted the confining pins and insisted upon escaping about her forehead and neck. There was no time to take it down and start all over, for there was another tap on her door. It would be Malcolm with the coffee.

Starting down the long hallway at his side, Blythe smoothed the folds of her skirt, touched the neckline. "I hope your mother will like me," she said, desperate for some small reassurance.

"She doesn't know you." His tone was civil, if curt. "It will take time. Remember, all this . . . our coming . . . was very unexpected."

Eager to meet Malcolm's mother and hopeful of her approval, Blythe stepped into the sitting room with an expectant smile. To her dismay her new mother-in-law's first words were "Oh my! That dreadful dress! "Black is so depressing! It reminds me of death and funerals, and we've had too much of death and dying here. Please, child, never wear that in my presence again!"

Blythe turned a stricken look on Malcolm. "I'm . . . so very sorry," she murmured.

"Blythe could not know your aversion to black, Mama," Malcolm intervened in a diffident manner. "She was able to bring only a few things with her. But, I'm sure, in the future she will wear . . . happier . . . colors." Malcolm quickly dismissed the subject.

But Sara had not concluded the matter. "Do excuse my impulsive reaction, my dear," Sara said sweetly to Blythe. "My nerves are frayed, I fear, and thus I sometimes speak before I think. I didn't mean to frighten you. Do come closer so I can see you and greet you properly." She held out both thin hands to Blythe.

As Blythe moved hesitantly forward, Sara sighed, "Why, Malcolm, she's hardly more than a child!"

Blythe felt her face grow hot under the older woman's assessing gaze.

The woman, propped against a profusion of ruffled lace pillows, had once been a great beauty. Blythe had seen the proof in her magnificent portrait. Even now, the fine bone structure was evident, although deep lines flanked either side of her delicately arched nose, stopping short of a mouth whose downward curve pronounced petulance. Two wings of stark white accentuated the dark hair swept back from her face. The

70

large mauve-shadowed eyes that might once have sparkled as brilliantly as sapphires had faded to an icy blue. Sara Montrose had a brittle fragility, but Blythe sensed that under that frail beauty was an iron will, a survivor's strength.

"Sit down, child. Malcolm, the coffee," Sara directed, gesturing with an arm covered in creamy velvet, ruffles of ecru lace edging the sleeve.

Blythe took a chair opposite Mrs. Montrose's chaise lounge, politely answering Sara's questions about her life—first at the boarding school in Sacramento, then the isolated existence of the ranch in Lucas Valley. Sara listened intently, nodding her head at intervals.

"It seems even you, at your tender age, have had your share of loss and tragedy," she said. "I, too, lost my mother in early childhood—a loss, I might say, that is never fully assuaged, no matter how much love one receives in later life."

As their gaze met, Blythe was aware that Malcolm's mother was taking her measure and that some bargain had been struck. It was as if Sara Montrose had decided to accommodate the differences in their backgrounds and that, with Malcolm as their common denominator, they could live as allies, if not friends.

When Sara's attention drifted from Blythe back to Malcolm, and the conversation gradually shifted to people and places that held no meaning for Blythe, she looked about her with interest, absorbing the ambience of the room. She had been told that Sara Montrose had spent most of her adult life, at least since the accident, in this wing of the house.

Oddly enough, this suite showed less damage than the other rooms at Montclair. Everything was pastel, whether by design or simply with the passage of time. The walls were a dusty rose, the moiré draperies pale blue, the furnishings as delicate as the woman who lived within these walls.

Blythe sipped her coffee from the egg-shell thin cups while Malcolm and Sara talked quietly. Observing the devotion of mother and son, she felt a tiny tug of longing, a little envy. Would she ever become part of the small circle of shared intimacy here?

At length Malcolm rose. "We shouldn't tire you, Mama. We'll go now, and I'll come back later and read to you for a while." He leaned over and kissed the hand he had been holding.

"All right, sweet boy. You know how I'd enjoy that." Sara patted his cheek affectionately. Then she turned to Blythe, "We'll have plenty of

71

time to get to know each other, my dear." She smiled and, in that moment, Blythe saw the magic that must have once been Sara's to charm and fascinate.

As they left Sara's rooms, Blythe said, "I think I'll go change my dress. It is rather warm for this climate besides being *black*," she added with a smile.

But Malcolm did not seem to catch her joke, just nodded disinterestedly. "Good. I'll take the tray downstairs, then I'm going for a walk."

He didn't ask her to accompany him, though she would have loved to tour the grounds with Malcolm as her escort. So she walked toward the room she had occupied last night, and Malcolm continued down the stairs without another word to her.

Taking off the offensive black dress, she put on the skirt to her ill-fated traveling suit and took out one of the cotton blouses of flowered calico that Mrs. Coppley had made.

Hearing voices outside, she went to the window and looked out to see Malcolm greeting a group of black men, farm workers judging by their garb. He stood talking with them for a few minutes, then they parted, and Malcolm went on alone. Blythe watched him go through a gate and proceed up a little hillside until he disappeared from view.

She was hungry. She had had only coffee, and her healthy appetite was asserting itself. She wondered if it would be proper to go down to the kitchen and find something to eat. She should have asked Malcolm.

Self-reliant since childhood, Blythe did not hesitate long. She went down the circular staircase, pausing every so often to gaze at one of the portraits.

As she reached the bottom step, she noticed a pile of luggage—a trunk, a wicker basket, and two hatboxes—standing by the door. Seeing these weren't hers and Malcolm's, which he had arranged to be sent out from the Mayfield freight office, Blythe wondered briefly whose they were, then went on toward the pantry.

There she found Garnet sitting at the table.

"Good morning, Blythe," she said, looking up from a list she was writing. "I'm glad you're here. I have quite a few things to go over with you. For instance, show you how Sara likes her tray set up. She's very particular, so you'll have to listen carefully, or else she'll fuss." Garnet spoke matter-of-factly. "She prefers the lily-of-the-valley china for breakfast, but the set with yellow buttercups at lunch."

Blythe was puzzled. Why was Garnet telling her all this when she had been in the house barely twenty-four hours and had only just met Mrs. Montrose?

"It's not that she means to be difficult," Garnet continued. "It's just that she has come to expect having things as she wishes them. I suppose we've all indulged her. She's had so much to bear . . . the accident . . . the War. . . . Even then, we—" Garnet's voice trailed off momentarily. "When Lizzie left, Sara was inconsolable. Lizzie was her personal maid, trained from childhood, and none of the other servants ever measured up. They were clumsy or forgot how she liked things . . . or just made her nervous—"

"But since you know her so well, know how to please her, why are you showing *me?*" Blythe asked bluntly.

Garnet paused and stared at her for fully half-a-minute. Then she spoke evenly, "Because, from now on, it will be your responsibility."

"But I've never done anything like this, I mean . . . taken care of an invalid. I may be every bit as clumsy and awkward as any of the servants, not please her any better. She may even resent me," protested Blythe.

"She'll have to accept you, won't she? You're Malcolm's wife. Besides, I won't be here."

Blythe looked at her blankly. "You won't be here?" she echoed.

"No, I'm leaving. This afternoon. They're sending the carriage for me. I'm going home to Cameron Hall, where I grew up and lived before I married Bryce . . . before the War. I'm needed there more than I am here . . . now." She spoke with an air of finality. "My mother runs a boarding school. My sister-in-law, Dove, has been helping, but with more students expected . . . well, they're short-handed." She stopped suddenly as if there were nothing more to say. "Come along. I want to show you about the linens. Suzie or Lonnie will come for the laundry. They do it out in the laundry shed, but you need to know how to count it and sort it and where it all goes."

In a kind of daze, Blythe followed Garnet as she led her through a variety of explanations, showing her the pantry, the cupboards, the storage bins for flour, corn, rice, grits, instructing her on what to direct the cook to prepare in quantities, and how to fix the family meals.

"There is really not much to that. Mrs. Montrose has the appetite of a bird. And when Mr. Montrose is here . . . well, he never really knows, or cares what he's eating. I—I don't know about Malcolm—" Her voice drifted off indefinitely. Then she sighed wearily. "I guess that's about all. You'll have to find your own way just as I did when it was all thrust upon me after Rose died."

Blythe drew a deep breath, gathering up as much poise and courage as she could muster. "I kept house for my father. I think I can manage. At least I'll do my best."

She felt overwhelmed by this sudden change. More puzzled, still, by the fact that Garnet was not staying to help her make the transition.

During Garnet's careful instructions about Sara's dosage of laudanum, the sound of the brass knocker at the front door resounded throughout the house.

"That's probably Josiah," Garnet said briskly, and hurried to open the door.

A black man stood there. He swept off his hat and flashed a wide, toothy smile. "Mawnin', Miss Garnet. Yo' mama, Miss Kate, say you want me here promp'ly at noon, so here I is."

"Thank you, Josiah. There are my things. I'll be along in a few minutes."

Blythe felt momentary panic. Garnet was actually going, and Blythe was not at all sure she could remember everything Garnet had told her that morning.

"Garnet, wait! Does Malcolm know you're leaving?"

Garnet was busy tying her bonnet strings. "Not yet."

"He's taking a walk. Why don't you wait until he comes back?"

Garnet turned around. For a moment, a look of sympathy passed across her face. "Malcolm may be gone for hours," she said. "He's up on the hillside . . . visiting Rose's grave."

Desperate, Blythe persisted, "But why must you leave?"

Slowly Garnet turned to face Blythe, those amber eyes riveted upon her. Instinctively Blythe knew that steadfast gaze was meant to communicate something significant. But what?

Then Garnet spoke. "Surely, you do not expect me to stay. As Malcolm's wife, *you* are the Mistress of Montclair *now*."

74

chapter
10

COMING DOWN from Malcolm's mother's room with her breakfast tray, Blythe fought tears of discouragement. It seemed hopeless that she would ever be able to please Sara as had Garnet or even the constantly lamented Lizzie.

She set the tray down on the hall table, sighed, and looked longingly out through the tall windows at the lovely May morning.

Today Sara had been particularly difficult. She had drawn her finely etched brows together and said crossly, "I don't see why Garnet felt she had to leave. After all, Montclair is as much her home as Cameron Hall. She came here as Bryce's bride when she was just a girl. . . . Oh, it's really quite vexing! I need her as much or more than her mother does. Just when I get used to someone, off they go. And Lizzie! I shall never forgive such ingratitude. Lizzie had all sorts of special privileges the other servants didn't have—"

Blythe wondered when Lizzie would have had time to enjoy "special privileges," what with anticipating her mistress's every need, catering to her every whim.

At last Blythe had settled Sara on her chaise with her writing portfolio on her lap, the pillows arranged just so, and with her languid permission to leave. *Oh, well, it will get better soon,* Blythe told herself optimistically. *I'll learn what suits her . . . and what doesn't!*

Blythe had taken on the care of Sara with a good heart. She wanted Malcolm's mother to love her, of course, but she also tried to treat her as tenderly as if Sara had been her own mother.

Still, there was so much to managing such a large house—one that used to keep twenty or more servants busy. Now she had only the two black women who came to help with the laundry and cleaning a few days a week.

A soft flower-scented breeze wafted through the open front door and, unable to resist, Blythe walked out onto the wide pillared veranda.

The air was sweet with the fragrance from the apple orchard, those trees with their delicate pink petals mingled with the white lacy blossoms of the pear trees nearby. A soft wind sent them scattering as Blythe watched.

How beautiful Montclair must have been before the ravages of war, time, and neglect had left their mark. No wonder Malcolm was heartsick and keeping more to himself with each passing day. He had come back to find a very different picture from the one he had carried in his mind so long. He had found the house falling apart, the fields unplowed and unplanted, no longer yielding the corn and tobacco that had provided the vast fortune needed to maintain Montclair.

Blythe had expected that, when Malcolm's father returned, the two men would work together to bring the plantation back to some semblance of its former productivity. But it took only a few days after meeting Mr. Montrose to realize that here was a broken man. Despite his courteous and gracious manner, his eyes were haunted, his face deeply lined with the sorrows and defeats he had known. Although he was not yet sixty, he moved and spoke like a very old man, without energy or enthusiasm.

Blythe tucked her skirts about her and sat down on the top step of the porch. The roses, blooming at random in the untended gardens, were still rich and lovely. She must cut some of the buds for Sara's dinner tray.

Just then her attention was diverted by the sight of a graceful figure on horseback, cantering up the driveway. Shielding her eyes with her hand, she recognized the approaching rider. It was Garnet.

Blythe watched her as she flung the reins over the iron hitching post, admiring the grace of her movements, her figure, accentuated by the nipped-in jacket and the softly flared skirt of her dark blue riding habit.

Garnet, seeing Blythe, seemed to hesitate slightly. She stood for a moment, slowly pulling off her leather gloves.

The woman looked glowing, Blythe noted, not as thin and pale as she had been when they first met. Her red-gold hair under the small-brimmed pancake of a blue hat was bundled into a netted snood.

"Good morning! I've come to see Miss Sara," she explained, fastening the edge of her skirt into a loop at the side. "I hope she's not resting."

Blythe scrambled to her feet, genuinely glad for Garnet's company. "Oh, she'll be so happy to see you! She's missed you." She almost added, "We all have," but something in Garnet's cool gaze stopped her.

"Then I'll just go on up," she said and started up the porch steps. As she passed, Blythe caught an intriguing spicy scent.

She followed Garnet into the house in time to see her skim up the winding staircase with quick, light steps and all the confidence of one who belongs. At once Blythe felt that feeling of isolation. How long would it take *her* to feel a part of life at Montclair?

Still, she was glad Garnet had come. Her visit would be sure to cheer Sara.

Blythe hurried out to the pantry. She would surprise them with a tea tray, she decided. Surely Mrs. Montrose would be pleased with a tray of fresh tea and some of the dainty ginger cookies she liked.

Blythe arranged the tray, and when the water boiled, she poured it over crushed jasmine leaves, let it steep thoroughly, then put the top on the china teapot and, over it, the quilted cosy.

Satisfied that she had followed Garnet's instructions to the letter and that even Sara would approve, she lifted the tray and moved confidently up the stairs and down the hallway toward Sara's wing of the house.

Nearing the closed door, she could hear the murmur of voices. She paused outside and shifted the tray slightly to free one hand. But as she started to knock, she heard her name mentioned. Instantly, she halted.

"Blythe? But Blythe doesn't matter." That was Garnet speaking.

"If only Malcolm hadn't made this terrible mistake. If only he had waited—" Sara's voice was anguished.

Mistake? Malcolm's mistake? What mistake? Then very slowly, the truth dawned upon Blythe. They meant *her! She* was Malcolm's mistake.

Rooted to the spot, she stood unable to move, an unwilling eavesdropper. Then she heard her name again.

"Blythe? She makes no difference. We all know Malcolm can never fully give his heart to anyone but Rose." Garnet's voice was tinged with a bitter sadness. "Sara, believe me, it would not have changed things if I had waited for a hundred years. But now I have a second chance for happiness, and I'm going to take it. Please . . . be happy for me," she pleaded.

Blythe had heard enough. Too much. Gripping the tray firmly, she turned away. Garnet's voice followed her as she tiptoed back down the hall. She was not sure where she was going, what she would do. All she knew was that she must get hold of herself before she could risk going into Sara's room, facing both women as though she had not just heard news that had shaken her world on two fronts. Garnet loved Malcolm! Malcolm still loved Rose!

Blythe just reached the top of the stairs when she saw Malcolm coming in the front door. She whirled around, but not in time.

Looking up, he saw her and bounded up. "Oh, you're taking Mama's tray in to her. Good! I was just going in to visit for a while. Didn't I see one of the Cameron horses hitched outside?"

"Yes, Garnet is visiting your mother," Blythe managed through stiff lips.

"Garnet? Wonderful!" Malcolm's eyes lighted up. "She should be a real tonic for Mama. Here, I'll take that in."

She relinquished the tray, then let her hands drop limply to her sides. She half-turned and watched him, his step livelier than she had seen it in a long time, as he walked along the hall to his mother's room.

It did not strike her at first that she had not been asked to join them. Her senses were too frozen for reaction. She went down the stairs, holding onto the banister, and without any real idea of where she was going, walked out of the house. Outside, she took the path through the kitchen garden along the meadow and down toward a spot where the woods began at the edge of the lawn.

The breeze felt mercifully cool to her flushed cheeks, and she closed her eyes, trying to calm herself. It wasn't what she had overheard that hurt so much as the realization that all she had instinctively felt since coming to Montclair was true. The only thing she hadn't understood was Garnet's role. Now that, too, was clear. Garnet had been in love with Malcolm, expected to marry him when he returned. That explained her abrupt departure from Montclair upon their arrival.

Yet, the thing that saddened Blythe most was that her dreams of happiness with Malcolm had faded as quickly as a rainbow after summer rain. Now it seemed hopeless to cling to her vision of a marriage that would take the normal course of others she had observed in the small community of Lucas Valley. There, young couples got married, and as babies began to arrive, they became a family. Innocent as she was, Blythe was not ignorant.

In all the weeks since they had arrived, Malcolm's behavior had bewildered her as he continued to sleep downstairs, never approaching the bedroom she occupied. Now she knew why. Garnet had put it into words. Malcolm could not love her, or any other woman, because he was still in love with Rose. His daily pilgrimages to the hillside cemetery proved that his heart was buried there with her.

Dreams die hard. A small sob escaped Blythe's throat as her own dreams of love and the hope of motherhood dissolved.

chapter

11

"BUT, OF COURSE, you must go, Malcolm!" Sara was insistent. "Garnet is your sister-in-law, your brother's widow. And the Camerons are our oldest and dearest friends. Kate would be terribly offended if the Montrose family were not represented at the wedding."

"But, Mama—" Malcolm's mild protest was weary.

"Now, I'll not hear another word. You and Blythe must be there. What would people think if none of us showed up? They would think we didn't approve." Sara paused, adding, "Not that I really do. At first I thought Garnet had lost her head marrying a Yankee. But when Major Devlin was so very helpful during our humiliation at the hands of those undisciplined troopers—" She shuddered with the memory. "Well, I must say he conducted himself like a gentleman. And I understand"— she brightened perceptibly— "that he is well-educated and wealthy besides!"

"All right, Mama," Malcolm interrupted, getting up from the chair beside his mother's bed. Passing a hand across his forehead as though it ached, he sighed. "I'll go. *We'll* go." He glanced over at Blythe who was putting Sara's freshly laundered nightgowns into satin bags, placing them in the sacheted drawers of the bureau.

Coming as she did from the West, and having been unaware of the bitterness that still existed in the South toward all Northerners, Blythe was astonished to learn that Garnet's marriage to Jeremy Devlin had caused such a flurry of gossip in Mayfield. Personally, of course, she was delighted—not just because the young woman posed some kind of threat to her happiness with Malcolm, but because she genuinely liked Garnet despite the cool reception she had been given upon her arrival.

Not only that, but ever since she had passed the tall, wrought-iron gates guarding the entrance to Cameron Hall, she had been curious about the great house at the end of the drive. Now she would see it for herself.

Blythe looked over at Malcolm, wondering about his grudging consent to attend Garnet's wedding. Was he reluctant because he did, indeed, care for his brother's widow? She pushed away the thought. It was like so many other questions begging answers, questions she dared not ask.

After Malcolm left the room, Blythe turned to Sara and asked shyly, "Whatever should I wear to such an occasion?"

Sara turned a critical eye upon her. "Well, it will be an afternoon ceremony, so it doesn't call for formal attire. And goodness knows, few of us have any money anymore for new gowns, so I don't suspect the guests will be too fashionably dressed." She surveyed Blythe for a long moment. "I suppose nothing you have is suitable." The comment was phrased more as a statement of fact rather than a question. "Come here, child, let me see—"

Blythe obeyed.

"Perhaps, with a bit of altering . . . you do sew, I take it?"

"Yes, ma'am."

"Then go over to the armoire." She waved an imperious hand in the direction of the large, ornately carved fruitwood closet. "I have a gown that might just do."

Blythe did as she was told. Opening the doors of the large French clothes closet, she caught the scent of the sweet, subtle fragrance of the potpourri balls hanging there.

"The blue taffeta, the one with ruching . . . bring that out and let's take a look at it. It's not the latest style, of course, being over ten years old, but then, as I said, no one else will be wearing *le dernier cri* either." She fingered the material. "Hold it up to yourself. Ah, yes. The color is perfect with your hair. I think it might do nicely. Sadly, I only wore it but once myself. But no one is likely to remember. Try it on, and we shall see."

Blythe quickly slipped off her pinafore and the calico dress and into the beautiful silk gown that felt cool against her skin and rippled deliciously over her petticoats.

Standing in front of the three-sided, full-length mirror in Sara's dressing room, Blythe turned this way and that. Even if the style was outdated, to her, this was the finest, the most elegant dress she had ever seen. She turned happily toward Sara Montrose, waiting anxiously for her decision.

Sara did not speak for a full moment. For the first time, she saw the perfect proportions of Blythe's tall figure. The girl's magnificent hair wreathed her face in a flaming aureole, and her eyes sparkled. She was a beauty!

Not given to flattery, Sara pursed her lips and nodded slowly. "Yes, I think that shall do nicely. Very nicely, indeed."

Blythe felt heads turning and curious eyes upon her as she and Malcolm entered the drawing room at Cameron Hall. Word had circulated quickly in Mayfield that Malcolm Montrose had brought home a bride from the far West, and everyone was eager to see her and make their own evaluation. Malcolm had told her that most of the men felt there was no need to go farther than the state of Virginia to find a pretty and talented wife. But this was the second time, she knew, that Malcolm had broken this unwritten code.

Knowing that she was the object of avid interest, Blythe's hand tightened on Malcolm's arm, although she felt reasonably sure she looked presentable in the periwinkle blue dress. She was taller than Sara, so they had cut off the train and made it into a fluted flounce for added length. Sara had loaned her a charming blue velvet Empress Eugenie hat with a pale blue feather that curled forward over her ear.

"Welcome to Cameron Hall, my dear." Kate Cameron held out both her hands as Malcolm presented her. "We're delighted you could come. And you, too, Malcolm dear. You're quite the stranger since bringing home such a lovely bride." She held her cheek upward for his kiss. Then she turned again to Blythe. "And you've come all the way from California!" She shook her head as if the idea were incredible. "Do take seats, won't you. The ceremony will be starting in just a few minutes."

What a lovely woman, thought Blythe. Slim as a girl, Mrs. Cameron's dark auburn hair was threaded with silver, but the gray eyes were clear and shining as a child's as she moved among her guests, graciously greeting one, then another.

Blythe and Malcolm took their seats in one of the rows of chairs placed in a semi-circular fashion in two sections facing a white marble fireplace banked with yellow and creamy ivory roses. Above the mantelpiece hung crossed sabers and a portrait of the Cameron family, painted when the children were young. The handsome parents were seated on a curved-back velvet sofa. Standing on either side were two red-haired boys, who must be Rod and his twin, Stewart, while the pixie-faced little girl with red-gold ringlets sitting in her father's lap was surely Garnet.

Even as Blythe gazed at the charming portrait, a piano in the adjoining parlor began to play softly. There was a rustle of movement as the guests turned toward the center hall where Garnet, on her brother's arm, was slowly descending the wide staircase.

All around came murmurs of approbation—"Radiant!" "Never saw her look lovelier."

Garnet was dressed in an almond moiré-silk, demure yet elegant in its simplicity. Her tawny hair was worn high, swept back from her face, and a sprig of ivory roses nestled in the coiled chignon at the nape of her neck. As she passed, the afternoon sunlight streaming through the tall windows made her gown shimmer with iridescent lights.

Although Garnet was not beautiful, she was undeniably attractive, and she moved with the confidence of someone who has always been loved and pampered. Everything about her seemed to glow—her skin, her eyes, her hair.

A tall, darkly handsome man waited at the side of the fireplace. There was a poignant moment when Garnet lifted her face for her brother's kiss before he handed her over to Jeremy Devlin.

Garnet looked happy as she met her bridegroom's adoring gaze. Perhaps, Blythe sincerely hoped, whatever Garnet had once felt for Malcolm had been replaced by this new, and obviously satisfying love.

"Dearly beloved—" The minister began the ceremony.

Blythe risked a glance at Malcolm, wondering if he were remembering the day only a few months ago when they had stood together in the little church in Lucas Valley, exchanging these same vows. But she was shocked to see his face set in stony lines. With a flash of unflinching honesty, Blythe realized it was another wedding day, another bride—*Rose*—he was thinking of.

She turned back quickly, focusing her attention on the intimate scene at the improvised altar. As she did so, she was suddenly aware that Rod, from his seat across the aisle, was looking at her. She met his thoughtful glance. Could he have possibly read in her expression the longing, then the dismay she felt?

Determinedly, Blythe concentrated on the marriage service taking place, even though each word struck a blow to her wounded heart.

"May God, the Author of all good things, give you steadfast love to live together in such mutual harmony and full sympathy with one another, in accord with Christ Jesus, that your hearts would be united in praise to Him and your lives would glorify him. Now, receive and welcome each other as Christ has welcomed and received each of us, by the exchange of these rings."

When the final benediction was pronounced, the couple turned to the friends and family who clustered about them with embraces and congratulations.

Throughout the room, the mood of solemnity shifted to one of light-heartedness. The doors of the dining room had been thrown open, and Mrs. Cameron was inviting everyone in where a magnificent three-tiered wedding cake stood waiting to be cut as soon as toasts were made to the bride and groom.

As Blythe moved with the crowd across the hall toward the high-ceilinged dining room, she felt Malcolm's fingers press into her upper arm. Surprised, she turned to hear him whisper, "As soon as we've paid our respects to Garnet and her husband, we're leaving."

Words of protest died on her lips as she saw the thin line of his lips, the clenched jaw. Why would Malcolm want to rush off just as the celebration was starting? These were his friends, people with whom he shared bonds of childhood, wartime comradeship, affection. Surely it would be impolite to leave so soon.

He made no reply to her unspoken question, merely propelled her into the room with its flower-decked, festooned bridal table.

Was it because Jeremy Devlin had been an officer in the Union Army that Malcolm did not want to stay for the festivities? Blythe recalled the embarrassing scene in New Orleans when Malcolm had refused to shake hands with Captain Thompson.

"Miss Blythe." A mellow voice greeted Blythe, bringing her back into the present moment. She looked up into the kind face of Rod Cameron. "Good to see you again, and you, old friend." He nodded to Malcolm.

Mrs. Cameron joined them. At her side was a fragile, dark-eyed woman, whose hair was nearly white in spite of her youthful, peach-bloom complexion.

"Blythe, my dear, I wanted you to meet our Dove. I just realized you two are sisters-in-law. Dove's husband was Malcolm's youngest brother, Leighton."

Dove held out a tiny hand and smiled. "I'm so happy to meet you. My Lee adored his older brother Malcolm."

Blythe was touched by Dove's gentle warmth.

"It was Dove who provided the lovely background music for the ceremony. She's the music teacher for our school," explained Kate, putting an affectionate arm around the young woman. "There will be more music later and dancing once the toasts are over. Do you like to dance, my dear?" she asked Blythe.

"Oh, yes, very much!"

"Then I shall claim a dance right away before you are swept away by the rest of the gentlemen who have taken note of the newcomer in our midst," Rod teased.

At his words, Blythe blushed with pleasure.

But there was to be no dance with Rod . . . or with anyone else. As soon as the series of toasts were given to the bridal couple and the ceremonial cake-cutting had taken place, Malcolm grasped Blythe's arm and, gripping it tightly, steered her through the open French windows and out onto the terrace. There, he dropped her arm and strode over to the horse and small wagon in which they had ridden to Cameron Hall.

Blythe had no alternative but to follow. With the sound of dance music tantalizing her ears, she climbed silently into the seat beside Malcolm. Without another word, he flicked the reins, turned the horse, and started down the long tree-lined drive to the gates.

Only once on the way back to Montclair did Blythe glance over at Malcolm's stern profile. Her heart ached with pity for him, and a little for herself.

Had everything gone out of life for him—all the bright happiness of music, gaiety and laughter? Would he ever enjoy a time, an occasion, a world—without Rose?

chapter

12

THE EARLY July heat was stifling, and only a random sultry breeze drifting in the open kitchen windows stirred the curtains listlessly.

Blythe lifted her head from the bubbling kettles and turned toward the window. All morning, she had supervised Lonnie and Suzie as they made jelly and pickling sauce from the wild berries and crabapples they had gathered in baskets. But the women had gone home at noon, leaving Blythe to watch the thick liquid so it did not burn while it simmered.

She wiped her damp forehead with the hem of her apron. Her hair was plastered against her cheeks in tight little tendrils from the steam.

"I must get some fresh air," she said aloud and placed the lid on the kettles.

She could not see the front drive from the kitchen, but as she came through the house toward the veranda, she thought she heard hoofbeats on the crushed shell. When she walked out onto the porch, she was just in time to see Rod dismounting.

She had not seen any of the Camerons since Garnet's wedding, hearing only through the inter-plantation grapevine that, after a honeymoon at White Sulphur Springs, the newlyweds had returned to Cameron Hall for a visit before leaving for an extended honeymoon trip to Europe. Since the Academy was in session until late June, Blythe guessed they must all be very busy.

Not that she had really expected to see any of them. She had loved both Mrs. Cameron and Dove at once and longed for the chance to become friends. But there was slim hope of that. So, Rod's coming was a happy surprise.

I must look a sight! she thought, wiping her hands on her apron, then brushing back her hair from her flushed face.

But Rod did not seem to notice. He swept off his broad-brimmed straw hat, made her a little bow, and smiled up at her. "This Virginia summer hot enough for you, Miss Blythe?"

"Plenty hot, Mr. Cameron," she replied with a smile.

She couldn't help admiring Rodrick Cameron. No matter the circumstances, he was always pleasant, good-natured. Unlike Malcolm, he did not seem embittered by the tragedies that had touched his family—the loss of his twin, his own wound, his diminished fortune. He seemed to have risen above the adversities, become stronger, made the most of what was left.

The sun glinted on his red-gold hair, giving it a fiery sheen, as he moved into the shadow of the porch and seated himself a step below Blythe.

"Too hot for man or beast." He laughed. "But I came with a purpose."

"I'm sorry Malcolm isn't here—" began Blythe.

"My mission doesn't involve Malcolm, ma'am. It involves you."

"*Me?*"

"I came to deliver a note from my mother." He withdrew an envelope from his linen coat jacket and handed it to her.

She accepted the cream-colored square, sealed with a tiny blob of blue wax and stamped with a crest, staring at the beautiful script.

"Open it," he encouraged. "It's an invitation. Now that our school has been dismissed for the summer, and Garnet is safely wed and off on a European honeymoon, Mama has time to do some entertaining. She wants you to come to tea next Thursday. I'll come for you myself in our refurbished phaeton."

"Why, thank you. How nice of your mother to ask me."

"She's wanted to have you over before this, but the school has kept her busy. Getting twenty young ladies packed up and off to their homes after the winter is quite a project." He grinned mischievously. "Even with my help!"

"And do you teach, too?" Blythe asked. Rod did not strike her as the schoolmaster type.

"Me? Teach? No, ma'am. I'm the riding instructor. And all these little students seem determined to become proficient horsewomen. Since their parents are willing to pay extra for the privilege, I'm more than willing to do my best to instruct them."

"They're lucky," said Blythe a little wistfully, thinking of her mare Milly, who had been sold along with the rest of the ranch horses after Pa's death.

"Well, I'm going to be hard put to keep our horses exercised until fall." He paused, eyed her quizzically. "Do you ride?"

"Oh, yes. At least, I used to. On the ranch. Mostly bareback, of course. No formal instruction."

"You probably don't need it."

Just then Mr. Montrose came out on the porch. "I thought I heard voices," he said. "Rod, my boy, it's good to see you! We don't have much company anymore. Where's Malcolm, my dear?"

"He's taking a walk . . . I think," Blythe replied in a small voice.

"Ah, yes. To the cemetery." Mr. Montrose shook his head. "He goes every day. I wonder if it's good for him—"

Blythe felt Rod's eyes upon her, and she asked quickly. "You will stay for a while, won't you, Rod? Malcolm may be back any minute, I'm sure, and he'd be disappointed if he missed you."

"Well, thank you, I will then."

The two men settled into rocking chairs, and Blythe cast Rod a grateful glance. It would be good for Mr. Montrose to have someone to talk to, someone who understood the old days.

"I'll make some lemonade," she offered, rising to go into the house.

"That would be splendid, my dear," said her father-in-law

Reaching the pantry, Blythe was glad she had had Suzie squeeze some lemon juice earlier, thinking Sara would like a cooling drink when she awoke from her nap. She put some of the juice in a pitcher, mixed in sugar, added water, then arranged it on a tray with tall glasses garnished with sprigs of mint.

As she was bringing it out to the porch, she overheard Mr. Montrose say to Rod, "So Garnet is married."

"Yes, sir. By now, the happy couple should be well on their way to Europe."

"Well . . . we can only *hope* she'll be happy. All we can hope for anyone is happiness," Mr. Montrose said.

Rod's eyes narrowed slightly. "Well, sir, I've heard it said, 'Happiness can be getting what you want or wanting what you get.' The trick is knowing what will really make you happy."

"That may be true, boy, if one is wise enough to recognize it." The older man sighed.

The following Thursday, before getting ready for her visit to Cameron Hall, Blythe prepared Sara's tray. Always meticulously following the instructions Garnet had given her, Blythe covered it with the freshly ironed linen cloth with its drawn-work edging and monogram. Next, she folded the matching napkin into a precise triangle, then placed the hand-painted china cup and saucer beside it. She would make the tea last of all, making sure the water was boiling vigorously before pouring it over the tea leaves. Then the small silver pot must be covered so the steaming brew was kept hot.

Her last task was to measure out exactly two spoonfuls of laudanum into the tiny crystal glass to ensure Sara a restful nap while she was away.

Malcolm had told Blythe to accept Mrs. Cameron's invitation, but Sara had fretted. "You won't be gone long, will you? I don't like to awaken with no one to come when I ring." With one frail hand, she gestured toward the small silver bell on the table beside her chaise, a summons Blythe had learned to answer speedily.

"Oh, I'll be back in plenty of time to bring your tea," Blythe assured her.

"Well, I know how visits can go on and on without noticing the time—" Sara's voice had trailed away with a hint of self-pity.

Still, aside from her surface pettiness, Sara was to be admired, Blythe felt. Overall, the invalid bore her physical disability with courage and poise and had managed to build a life for herself within its narrow confines. She had somehow been able to survive the blows fate had dealt her—the death of two sons, watching her once strong, proud husband come home in defeat to a ravaged plantation and diminished fortune. Yet Sara had not given in to despair. She read voraciously, wrote dozens of letters to friends and relatives, maintained her appearance.

Malcolm's homecoming had obviously done wonders for Sara, so Blythe harbored no resentment of their loving bond. At times, however, she could not help wondering if Rose had ever suffered this same feeling of exclusion. But no one ever spoke to her of Rose.

Hearing the grandfather clock in the hall chime the quarter hour, she hurried upstairs to get dressed. With much thought and trying-on the night before, she had resolved the matter of what to wear. She had chosen a light-weight cotton print in a tiny bluebell pattern with puffed sleeves and a collar of crocheted lace.

Mrs. Coppley had given Blythe the dress along with a confession. "I made it for my niece, Sally, before she married. But with three babies in as many years, it don't fit no more. It ain't hardly been worn."

Again, it was her hair that posed the biggest problem. The humidity forced the curls tighter, and Blythe fought to smooth them into the neat roll she had practiced. Before she was satisfied with her efforts, however, she heard the sound of Rod's horse and buggy on the drive below. Not wanting to keep him waiting, she grabbed her wedding bonnet and was tying its strings as he pulled up in front of the house.

Blythe ran down the veranda steps to meet him, her skirts billowing out from her tiny waist. She was unaware of the pretty picture she made . . . or that the man observing her envied Malcolm Montrose his uncanny good luck. Rose had been a stunning brunette, but this young woman had a fresh, innocent beauty of her own.

The ride to Cameron Hall passed pleasantly. Blythe believed Rod Cameron to be one of the most relaxing persons she had met since coming to Virginia. With Mr. and Mrs. Montrose, she often felt shy; with Malcolm, uncertain of what to do or say, awkward in the extreme.

Kate Cameron came out on the porch to greet them. "Welcome again, Blythe, dear! It's been much too long since we've seen you, but with the wedding and graduation . . . well, things around here have been busy, to say the least." She broke off with a light, lilting laugh. "We'll begin today to remedy all that. I'm longing to get better acquainted."

Blythe felt instantly at home. So this was a true Southern lady— this model of charm and decorum and genuine warmth. Up close, Kate looked older than her slim, girlish figure would imply from a distance. But although her face was lined, her manner was serene, and she seemed much more interested in others than in herself. She knew exactly what to say and do to set each person at ease. And she did it without affectation or effort.

"We'll sit out here where we can catch some breeze." She led Blythe over to a shady corner of the side porch. "Dove is planning something cool and lovely for us to drink."

Blythe settled gratefully into a white wicker chair. Nearby, a round table was covered in pink linen. On it, a cut-glass vase held a fragrant bouquet of roses.

"What beautiful flowers," Blythe said admiringly.

"Yes. I love roses, too," Kate agreed. "The gardens are just coming back. They were ruined during the War. Those Yankees rode their horses right through them, trampling everything—" She broke off, her mouth tightening slightly as if remembering the desecration. "After that, I concentrated for a while on growing vegetables. But, let's not dwell on unpleasant things." She waved a slender hand in dismissal. "This afternoon I just want to get to know you." She smiled at Blythe. "Now, do tell us all about California. Since I doubt I shall ever see it myself, I'd like to hear from one who has lived there."

Before Blythe could even wonder how to begin, Dove appeared. Once more Blythe was struck at the contrast of her snow-white hair and youthful features. Her hair must have turned white as the result of some great shock, probably the death of her husband Lee.

"Here's our Dove now. Come sit here by me." Kate said, patting the flowered cushion of one of the chairs nearest her. Turning again to Blythe, she asked, "How is Malcolm these days? We miss him. We thought he'd be over more once he got back from the West. But we haven't seen him since Garnet's wedding. When he was a little boy, he practically lived at this house. He was great friends with the twins, of course, and Garnet worshipped him. We always considered him part of the family."

"He spends a lot of time with his mother," murmured Blythe, realizing this to be a poor excuse for neglecting old friends. But how could she explain Malcolm's reclusiveness when she couldn't understand it herself?

"I suppose, like so many others, he has some adjusting to do. Seeing the damage at Montclair must have been a terrible blow," suggested Kate. "Those of us who lived through the Yankee invasion and occupation saw it all crumble, bit by bit. And we've spent a great deal of time trying to recover, rebuild. But for someone who didn't see it happen . . . only the aftermath . . . well, I'm sure Malcolm needs time to put things into perspective."

Just then, a little girl of about six or seven years of age peered around the corner of the porch.

Seeing her, Kate called, "Don't play shy, little Dru! Come on out, precious, and meet our company."

Right away the child ran to Dove, who put an arm around her and drew her close. From this safe haven, the little girl peeked at Blythe's mischievous blue eyes.

Her masses of dark curls were tied back with wide, white satin ribbon, and she was wearing a starched, ruffled pinafore over a pink candy-striped dress. Blythe thought she had never seen such an enchanting child.

"This is Druscilla Montrose, Leighton and Dove's little one. Say 'hello' to your new Auntie Blythe," Kate instructed.

The child dimpled and put one finger to her mouth, squirmed a little, but managed the greeting as she had been asked. Then she whispered something in Kate's ear.

"Where are your manners, sweet?" admonished Dove. "We don't whisper in front of company."

Kate laughed indulgently. "She just wanted to know when the tea party was going to be. Very soon, darling," she told the child. "I see Mina coming with the tray now."

An elderly black woman shuffled out onto the porch, and Rod rose to help her with the tray of refreshments.

"Mina," Kate said, "this pretty young lady is Mr. Malcolm's new bride."

The old woman grinned a toothless smile and bobbed a little curtsy toward Blythe. "Pleased to meet you, ma'am. Mistuh Malcolm is a fine gen'lmun."

After Mina had made a painfully slow exit, Dove poured tea, adding lemon, sugar, and sprigs of fresh mint as she passed the cups. "We—Dru and I—lived at Montclair during the War," Dove explained to Blythe. "Of course Dru was just a baby and doesn't remember much about it. But the three of us—Cousin Harmony Chance, her little girl, Alair, Garnet, and I—and Miss Sara, of course, all stayed there together while the men were off fighting."

"And how is Sara?" Kate asked Blythe.

"I suppose she is as well as possible . . . under the circumstances," Blythe replied cautiously. "Of course, I've only known her a short time . . . and not at all before the accident—"

"Oh, very few did. That happened years and years ago. Malcolm was only five or six at the time." Kate shook her head sadly. "Sara was the most beautiful young woman I've ever seen—a charming hostess, an excellent horsewoman. That's why the accident was so devastating! You know Malcolm witnessed it, don't you? A very shocking thing for a child. I believe that to be the basis for his absolute devotion to his mother."

"Are you taking care of her then?" asked Dove. "I know how she depended so on Rose—" Dove stopped mid-sentence, her face going pink. "Oh, dear! Forgive me, Blythe."

"There's nothing to forgive. Of course, I know about Rose," she said, flushing a little herself as three pairs of eyes regarded her.

"Well, of course, you would," Kate interjected smoothly. "Sara has a habit of making people her slaves. Maybe I shouldn't say that, but after her maid Lizzie left—ran off up North by the Underground Railroad, some think—Rose took over. Then, after poor Rose died, Garnet stepped in, so I know how demanding Sara can be. Not to be uncharitable, but just to warn you, dear Blythe . . . you must not let yourself be trapped into becoming her maidservant. If you're not careful, Sara will monopolize both of you, and you and Malcolm must have a life of your own."

At that moment little Dru, jiggling in her chair, tipped it precariously, and the ensuing scramble to keep her from spilling the contents of her glass provided a distraction that ended the discussion, to Blythe's immense relief.

The little girl seemed to be the joy of the three adults and, without being the least spoiled, added a sparkle to the afternoon. Blythe could not help thinking wistfully how different things might be at Montclair if there were a child.

But how could that ever be? Malcolm would never be a true husband to her as long as he was obsessed with Rose. Even in death, Rose was the true mistress of Montclair . . . and of her husband's heart.

Unconsciously, Blythe shivered.

"Are you getting cold, dear?" Kate asked solicitously. "Perhaps it is getting too shady on this side of the porch. Suppose we move our chairs into the sunshine."

Jolted from her morbid thoughts, Blythe said quickly, "Oh, no, I'm fine! But I think I'd best be going. I promised Malcolm's mother I would be back by four."

Rod got to his feet, followed by the ladies.

Spontaneously, Kate hugged Blythe. "I'm so glad you came. I feel I'm beginning to know you already. Please come anytime and . . . if you ever need to talk—" Her kind eyes held Blythe's for a long moment. "It must be lonely for you sometimes. Montclair is the most isolated plantation in this part of the county. But we shan't let you be a stranger here. Do remember that."

chapter
13

Kate Cameron's parting words remained with Blythe as Rod handed her into the carriage and they started down the drive back to Montclair.

"Your mother's so lovely and so kind," she said. "She made me feel very much at home . . . me . . . a *stranger!*" Blythe shook her head wonderingly.

Something curious flickered in Rod's eyes as he asked, "Haven't you ever heard the biblical admonition, 'Do not forget to entertain strangers for by doing so, some have entertained angels unaware'? Maybe my mother thinks you're an angel."

Blythe blushed, knowing he was teasing her. "Well, all the same, it makes me feel very warm and happy," she replied. "You're very lucky, you know, to have your mother still. My mother died when I was just a little girl, younger than Dru."

"I'm sorry," Rod spoke gently.

"But, of course, I barely remember her," she hurried on, hoping he had not thought her self-pitying. "Pa was wonderful, and the women in Lucas Valley were all real good to me—helping him out with my clothes, teaching me to sew and cook—"

Rod nodded, and a little smile tugged at the corners of his mouth. "All very useful knowledge, I'm sure."

"Oh, yes. Every woman, no matter how privileged, should know how to cook and sew and run a household." She stopped, realizing she was engaging in "prattle," in Malcolm's words. Then, "I liked Dove right away, too. They were both so nice to me."

"Why wouldn't they be? You're easy to be nice to."

Blythe glanced at Rod, then down at her hands folded in her lap, not certain how to reply.

They jogged along the road without talking for a time before Rod asked, "Tell me, did Malcolm find any gold out there?"

Surprised that this had not been discussed on the first night he and Malcolm had stayed up so late talking, she answered, "Well, not much anyway. And what he did find was stolen."

Rod shook his head. "Too bad."

She nodded. "Gold fever! That's what Pa called it. It makes people crazy, he said. They'll do anything—steal, lie, even kill for it."

"But your own father was a miner, wasn't he?"

"Yes, but Pa was one of the lucky ones," Blythe said. "He came to California not long after they found gold at Sutter's Mill. After my mother died, he had a couple of good claims, both rich. So he took me to Sacramento, put me in a convent boarding school there, then went back to the gold fields. He stayed three years working his claims and saved enough to buy the land and some livestock and build the house."

"Your father was wise. I've heard tales of so many who struck it rich, then squandered it all."

"I know. I heard him tell Sister Helena when he came to take me home with him, 'There's the gambler's risk and there's being a fool, and I'm neither one. Sure, I could go on prospecting. There're still untapped mines in those mountains. But I've got my health, and this little daughter of mine to think about.'" She paused, looking at Rod, wondering if she had said too much. "Anyway . . . that's how we came to be in Lucas Valley."

"And Malcolm stayed on with you?"

She explained how her Pa had taken a liking to Malcolm from the beginning, how they had sat for hours on winter evenings, drawn up in front of the pot-belly stove talking about books while she listened. She felt the familiar twinge of homesickness, a fresh wave of grief.

"Then what happened? When he was well, why didn't Malcolm go back to his mine or come home to Virginia?"

Blythe shook her head. "I don't know. Sometimes he'd talk about Virginia. Montclair. He said it had been his dream to find gold, make his fortune, and come back here to rebuild the plantation. Well . . . after all that happened, and with so little family left . . . I guess he thought he hadn't anything to come home to. That's when he told us about his wife and little boy."

Rod deliberately slowed the horse from a trot to a walk as they neared the turn-off to Montclair. "What changed his mind?"

"Pa's death, I think," Blythe answered. Rod seemed to be waiting for her to continue, so she took a long breath and told him about the accident, about her need for Malcolm's help on the ranch. "A few weeks before Pa died, Doc Sanderson tried to prepare me, even suggested a place in town where I could live. But, of course, that wasn't necessary."

"How was that?" Rod asked.

Blythe turned to him, her eyes wide. "Why, there was Malcolm! He wanted to marry me, to take care of me."

There was a long pause, then Rod slapped the reins and the horse trotted obediently up the road leading to Montclair. "I see."

Blythe felt a sense of uneasiness. Maybe she had said too much. Malcolm might not be pleased. But Rod was so kind, so caring, and she had not had anyone to talk to in such a long time—

Long shadows were criss-crossing the overgrown yard in front of Montclair as Rod reined to a stop in front. Blythe hopped down without waiting for him to come around and assist her.

"Thank you so much. I had such a good time. Please tell your mother again how much I enjoyed the afternoon."

"Our pleasure," Rod said, lifting the brim of his hat slightly. "Regards to Malcolm . . . and to Mr. and Mrs. Montrose."

"I'll tell them," she promised and then turned and ran lightly up the steps and into the house.

The first thing Blythe saw upon entering was Malcolm's trunk to the left of the front door. The second was Malcolm himself, coming down the stairs with Sara's tray in his hands.

"You're late," he said in mild reproval.

Blythe darted a glance at the grandfather clock in the corner of the hall. The hands pointed to nearly five.

"I'm sorry!" she apologized, knowing that, if Rod hadn't slowed down while she was telling her story, they would have arrived on time. "Was your mother upset?"

"No, I was in her room at four, so I just came down and prepared her tea myself."

"It won't happen again," Blythe said contritely. She had so wanted to be dependable, to fulfill her duties to her mother-in-law so Malcolm would be pleased.

"Fortunately, I was here . . . *today*. But you must make sure to be here when she needs you while I'm away."

"Away?" Blythe was stunned. Then she looked at the trunk by the door. "Are you going away?"

"Yes. I've decided to go to Massachusetts, to Milford. I'm catching the early train to Richmond in the morning, then on to Boston. I'll be seeing Jonathan."

"Jonathan! Oh, Malcolm, I'm so glad for you. I know how eager you must be to see him!" Blythe clasped her hands together with delight. Then she saw Malcolm's expression. He looked neither eager nor happy.

"You *are* happy, aren't you?" she persisted.

She saw the familiar tightening of his cheek muscle. "I'm not sure. I'm afraid he won't know me."

"But you're his father! Surely, he remembers. My mother died when I was very small, but I remember—" she said and moved to touch Malcolm's arm.

He flinched and shook his head slowly. "Well . . . we'll see."

"Will you bring him back to Montclair?"

A shadow darkened Malcolm's expression. "To what?" he asked. "What do I have to offer him now?"

"But a little boy should be with his father."

"His uncle—Rose's brother—has been like a father to him all these years I've been gone."

"But that's not the same."

Malcolm shrugged, and his broad shoulders sagged visibly.

Sensing his fear of disappointment, of what might await him in Massachusetts, Blythe spoke impulsively out of a heart longing to comfort him. "Malcolm, would you like me to come with you?"

He gave a short laugh. "Do you honestly think I could show up at Rose's family home with a new bride?"

Blythe felt the stinging rebuke as if it had been delivered by a slap of his open hand, but she masked the pain. "No, I suppose not. I didn't think—" she said quietly, then started toward the staircase. "I'll go up and explain to your mother why I was late, tell her about my tea with the Camerons."

But Malcolm's words halted her. "There's no need for you to do that. She was restless while you were gone, so I sat with her and we talked.

Then when I gave her tea, she took her laudanum, and I stayed with her until she fell asleep. You'll only disturb her if you go in now."

Her foot on the first step, Blythe's hand gripped the banister tightly. A sense of hopelessness dropped like a leaden weight upon her. What Malcolm was saying was that she wasn't needed . . . not by him nor by anyone else at Montclair.

chapter
14

BLYTHE STOOD at her bedroom window, looking out into the starless night. It was the second week of Malcolm's absence and she was achingly lonely.

The house was quiet, Sara settled for the night and Mr. Montrose, shut up in the library, either lost in his memories, reading, or playing endless games of "Patience."

Bravely, Blythe battled self-pity. Today was her seventeenth birthday, and no one knew or cared. Pa had never forgotten her birthday. She fingered the gold locket he had given her two years ago. Inside, were pictures of himself and her beautiful young mother. These were only copies from the daguerrotype they had had taken on their wedding day. Both looked heartbreakingly young and happy, smilingly unaware of what life held for them.

And what does life hold for me? she asked herself. *What is to become of me?* Would her life go on and on in the same dreary pattern of days here at Montclair? Unchecked, two tears rolled out of her eyes and down her cheeks.

Ever since the afternoon she had spent with the Camerons, after glimpsing the gracious kind of life they led even in their reduced financial circumstances, Blythe could picture what life at Montclair must have been. She also realized how different *she* was from Kate Cameron and Dove, and probably Rose, too.

Blythe envied these women their inborn elegance, their poise, their easy confidence in their position. She was overwhelmed with all the things she did not know, the things instinctive in any true lady. Seeing the contrast, it was no wonder that Malcolm could not love her.

It wasn't just his obsession with the past, his continual mourning, that bothered Blythe. Somehow she knew she must change, must become like the other women in his life—not to replace Rose, but to earn her own right to his love and to give him back some joy, some reason to hope again. Surely they could build a life together . . . with Jonathan . . . and, perhaps someday, children of their own.

Finally, Blythe went to bed, the bed in which she had slept alone ever since her arrival at Montclair. Before she turned down the covers, she knelt at the foot and prayed, "Dear Lord, show me how to make Malcolm happy. Help me be a good wife, and a good mother to Jonathan if Malcolm brings him here. And bring Malcolm home soon."

The next morning, Blythe awoke to sunshine, and her natural good spirits and optimism returned. She was cheerful as she took Sara's breakfast tray up and helped her get settled on the sunny balcony opening off her bedroom. She listened to her mother-in-law's complaints with patient good humor.

As Blythe was coming downstairs, Mr. Montrose emerged from the library. He gazed at her with a puzzled expression for a moment as if he could not recall who she was. Then he seemed to remember. "Good morning, my dear. I was just going up to read to Sara for a while. But now that you're here, I'd like to speak to you, if you have time."

"Yes, of course, Mr. Montrose," Blythe said, setting down the wicker basket she was carrying and following him into the library.

She was always impressed with the man's dignity and bearing. Although stooped of shoulder now and walking with the stiffness of premature aging and arthritis, he was still a handsome man. From his portrait on the hall alongside that of Sara, she knew he had been robust, bursting with health and vigor. His thick wavy hair was now snowy, and the face deeply lined. He was meticulously groomed, his thin white shirts always immaculate and his shoes shined, even though his clothes were shabby and worn.

She could not forget that this man was the father of three brave sons. He had once owned two hundred slaves, acres of productive land, a stable filled with fine-blooded horses, presided over a home known for its lavish entertaining and gracious hospitality. He had served his nation and then his state within the Confederacy, loyally and bravely . . . and he had lost it all.

Blythe was reminded of Job, and the verse from the Scriptures flashed through her mind: "I will restore the years the locusts have eaten." Would the Montrose family be restored, the years of deprivation, poverty, and loss assuaged? Not in Clayborn Montrose's lifetime, she sadly feared.

"I was planning to wait until Malcolm returned, but since consulting with Dr. Myles, I decided it would be better to tell you now so that you can help prepare Sara and our son for their parting."

"Parting?"

"Yes, it has come to that, I'm afraid. Sara's health is deteriorating. Of course, none of us ever entertained the illusion that she would regain the use of her legs. But now the prolonged immobility has caused other problems. No need to explain the details, but the fact remains that eventually she will need round-the-clock attendance. As you undoubtedly have observed, her emotional health is also fragile—" He paused and looked off into the distance, as if trying to recall the Sara of his youth. "She and Malcolm have always been unusually close, and, during his long absence, she . . . well, she became dependent on laudanum." He rubbed a blue-veined hand across his forehead as if it pained him to say all this. "A dependency, I might add, that was increased by bouts of despondency . . . melancholia, I think is the medical term. Dr. Myles believes Sara would be better off in a less isolated environment. That is why I'm planning to take her to Savannah."

"Savannah?"

"Yes. Her younger sister lives there, and there are many other relatives as well, cousins and so on. We can live nearby, and she will be surrounded with sociability, young people, visits from old friends. It will give her a new lease on life. At least that is what Dr. Myles thinks . . . hopes . . . and I concur. Especially, since—if anything happened to me—she would have no one but Malcolm."

"But you have me now!" Blythe said. "You know I would help in any way."

"Of course, my dear. I'm sure you would. You have shown yourself to be very willing, very helpful, but you must see that this would be a far better plan . . . for Sara, for me, for all of us. You and Malcolm need to get on with your own lives. Montclair belongs to Malcolm now." He sighed heavily. "I'm afraid I haven't the heart for it."

Blythe's own heart went out in compassion to this still proud man.

"I can't deal with the new order—all this—" He gestured toward the window where they could see the fields unplowed, left to brush and

105

weeds, the fences unmended. "Every day I look out and feel all the disillusionment and discouragement sweep over me. No, it will take a younger man—someone with energy and enthusiasm and vision to rebuild Montclair."

Blythe felt a sinking sensation. Malcolm was not the man Mr. Montrose was describing. In fact, Malcolm's own view of Montclair and the future was equally as depressing as his father's.

"When will you go?" she asked.

"I talked with Sara's sister when I was in Savannah a few months ago. There had been some provision made for Sara in her stepmother's will, only a small sum, but it should provide for her reasonably well for the rest of her life. And of course, she will be near close relatives who would be there to care for her if—"

He left the sentence unfinished, and with a little thrust of alarm, Blythe wondered about the state of his own health.

"Malcolm will be sad to see you go. He spoke so affectionately of his parents, of his home here when he was out West with us," she said softly.

Mr. Montrose turned, so, she suspected, she could not see the sudden brightness of tears. "Yes, well those were happy days when the boys were young—Malcolm, Bryce, and Leighton, all of them and their friends. Yes, indeed. But that was long ago . . . and life goes on, however much we would hold on to it." He lowered his voice to a husky whisper. "If only our minds, our memories would retain what the inscription on the sundial in Noramary's garden declares: 'I count only the sunny hours.'"

Blythe knew he referred to the first Montrose bride, Noramary Marsh, the English beauty who had laid out a garden here like one at her childhood home in Kent.

A silence fell over the room as Mr. Montrose composed himself. Turning to face Blythe once again, he said, "I think we will take Sara's maid and Joseph with us. Joseph has been with me since boyhood. All these details will be settled. The move must be made as easy for Sara as possible, of course."

Blythe, feeling herself dismissed, stood. "I will do all I can to help."

"Yes, child, I know." Then he looked at her, his gaze seeming to focus clearly on her. "When we are gone . . . when you and Malcolm are here alone together . . . try to be happy."

It seemed a strange thing for him to say, and Blythe felt her throat constrict. It was as if, in spite of his distracted air most of the time, Mr. Montrose had sensed that there was something wrong, something disturbing about his son's relationship with his new bride. But there was nothing he could do about it . . . nothing at all.

chapter
15

As soon as Sara was told about the plans to go to Savannah, she vacillated between excitement and tears. Although Mr. Montrose had assured her that they were only going for an extended visit, day by day she grew increasingly agitated—as if sensing the permanence of the move and all that it implied.

She had Blythe remove the drawers from her bureau and bring them to her, one after the other, so she could go over the contents. She folded and put some things aside, directing Blythe as to which things should be packed in the deep, hump-backed leather trunk that stood open beside the chaise lounge.

Then, one morning after Cora had finished her cleaning chores and left the room, Sara whispered, "Blythe, I want my jewel case. We devised a hiding place during the War when we lived in fear that those awful Yankees might come back at any moment. It was a good thing, too, because they raided here several times and ransacked and stole almost everything! Oh, it was dreadful!" Sara paled at the memory. Then she beckoned Blythe nearer. "In my dressing room, under the rug, there are a few loose boards in the flooring. With a little pressure, one end will tip up. The case is under there."

Blythe did as she was told and found a large, square leather box. It was quite heavy, but she managed to lift it out, then wiped off the dust and brought it over to Mrs. Montrose.

Sara took a tiny key from a chain she wore around her neck under her ruffled peignoir and unlocked the box. She opened the lid then said, in a trembling voice, "Imagine! These might have fallen into the hands of those rascals!"

With that, she drew out a rectangular dark blue velvet case from the depths of the box and touched a spring lock that flipped back to reveal an exquisite ruby and diamond brooch and matching pendant earrings. The jewels sparkled into Blythe's dazzled eyes.

"Have you ever seen such a magnificent set?" asked Sara, watching Blythe's reaction. "It is called the Montrose bridal set, passed from generation to generation and worn on only the most special occasions . . . although, I must confess, I wore it often. Clay wanted me to—" The faded blue eyes took on a dreamy quality as if peering into the past. "He loved showing them off, and showing me off as well. Perhaps you wouldn't believe it now, but I was once very beautiful—" A note of melancholy crept into Sara's voice, and one thin hand went to her face as if to recall its once smooth, unlined perfection.

Blythe quickly contradicted her. "But you still *are*."

Sara shook her head impatiently. "I have mirrors, child, and I'm not blind. All that is past, and I hope I am past the vanity of my youth." She gave a little toss of her head. "You, of course, will now have the privilege of wearing them . . . one day when Montclair again throws open its doors."

This prediction had a particularly hollow ring, Blythe thought. She knew that, given its present condition, its present master, that day might be long in coming.

Sara closed the jewel case and replaced it. Then, one by one, she showed Blythe her other treasures—a strand of lustrous pearls, earrings with pear-shaped pearls, a filigreed necklace of delicate gold and opals. There were enameled bangles and flower-shaped pins and a mourning set of shiny jets, which Sara held up with a half-jesting remark. "This I should probably wear all the time."

Finally, Sara took something from the very bottom of the box, and held it cupped in both hands for a moment before she opened her palm and held it out to Blythe.

"This, my dear, is the legendary Montrose betrothal ring, crafted to order long ago in Scotland for Montrose men to give to their chosen brides." Sara placed the ring in Blythe's hand, and she took it, examining the mellow gold heart-shaped setting in which a deep purple amethyst was held by two tiny sculptured hands. "In those days, there was a betrothal ceremony almost as binding as the wedding service itself. In fact, if a betrothal pact was broken on either side, it sometimes resulted in clan wars or, in later days, a duel or blood feud," Sara said dramatically.

"Of course, even in more civilized times, betrothals have been regarded as sacred and, if an official engagement is broken for any reason, it constitutes a betrayal of trust, a blot on the family name. In fact—" Sara warmed to her role as storyteller, her voice growing stronger with the telling— "the story goes that the first bride to come here to Montclair came as the result of a broken engagement— Noramary Marsh. Her cousin, Winifred Barnwell, was Duncan Montrose's intended bride, but she ran off with her French tutor practically on the eve of the wedding, it is said. Anyway, I myself never wore that ring. Clayborn gave me this ruby and diamond ring before we were married, and it seemed more suitable . . . for *me*."

Blythe's glance moved to the huge glowing red stone surrounded with brilliant diamonds flashing on Sara's slender finger.

"But . . . you surely don't mean for me to have this, do you?" Blythe asked in awe, looking from the betrothal ring back to Sara.

"Indeed I do. I notice you are wearing only a simple band. And I know dear Malcolm did not make the fortune he sought in the West and has come back here with no means at all." She made a hopeless gesture. "And if he came into any money, there is so much that has to be done to refurbish this house, reclaim the land—" Her voice trailed away significantly. "Besides, who is to inherit it, if not you?"

At this question, Sara's eyes filled with tears. "Malcolm is the last of the Montrose men. Don't you realize that with him the family will end unless . . . unless you have children . . . a son?"

"But what about Jonathan?" Blythe asked. "Don't you think Malcolm will bring Jonathan back with him to Montclair?"

Sara's mouth twisted, and she shook her head. "I doubt it. Garnet and I discussed it many times while Malcolm was away . . . not hearing from him in so long, not knowing if he'd ever return—" She paused for a moment, thoughtfully fingering some of the jewelry as she began to put the pieces back into the box. "The Merediths—Rose's family, her brother actually—are enormously wealthy—own mills. They made a fortune during the War, manufacturing uniforms for the Yankee Army." Her mouth curled in contempt. "After the War, John Meredith wrote Garnet that it was his sister's wish that Jonathan come North. Her father was getting on in years, and he had only seen his grandchild once when Rose took him there as a baby."

"After Rose died and Malcolm went West," she went on, "Garnet felt honor-bound to carry out Rose's wish, so she took the boy to meet his uncle. That was over three years ago. I'm sure Jonathan has almost forgotten his life here, his Southern relatives."

Sara wiped away the tears with the edge of a lace-trimmed handkerchief and said evenly, "Malcolm is a changed man, Blythe. You would have had to know him before to understand how drastically different he is now. I hesitate to say 'broken,' but defeat was never in his experience . . . and it is bitter. Perhaps, if Malcolm had been . . . lucky . . . out West? Perhaps if he had been able to do for Montclair all he had dreamed—" Again Sara sighed, lifting her shoulders helplessly. "It would take a miracle, I believe, to bring Malcolm back, to give him the incentive to begin again." Sara's gaze fastened on Blythe. "Maybe *you* could bring it about. You're young, full of life, and I know you love him. Love can sometimes work miracles. But . . . I don't know . . . perhaps it is too late, even for that—"

The silence that fell between the two women was heavy with unspoken doubts. Blythe felt the weight of the task Sara had bequeathed her, knowing her inadequacy.

"The only reason I agreed with Clay to go to Savannah, you know, was because I saw him growing older every day." Sara broke the silence at last. "Living here at Montclair the way it is now is like rubbing salt in his wounds. Why else would I leave all this? I am perfectly comfortable here. Oh, yes, I know I complain . . . a pampered invalid's old habits." She waved aside an imaginary rebuff. "But now I am to uproot myself, accommodate myself to other people, a different routine, a strange place . . . yes, strange, for I've been away from Savannah for over thirty years. It is for Clay I'm doing this."

Blythe was amazed. She had observed Clayborn Montrose's devotion to Sara, but she had not suspected his wife's deep love for *him*.

Suddenly Sara looked very weary; the animation had left her expression, and the lines deepened in her face. "Put this back now," she sighed. "I feel very tired. I think I need to rest a little."

Blythe returned the box to its hiding place. She had slipped the betrothal ring into her apron pocket, not wanting to place it on her finger until she spoke to Malcolm about it. She was not even sure it would fit . . . or that she herself would ever fit the image of former Montrose brides.

As she arranged Sara's pillows more comfortably behind her head,

Sara grasped her wrist with one thin hand. Looking up at Blythe with an expression of sympathy, she said, "Poor unsuspecting child. What have you walked into? But soon you will be rid of two burdens—a helpless invalid and a melancholy old man."

Blythe started to protest, but Sara interrupted. "Oh, my dear, I know, I understand. I came to this house as a bride, too, but it was so very different then. Montclair was blooming like the orchards and the gardens . . . ah, you've never seen such flowers. And the house was so splendid . . . everything in readiness for Clay's bride. A whole new world of luxury awaited me here. Nothing was forbidden to me, everything was possible. My word, my slightest whim was law. Every young woman should know such love, such happiness, such sweetness. . . . Even though it has all passed away now, and I've gone through the valley—" her voice broke a little— "I shall always have my memories . . . but what will you have? Poor, poor child."

When Blythe left her mother-in-law's suite, she felt strangely subdued. A lingering sadness followed her downstairs. She wandered directionless through the rooms, trying to imagine what it must have been like when Sara first came here. Sara and the others . . . Garnet and . . . Rose.

Suddenly, Blythe was gripped with a curious restlessness. She left the house, walking through the untended gardens, past the orchards, and along a worn path leading up a hillside. It led to a small graveyard. The Montrose family's burial ground!

Blythe pushed open the ornate black iron gate and walked in. Stepping reverently between the headstones, she found the one she was looking for:

ROSE MEREDITH MONTROSE
1839–1862
Beloved Wife of Malcolm
Mother of Jonathan
"Love Is As Strong As Death"

She stood for a long time reading the words engraved on the tomb, over which hovered the stone figure of a brooding angel.

A little vase of wilted black-eyed Susans had been placed at its base. By Malcolm before he left for Massachusetts?

Blythe picked up the arrangement, took it over to the edge of the cemetery, emptied it. Then she plucked some Queen Anne's lace growing wild nearby, filled the vase, and brought it back, placing it gently on top of the slab.

Kneeling, she began to whisper a prayer . . . no, it was more like a conversation: "Rose, I want to help Malcolm. I know he loved you and mourns you still. You'll always come first in his heart. I can accept that. And if he brings Jonathan home, I promise you I'll do all I can to make up to both of them for losing you."

chapter
16

STEPPING OUT onto the side porch one morning, Blythe felt a slight nip in the air that signaled the approach of fall, although it was only the first week in September.

Malcolm had been away for nearly a month. No one knew when he would be back. Not even his father had heard from him. Of course, Massachusetts was a long way, Blythe comforted herself, and travel difficult.

Suppressing a longing to escape the house and the overflowing basket of clothes waiting to be ironed, Blythe went back inside. There was no use waiting for Suzie to come or Cora, for that matter. They came whenever it suited them. Not that Blythe blamed them. They were paid very little, and they had their own families to care for, besides working alongside their husbands in the small plots of land former Montrose slaves had been given for their own use.

Lonnie was different. She came as regularly as clockwork to tend to Sara's rooms. She had been trained under the "late-lamented" Lizzie, she told Blythe, and her loyalty to the "Missus" ran deep.

Anyway, Blythe did not really mind the ironing. In fact, she rather enjoyed it when the weather wasn't too hot. She had always done up her Pa's shirts.

She set the flat irons on the small stove in the kitchen annex to heat. One thing about ironing, she thought, it left her mind free to wander at will. And, lately, there had been a great deal to think about—mostly about Malcolm and how things would be when he returned. If he brought Jonathan with him—and she sincerely hoped he would—she felt that the whole atmosphere of the house would take on a new vibrance and joy. Yes, Jonathan might be the answer. His coming would bring life and laughter to a house that had long been waiting for something . . . someone.

She picked up one of the irons, pressing the heel across the dampened, starched shirt, seeing the wrinkles vanish. *If only life's wrinkles could be smoothed out half so easily*, she mused. She turned the garment, again lifting the flatiron from the stove and banging it, hissing, against the collar of the shirt. As she worked, her constant question repeated itself. How could she become a woman Malcolm could respect, admire and, perhaps someday, even love?

Achingly anxious to please him, Blythe had observed Kate Cameron and Dove, tried to practice—when she was alone—how they moved, carried themselves, sat, lifted a teacup.

She had found a book on the shelves in the library, *The Lexicon of Correct English Usage,* had borrowed it and studied it when she was alone in her bedroom. She loved the library, not only because of the books, but because there was a portrait of Malcolm, standing proudly, handsome in his Confederate uniform, the gold epaulets and braid, the saber at his side.

It was a Malcolm Blythe had never known—young, vibrant, eyes full of hope, dark wavy hair untouched by silver. *This was the Malcolm both Garnet and Rose had known and loved*, she thought wistfully.

But Blythe tried not to dwell on these things. From early childhood, she had been taught three things that stood her in good stead during these difficult and often confusing days—to take things with a brave face, refusing self-pity; to follow through on all endeavors ventured; and, above all else, to be kind and cheerful.

It was the latter quality that was so much a part of Blythe's outlook that she was able to bring sunshine to the darkest days at Montclair. Buoying her spirits was a habit instilled at the convent school, that of beginning each day by asking God's blessing, reading a passage from her Bible, and praying. She had learned, from this practice, to anticipate answers to her prayers, thus building hope, strengthening faith. Indeed, the days did seem to pass much more happily.

Preoccupied with her own thoughts, a voice behind her saying, "It's much too nice a day to be inside!" made her jump.

Startled, she set down the iron, burning her finger in the process, and saw Rod Cameron at the open back door.

"Come on!" He motioned her out. "I've something to show you, a surprise!"

"A surprise?" she repeated, the burned finger at her mouth. Her eyes, alight with childish excitement, were damp. She pushed back the coppery curls clinging to her forehead and smiled at Rod expectantly. "What kind of surprise?"

"Come with me and you'll see," he urged, holding out his hand.

She whisked the half-done shirt off the ironing board and stood the iron on its end, then took Rod's hand and ran with him down the porch steps.

A sleek, chestnut-colored horse was tethered beside Rod's roan, its arched neck and flowing blond mane tossing skittishly.

"Oh, what a beauty!" she breathed in a soft voice, approaching it quietly, then gently stroking the velvety nose.

"I brought her over for you to ride," he told her.

"For me?"

"Yes, I remembered hearing you say that you rode into town to school from your ranch, and guessed you must miss riding. Since they don't stable horses at Montclair now, I thought you might enjoy a ride."

"Today?"

"Of course, today." He smiled at her.

"Oh, I don't know—"

"Why not? There's no reason, is there?"

"I was ironing—"

He dismissed the chore with a wave of his hand. "Oh, the ironing! The ironing can wait," he chided her gently. "Don't make excuses, Blythe. You know you want to come."

"But there's Mrs. Montrose—"

"Mrs. Montrose was a fine horsewoman in her day. She'd be the first to insist on your taking time out on such a fine day."

Tempted, Blythe still protested. "But, Rod, I see you have her saddled. I usually rode bareback on the ranch or sometimes—" she blushed— "astride. I'm not sure I could manage a side-saddle."

"I'll teach you. After all, that's my profession, you know." He made an elaborate bow. "Besides, my horses need exercising, so you'll be doing me a favor. Now, don't dream up any more excuses."

"Well . . . I'll go see if Mrs. Montrose needs anything first."

He smiled broadly. "All right, but hurry! We're wasting time."

To her surprise, Sara raised no objections, merely asked Blythe to fetch another shawl and a book and some fresh water before she left.

"I think you'll find an old riding habit of Garnet's somewhere and a pair of boots if you need them," she suggested. "You're about her size."

Within minutes, Blythe was buttoning on a riding skirt she found in the room Garnet had vacated in such a hurry. It was rather short, for she was an inch or two taller than Garnet, but the boots fit, and she hurried downstairs and out to the drive where Rod was waiting.

He gave her a hand up, showed her how to throw her leg over the saddle bar, and she picked up the reins, again following his direction.

"There, you see. It's easy. We'll take it slow at first and follow the path through the woods."

He swung up onto his own mount, then came alongside her, smiling his encouragement.

Keeping the horses to a walk, they went down the driveway, then cut over into the meadow, crossed a narrow rustic bridge, and moved into a gentle canter on a woodland bridle trail.

Blythe could not help smiling. Everything about this experience— the breeze on her face, the easy rocking motion of the horse beneath her, the sun playing on them in shifting light and shadow as they rode through the pine-scented woods, Rod at her side—all elicited a delicious warm glow.

Presently, they came to a clearing. Beside a mossy-banked stream overhung by willows, where water rushed over the rocks in a miniature fall, Rod dismounted. He covered the distance between them in an easy stride. She placed her hands on his shoulders, and he lifted her down.

This close to him, so close she could smell the leathery scent of his vest, the sun-warmed cotton shirt, Blythe's pulse quickened. She realized that she had never been this close to any man, except for her father . . . or Malcolm.

Not in months, however, even to Malcolm—not since the day Pa died and Malcolm, in comforting her, had put his arm around her shoulder and she had rested her head against him, sobbing. But never since had Malcolm embraced her, held her, kissed her. She had waited, hoping desperately that he might come to her—

Blythe thrust away these troubling thoughts, aware that she and Rod were still standing only inches apart. She stepped back, a little awkwardly and Rod simply moved over to the edge of the hill to look down at the stream.

As she followed, Blythe was newly aware of his rugged good looks. She wondered why he had never married. Had he left a sweetheart behind when he went away to the War and returned to find her, unwilling to wait for him, married to another?

Blythe's musings were diverted by Rod's beckoning motion. "Look. Here. The water is so clear you can see the fish," he said, pointing to a flash of silver in the sun-dappled stream below.

For a while they watched quietly, then Rod looked at her, saying, "Blythe is such a pretty name, unusual. How did you come by it?"

"It may sound silly but rather sweet, really. Did you ever hear the old rhyme—

> Monday's child is fair of face;
> Tuesday's child is full of grace;
> Wednesday's child is loving and giving;
> Thursday's child works hard for a living;
> Friday's child is full of woe;
> Saturday's child has far to go;
> But the child who is born on the Sabbath day
> Is blithe and bonnie and good and brave.

"And since I was born on a Sunday—"

"They called you Blythe," he finished for her. "'Blithe and bonnie and good and brave,'" he recited quietly. "It suits you," he said softly.

She was suddenly conscious of Rod's gentle gaze resting upon her. And something more. She saw in his eyes a look she had never seen before . . . nor in any man's eyes. All at once something swept over her, a breathless sensation of excitement and—danger!

Abruptly she turned away and started toward her horse, calling over her shoulder, "I must be getting back. Mrs. Montrose likes to have her tea and cake promptly at four."

Rod followed, holding the horse's head while she swung into the saddle.

"Well, there's always tomorrow," he said confidently. "With the students away for the summer holiday, I really need to keep these horses fit. You'd be rendering a great service . . . and a personal favor . . . to help me exercise them each day."

Blythe hesitated for some inexplicable reason, then looking into Rod's clear eyes, his direct expression, she thought, why not? Rod was

Malcolm's friend and now he was offering to be hers. And Blythe needed a friend. What harm could it do to accept? So she smiled and said, "Yes, I'd like that."

"Good. Then it's settled." Rod gave her a little salute before he swung into his own saddle, and they turned their horses toward Montclair.

chapter
17

THEREAFTER, Rod arrived every afternoon with two horses. Blythe was always waiting eagerly. Their daily ride had become the high point of the otherwise monotonous pattern of days at Montclair.

One afternoon, when Rod walked in through the kitchen door as had become his habit, he was carrying a bouquet of yellow roses.

"The last of Mama's roses until next year, I'm afraid." He held them out to her. "She picked them for you."

"Oh, how lovely!" Blythe gave a small cry of pleasure and came forward to take them. Their fragrance filled the room, and she buried her face in their dewy freshness. "Mmmm, how sweet they smell."

Rod watched with an unexpected little catch in his heart as she bent over them, then lifted her head to smile at him.

"Mrs. Montrose will enjoy having some in her room. It was thoughtful of your mother to send them, Rod." Still holding the bouquet, Blythe turned to the cabinet behind her. "One of the crystal vases should do nicely."

As she started to arrange the flowers, one of the top-heavy blossoms dropped onto the table, the stem breaking about halfway down. "Uh-oh!" She took it up, held it to her nose, breathing in its scent. She closed her eyes for a moment. "Too bad!" she said, laying it aside and putting the finishing touches on the arrangement.

Satisfied, Blythe picked up the vase. "I'll just take this up to Mrs. Montrose, then we can go for our ride," she said, and hurried out of the kitchen.

Once she was gone, Rod picked up the discarded rose still lying on the table, held it to his lips, then slipped it into his jacket pocket.

In Blythe's memory, that afternoon always shone with a particular brilliance—the sky, a cloudless blue; the woods and fields, breathtaking in their splendor; the gum and oak trees, a deep crimson; the maples, gleaming with gold.

They rode the ridge straddling both Montclair and Cameron Hall properties and commanding a view of the entire valley. It was from that vantage point she glimpsed a clearing, where the sun sent cathedral-like rays of light slanting through the tall trees. Nestled behind a clump of maples was a cottage, its sloping roof, dormer windows and columned porch reminiscent of another.

"Oh, look, Rod!" exclaimed Blythe, drawing rein. "What a darling little house! It looks just like—"

"Montclair." He nodded. "It was the model of the big house. They used to build them to scale in the olden days so that the owners could actually see how their mansions would look, and—" he added— "to make any changes at that time instead of having to correct them later, a process which would be both time-consuming and expensive. Of course, expense was relatively unimportant since most of the work was done with slave labor. Thank God, we have rid ourselves of that blight, at least."

"Can we go inside?" Blythe was fascinated with the doll-like house.

"I don't think so. It hasn't been used for years—not since before the War, I'm sure. That's why it's shuttered and probably locked."

They dismounted, and Rod tethered the horses loosely, allowing them to graze.

Blythe twisted the bottom of her skirt and knotted it to one side so that it wouldn't drag, then began to explore the grounds. What seemed to have been a planned rock garden was now overgrown, but abloom with colorful wildflowers—purple asters, goldenrod.

On one side of the cottage was a latticed arbor with clusters of golden grapes hanging from the vines.

"Oh, look, Rod! Grapes!" she called to him.

He followed her under the arching shelter. "Scuppernongs," he told her. "They've a marvelous flavor. I think they used these to make wine at Montclair." Rod took out his pocket knife, cut off a bunch, and handed it to Blythe, then cut another for himself. They seated themselves on the bench built around the inside of the arbor.

"Mmm, delicious," Blythe murmured as she popped one into her mouth, savoring its tangy-sweet juice. "I suppose it's all right for us to help ourselves!"

Rod held up the cluster, spinning it around in small circles so that the sunlight glistened off the rounded orbs.

"By all means! I even have scriptural permission," he said, looking at her with one eyebrow raised, mischief in his eyes.

"Scripture?" She tilted her head to one side and looked skeptical.

"Certainly. And I quote Deuteronomy 23:24: 'When thou comest into thy neighbour's vineyard, then thou mayest eat grapes, thy fill at thine own pleasure; but thou shalt not put any in thy vessel.' Well, I have no intention of taking any away!" he said in mock seriousness.

Blythe laughed merrily, the sound of her own laughter startling her. How long had it been since she had experienced anything so delightful?

"What a pity no one knows about them now. They would make wonderful jelly," she said, popping yet another into her mouth. She had spoken with her mouth full, and the juice spurted out from between her small white teeth and ran down her chin. "Whoops!" she said, trying to wipe away the juice with her fingers.

Rod took out his handkerchief and gently dabbed the trickles of grape juice while, with his other hand, he steadied her chin. The feel of his fingers on her face sent a curious tremor through her.

For a split-second Blythe looked into his eyes, so close she could see the iris. Then, she deliberately looked away, saying lightly, "So, then, you are a student of the Bible?"

"As a matter of fact, I am. But don't give me too much credit. You see, I was in a Yankee prison, captured after being wounded. And the only book in the whole miserable place was the Bible someone had left there. I'd always been a great reader and, until I got my hands on that book, I nearly went out of my mind! Reading it over and over, I memorized parts of it. You might say it not only saved my sanity . . . it saved my soul."

They sat there for a long time, eating grapes and talking easily. Blythe felt relaxed and comfortable, more herself than she had felt since coming to Virginia.

She leaned back against the latticework, relishing the warmth of the sun casting shadowy patterns on the uneven brick floor of the arbor, the softness of the breeze that stirred the leaves of the grapevines above, the sweet taste of the grapes still on her tongue. Everything shimmered with a very special beauty.

Time passed. Neither of them was aware of how long they had been sitting there until Blythe noticed the lengthening shadows and shivered in a subtle change in the wind.

"It must be getting late," she said. "I guess we should be starting back."

Rod sighed. "I suppose," he said reluctantly.

They rode silently along the alternate path that led to the road. At the gate to Montclair, Blythe dismounted and handed her reins to Rod.

"I'll walk up to the house from here," she told him.

"I hate to see this day end," Rod said.

"There's always tomorrow," Blythe reminded him.

"Yes . . . tomorrow," he agreed, but there was some doubt in his voice.

They said good-bye and Blythe wondered if he, too, had felt a kind of melancholy after they had ridden away from Eden Cottage. The small deserted house had held such promise of happiness in the past that seeing it abandoned made her feel somewhat sad. Like Rod, she wished the lovely glow of this day would never fade.

As she came in sight of Montclair, Blythe felt a sudden depression. She was just tired, she told herself. All she needed was to get her boots off and make herself some tea.

Then, just as she neared the porch steps, the front door opened, and Malcolm stepped out.

chapter

18

WITH ONE LOOK at Malcolm's gaunt face, Blythe's happy words of welcome died on her lips. He looked pale and deathly tired, his eyes more deep-set than usual, their clear blue darkened to the color of slate.

Before she could ask, he frowned and spoke sharply. "No, I didn't bring Jonathan. He's better off where he is . . . far better off. What do I have to offer him now?" The question was edged with despair.

A father's love, his grandparents, his heritage! Blythe stemmed her spontaneous answer. Even if Jonathan's wealthy uncle could provide him with many of the material advantages Malcolm could not, nothing could take the place of a parent's love. Blythe knew that so well herself. Even though she hardly remembered her beautiful, dark-eyed mother, her father's love had warmed, comforted, sheltered her all her growing-up years.

But Malcolm's stern expression halted any further discussion. "I've been up to see Mama," he told her. "She's ready for her tea."

He stood there for a moment, looking at her once again as if he were not sure who she was or what she was doing here. Then, abruptly, he turned and walked toward the library.

"It's good to have you back, Malcolm," Blythe called after him, but he did not reply. *Perhaps he didn't hear me,* she sighed, and went down the hall toward the kitchen to prepare Sara's tray.

Later, when she knocked at the library door to summon him to supper, Malcolm's voice sounded strangely slurred as he mumbled that he wasn't hungry.

Blythe, sitting opposite Mr. Montrose at the table, found it hard to swallow any food over the hard lump that kept rising in her throat. And her father-in-law seemed quieter, more distracted than usual. When he spoke, however, Blythe realized that he was keenly aware of this new tragedy in his son's life.

"What can we do?" he sighed, shaking his silvery head. His thoughts had simply found voice, for he looked at Blythe as though she knew exactly what was on his mind and heart. "We can't bring back the past, and that's where Malcolm is living. After the War . . . after Lee then Bryce . . . and for months we didn't know whether Malcolm was alive or dead . . . I told myself we had to go on. We are here for a purpose. God knows what it is. But we must go on!" He pounded on the table with his fist, nearly toppling the crystal tumbler near his plate.

Then he leaned forward, his blue eyes riveting on her. "You and Malcolm must have children, fill this house with the sound of happy voices, bring it to life again. Children would give Malcolm a reason to look to the future, to build Montclair again, to pass the heritage on—"

Blythe bit her lip to keep from blurting out her heartfelt cry. Yes, oh yes! But Malcolm never came near her!

"I must go up to Sara," murmured Mr. Montrose.

He rose, folded his napkin, and left it at his plate. Saddened, she watched as the tall man, his noble gray head bowed, walked away.

After she did up the dishes and put away the good linen cloth she had used to make the dinner hour special for Malcolm's return, Blythe took her lamp and slowly mounted the stairs to her bedroom. She paused for a minute outside the closed library door. Hearing nothing, she moved on.

In the bedroom, she poured water into her porcelain washbowl, undressed, and bathed. She put on a fresh nightgown and challis-flowered dressing gown, then took down her braids and began to brush her hair with slow, rhythmic strokes.

Brush in hand, Blythe moved over to the window and knelt down, her chin on the sill. Gazing out into the darkness, she thought of Mr. Montrose's impassioned words: "You and Malcolm must have children—"

She knelt a long time by the window. What was it all about? What was the meaning of it? Would she ever know . . . or understand?

This was one of those nights when the big bed seemed very lonely. She could not help wondering if Malcolm ever felt this same need to be held, comforted. He must feel this sense of incompleteness. Did it haunt his days and torment his nights? Of course, it must. *But it was Rose he longed for, not me,* Blythe sighed.

Downstairs, in the great library, a fire banked against the night chill, Malcolm relived his disastrous experience. He had left for Massachusetts with many misgivings and apprehensions. He had not seen the Meredith family since he and Rose had returned from their European honeymoon in 1858. In the meantime, she had died, killed in the tragic fire started by an accidental overturning of an oil lamp in her room at Montclair one night when she had gathered her servants there to teach them to read.

These lessons were conducted in utmost secrecy since it was against Virginia law to teach slaves to read and write. Malcolm had hated slavery as much as Rose had. But, until Rose's outrage forced him to do so, Malcolm would never have faced the issue. Then, when war came, his loyalty to family and state had impelled him to enlist in the Confederate Army. This had caused a bitter estrangement between himself and Rose. When he got word of the accident, he had rushed to her bedside, but it was too late.

All this, Malcolm knew, would be in the Merediths' minds when he arrived, bringing back all the senseless tragedy of Rose's death.

Added to that would be his reason for coming. Jonathan. This matter, too, would be fraught with old angers, for his son had been living with Rose's brother John, Malcolm's former classmate at Harvard and close friend. The sword of the states' conflict had severed their old friendship.

The journey north was slow and tedious. Meeting varying train schedules necessitated overnight stays along the route. To save expense, Malcolm had looked for the most economical accommodations and had often spent the night in shoddy hotels. The cost in discomfort, stress, and sleeplessness was great. Malcolm had forgotten the quickened pace of life in the North and felt affronted by the rudeness he seemed to encounter everywhere. The jostling crowds, the indifference of ticket agents, conductors, hotel clerks added to his disorientation. By the time he reached Boston, he was exhausted. Here he had to change trains again for the trip to Milford, where the Meredith family had lived for generations.

As the train rattled through the New England countryside, there was a glaring contrast between its unscathed loveliness and the battle-scarred, impoverished Southland he had left. When Malcolm arrived in Milford, he found the town enjoying a thriving prosperity, while in his mind were scenes of run-down plantations and deserted farmlands. Mayfield, the scene of many fierce skirmishes and occupations by both armies, had not yet recovered from its wounds. Nor had he.

As he walked along the tree-lined street of large, impressive homes set on well-kept lawns, his tensions mounted. Malcolm's heart was hammering, his mouth dry as he stopped before the gate of the Merediths' mellow brick Federal house. Here was Rose's home where he had first courted and come to love her.

He looked up at the imposing façade of the house, facing the green perfection of the town common. Its dark shutters framed the sparkling paned windows, hung with starched lace curtains. Seeing it again after all these years brought a rush of memories that left him weak.

How often he had hurried along this same street when he was visiting Rose from Harvard. For a few minutes Malcolm stood there, gathering his courage to open the gate, walk up the flagstone path to the shiny black door, and lift the polished brass knocker.

At last, conquering the urge to leave, he thrust himself through the gate with determined stride, walked up to the house, and knocked.

The door was opened by a rosy-cheeked young maid, wearing a black uniform. She took Malcolm's hat, asking in a decidedly Irish accent, "Who shall I say is callin', sir?" .

Obviously she was new. Always before he had been instantly recognized and welcomed by the Meredith servants.

"Malcolm Montrose," he replied.

At the name, her eyes widened noticeably. "Oh, yes, sir. Mr. John is expectin' you. You're to come into the parlor, and I'll be tellin' them you've come."

Leading the way through the hall, with its plush carpet and dark wainscoting, she opened double doors and ushered Malcolm into the elegantly furnished parlor. He might as well have been an unknown caller, an infrequent guest, a stranger, Malcolm thought with a trace of irony.

The maid closed the doors quietly behind her, leaving him standing alone in the center of the room.

Immediately his eyes fell on a portrait of Rose. Evidently it had been painted from a daguerreotype taken on their wedding day. His heart contracted as he beheld her once more in all the innocent radiance of that day, dressed in ivory silk, her dark hair covered with a filmy veil, held by a circlet of rosebuds. She smiled out of the picture, all hope and happiness shining out of those wonderful eyes.

His throat seemed to swell and his chest tightened until he felt he was suffocating. Unable to bear the pain, he looked away. As he did, he saw another gold-framed portrait of Rose's brother, John Meredith, resplendent in his blue Union Army uniform—sharply reminding Malcolm that he and his once close friend, his brother-in-law, had more recently been enemies.

The sound of the door opening brought Malcolm back to the present, and he turned to see his former classmate enter the room.

Expensively tailored, immaculately groomed, his handsome face smoothly shaven, John Meredith possessed all the poise and confidence that affluence and community status can give a man. Moreover, in the steel-gray eyes and carefully controlled expression, Malcolm could read the damage done to their relationship by time, distance, and conflict. All the camaraderie of their youthful friendship, even the closer ties brought about by his marriage to Rose were gone.

They met now as two men who had fought on opposite sides of the War that had deeply divided the country both their ancestors had fought to establish. Malcolm knew that the cords that had once bound them were irrevocably unraveled.

John's hand, when Malcolm offered his, was a brief handclasp with no warmth. His greeting, a simple, "Malcolm . . . a very long time. How was your journey?"

They exchanged a few irrelevant remarks about trains, travel in general, and the weather, then John cleared his throat. "I wanted to be here to greet you before you see Aunt Van and Father, prepare you . . . if that is the word. Of course they have both aged considerably since you last saw them. But more than that, the tragedy . . . Rose's death . . . has been a blow from which neither of them, I fear, will ever fully recover. You must expect that there will be some—no matter, how little-deserved—blame attached." John halted awkwardly. "We know, of course, it was an accident, one of those horrible twists of Fate. But they had both begged Rose to come home and bring Jonathan when the threat of war between our two . . . regions . . . was imminent. The fact that she stayed in the South. . . . Well, there is no use going into the sad outcome. I just wanted to warn you if anything is said inadvertently . . . you must allow them both the benefit of their years."

There was a significant pause before John continued. "They have agreed to receive you . . . for the sake of the memory of happier days . . . and, of course, as Jonathan's father."

"About Jonathan—" Malcolm interrupted. "May I see him now?"

"Jonathan is not here, Malcolm. He lives with my wife, Frances, and me in the country not too far from here, an hour's drive perhaps. We built a house near the lake. You will, of course, see him later after dinner with Father and Aunt Van."

There was a sound at the parlor door. "Here they are now," John said and went to admit two elderly people.

Mr. Meredith, once one of Malcolm's professors at Harvard, was now bent and fragile-looking, his hair a wispy white aura about his narrow balding head. He leaned heavily on the arm of his sister, Vanessa, who was still ramrod straight, holding herself with the same regal bearing Malcolm remembered, although she, too, was wrinkled and gray.

Afterwards, Malcolm wondered how he endured the next half-hour. The stiffly polite visit with Rose's father and the aunt who had reared her after her mother's death, was agonizing. Malcolm had been acutely aware of their cold reserve.

Thankfully, dinner was finally announced. But this proved even worse for Malcolm's already strained nerves. The fine meal was impeccably served by two white-gloved maids and expertly directed by the unsmiling butler standing by the Sheraton buffet. From that post, he orchestrated the passing of the silver platters of well-done roast, the fluted silver bowls of whipped potatoes, peas and pearl onions in creamy sauce. It was tediously long; and as course followed course, the conversation was stilted at best.

Malcolm tried to concentrate on the striped wallpaper with its alternating medallions and on the sculptured silver pheasants adorning the centerpiece. As graciously as possible, he answered the few questions targeted toward him, trying not to read into them any implications. Everyone behaved with absolute correctness. After all, the Merediths were guided by the same rules of etiquette, demeanor, and manners that Malcolm had been taught. That is what made it all so unbearable. Though both families had originally come from English nobility, linked by background and tradition, now the only thing that joined them was the common tragedy they had suffered—a tragedy, they all knew, would never have happened had Rose not been so foolish as to fall in love with a Southerner.

No one took more than a spoonful or two of the delicate caramelized cream dessert, and soon afterwards, Aunt Van excused herself, followed by Mr. Meredith, who advised Malcolm that his physician had ordered him to rest each afternoon.

Calling the butler over, John instructed him to serve coffee in the library and, rising, he said to Malcolm, "Let's go where we can talk privately."

When the butler had brought in the coffee service on an oval silver tray, poured the rich, fragrant brew into shell-thin Dubarry china cups, then discreetly disappeared, John began, in his well modulated, reasonable tone of voice. "Before you see Jonathan, I thought there were several things we should discuss. Frances and I have brought the boy up with our own two children, Ellen and Norvell, and love him equally. He is enrolled in Milford Academy, a fine preparatory school, and I have already registered him as a potential student at Harvard. Since he is an intelligent child, quick to learn, and good at sports as well, I have no doubt he will be accepted."

As John talked, Malcolm was acutely aware of the chasm between them. Despite their aristocratic roots, they now lived in different worlds—worlds that might as well be continents apart. Again, Malcolm felt the bitter gall of defeat—one more in the string of defeats he had experienced over the past ten years.

"So now that we understand each other," John was saying, "shall we drive out to the country? Frances has told Jonathan you're coming."

They maintained a stiff silence on the ride through the tranquil, New England countryside, which looked for all the world, Malcolm thought, exactly like one of the popular Currier & Ives prints. John's handsome landau was a deep maroon with gold trim, drawn by a high-spirited coal black horse. Malcolm knew good horseflesh, and this was one of the finest he had seen. Again, the goad of bitter resentment pricked painfully.

When they arrived, he saw that John's home was a "new" Victorian-style, three-story mansion, with veranda encircling the lower floor, and eaves and peaked roofs rising magnificently against the sky. The lawn was elaborately landscaped, with an iron stag in the center of the circular drive and manicured flowerbeds edging the smooth front lawn.

Frances Meredith met them at the door. She was tall and slim, with the same aloof, correct manner as Aunt Vanessa. Her fine features were set off by a lovely complexion, and her keen blue eyes were coolly appraising. As he bowed over the hand she extended, Malcolm sensed that she knew all about him and why he had come, and that she did not approve of either.

"I'll get Jonathan," she said after John made the introductions. "He's in the playroom upstairs with Ellen and Norvie." She turned and went swiftly up the winding, dark oak staircase, her pleated train swishing on the steps.

"Come. We'll wait in the front room." John led the way into a large, cheerful room, where a bright fire crackled in the wide fireplace.

Malcolm followed, looking about him with curiosity, noting the distinct difference between this house and the town house. Here, all was spacious and bright, with a plump, inviting sofa and comfortable chairs covered in a colorful fabric. There were pictures on the wall, and a spinet piano in one corner; bookshelves crammed with books, and windows all along one side of the room looking out on a tree-studded expanse of yard. It was a room that promised warm, congenial gatherings—a homey, happy place where children would be as welcome as adults.

This is where Jonathan was growing up, Malcolm realized, with a kind of painful relinquishment. Before he had even seen his son, Malcolm knew he could not take him away. What would Montclair seem like to someone who had lived *here*?

Lost in his own melancholy thoughts, Malcolm was unaware of anything else until he heard John say, "Come in, Jonathan."

Malcolm was attacked with a terrible fear, an emotion close to the panic he had once or twice experienced in battle. And then the slim, handsome boy entered, and Malcolm felt himself go weak with tenderness.

"Jonathan!" Malcolm spoke his name through stiff lips. With something like shock, he saw his own face at ten, looking back at him. But the eyes—oh, those eyes—were his mother's. Jonathan had Rose's enormous, dark eyes.

"Come in, Jonathan, and say 'hello' to your father," John coached as the boy looked at him anxiously.

Malcolm felt the drumbeat in his temple signaling the onset of one of the blinding headaches he had fallen prey to since his prison days. The throb became insistently sharper, bringing the accompanying blurring of vision, the agony of even the slightest turning of his head.

Somehow, the hour passed in an unreal spinning of time. John had considerately left him alone with Jonathan for a short period of time, but Malcolm had been too overcome to talk naturally or easily to his own son.

Gripped by the pain in his head and the waves of nausea, he declined Frances's invitation to stay for supper, but valiantly met the Meredith children—a pretty, shy little girl and a sturdy, tousle-headed boy. Then, refusing John's offer to drive him back into Milford, they looked up schedules instead, and John took him to the small train station to board an evening train back to Boston.

Malcolm slumped into the seat in the first compartment he stumbled into, and could scarcely remembered arriving at the huge, hollow Boston terminal, hiring a hack to his hotel, and falling into bed.

If anticipation of the trip to Massachusetts had been daunting, Malcolm's trip back to Virginia was worse. Depression replaced dread; remorse, anxiety, for the whole experience had confirmed his worst forebodings.

Malcolm delayed as long as possible his arrival in Montclair, staying overnight in Richmond, then forcing himself to travel on to Williamsburg for a visit to his Barnwell relatives, whom he had not seen since he had returned from California.

At the Mayfield train depot, when Malcolm arrived from Williamsburg, he spotted one of the black men, a sharecropper on Montrose land, loading supplies onto his wagon, and he hitched a ride with him out to Montclair.

As they came up the winding drive to the house, the whole disastrous journey hit in all its humiliating detail.

Blythe wasn't there when he walked into the house, a fact for which Malcolm was immensely grateful. He didn't want to face her right away with the news that he had not brought Jonathan with him. She had seemed so pitifully pleased with the idea. Poor thing. She was hardly more than a child herself, he thought ruefully. No doubt she had looked forward to having someone nearer her own age in the house—this house that was daily becoming more and more a mausoleum!

It was bad enough to have to tell his mother, who had thought it would be wonderful for Malcolm to have his son with him . . . and his father, who still lived with the impossible dream that the Montrose family would resume its proper position in the county . . . *as impossible as that the South would rise again*, he thought.

It had struck Malcolm anew as he had traveled through the small Southern towns outside Washington, how far from fulfillment that dream was for anyone who held it. All of these towns had the same downtrodden, battle-scarred look as Mayfield. There were no signs anywhere of pulling out of the war-imposed, impoverished state.

Malcolm came down the stairway after a long, wearying talk with his parents. Learning of their plans to move to Savannah, he felt bowed and burdened with all that meant—the full responsibility of restoring Montclair, of resurrecting its dying farmland, of life alone with a child bride with whom he had little or nothing in common.

He thought of Rose, and his inconsolable loneliness surged within, filling him with grief and regret. Rose, with her keen mind, her sparkling wit, her intelligence and beauty.

He banged his fist on the post of the banister as he reached the last step and walked out onto the porch, longing for some fresh air to clear his mind.

As he stepped outside, he saw Blythe coming up the drive. In the too-short riding skirt, her long hair swinging in braids, she looked about twelve years of age, and again Malcolm was wrenched with the improbability of his situation, his farcical marriage.

When she saw him, she broke into a run, calling his name. "Malcolm! Malcolm! I'm so glad you've come! Did you bring Jonathan?"

Later, he knew he had been unnecessarily harsh. He had answered her questions with cold abruptness and was ashamed when her eyes filled with tears.

But he couldn't handle her disappointment, her hurt. He had his own to deal with. He walked away from her and went into the library, shutting and locking the door behind him. He leaned against it, every muscle tense, every nerve twitching, biting his lip so as not to let the moan of despair emerge from his bruised and broken heart.

In the direct line of his vision stood the glass-fronted cabinet, some of its diamond-shaped panes smashed by the rifle butts of the Yankees who had raided Montclair. Its lock hung loose. Here, his father kept a few bottles of rare old brandy that had somehow escaped the horde of foragers who had emptied the wine cellar years before.

Malcolm stood for a long time staring at the cabinet, feeling the temptation for oblivion rising within him. Malcolm, who had never had more than an occasional glass of wine in a toast or champagne at a wedding, now felt the strong urge to lose himself in the bottle of amber liquid. He had had no taste for the raw whiskey swilled by the miners in the gold towns of the West, nor for the bourbon and branch sipped by his fellow card-players on the ship coming from California. But now the need to blot out the pain and emptiness stirred, becoming ever more demanding. He stood, fists clenched, hoping it would leave.

Then, impatiently, he walked across the room, yanked open the cabinet doors, reached in, brought out the decanter and removed the stopper.

chapter
19

AUTUMN CAME to Virginia in a blaze of brilliant color, turning the woods around Montclair into a glorious patchwork of russet, crimson and gold against the dark green background of cedars and spruce.

But in spite of the beautiful Indian summer, a pervasive melancholy persisted at Montclair. Ever since Malcolm had returned from his trip, he had become more reclusive, taking long solitary walks or shutting himself away in the library.

For Blythe, who loved people and had a natural capacity for gaiety and happiness and a longing to share it, this isolation was hard to bear. Helping Sara get ready for her move to Savannah came as a welcome diversion.

Mr. and Mrs. Montrose were to leave at the beginning of October while it was still warm so that Sara would not have to travel in inclement weather. Southern trains were still running unpredictably, with long delays at some stations, so every provision for her comfort along the way had to be arranged beforehand.

Malcolm would accompany his parents as far as Richmond, see them safely on the train, make sure their accommodations were adequate and that they would receive the best service available.

Blythe's daily rides with Rod had come to an end at the return of the students to Cameron Hall for the new term. If it had not been for Sara's constant demands, Blythe would have missed those afternoons even more because they had been the happiest she had known since coming to Virginia.

Blythe's days became busy assisting Sara with her preparations. Every item to take or leave was debated endlessly before a decision was made.

In this, Blythe proved indispensable. She listened with attention to all Sara's instructions, ran up and down stairs dozens of times every day to carry them out herself or to supervise some task. If Sara wanted something unpacked that had already been packed, Blythe complied without complaint, though she often had to bite her tongue to hold back a comment. Sara's nervousness was understandable, Blythe felt. After all, Montclair had been her home for thirty-five years.

Finally the day of their departure came. After Malcolm carried her out to the carriage for the first lap of their journey to Williamsburg, Sara called to Blythe, "Come here for a minute, child!" She beckoned her close.

Blythe leaned over, catching the scent of lilacs that always surrounded Sara like a delicate whisper. Framed by the shirred pink chiffon lining of her bonnet, Sara's complexion had taken on a youthful glow, and her eyes seemed again the deep violet-blue of the woman in her portrait.

"Take care of my darling Malcolm, won't you?" she asked. "I have lost my two other sons, and somehow I feel I have lost Malcolm, too. But maybe . . . maybe there is still a chance. . . . No matter how things look, there is always hope. Dear Rose taught me that. Perhaps I shouldn't mention that name, but I've always felt Rose was sent to give us all something, and I've come to believe her death that seemed so senseless had meaning, after all. She left her mark on all of us. So don't dwell in the past, Blythe, and don't let Malcolm do so, either."

Tears sparkled for a moment in Sara's eyes, making them glisten like sapphires. "It can't all have been for nothing, can it? The deaths . . . all the loss—" She touched Blythe's cheek briefly with one silk-gloved hand. "Good-bye, my dear, take care of yourself . . . and try to be happy."

Malcolm handed Blythe a ring of keys. "Have Lonnie stay overnight if you don't wish to be alone," he suggested. "I should be back within the week. After I see Mama and Father safely aboard the train, I may visit with some friends in Richmond . . . I can't be sure—"

From within the carriage, Sara's voice called, interrupting whatever else Malcolm was about to say. "Blythe, be sure Suzie and Cora come when they're supposed to and turn out my rooms. I want everything washed and cleaned thoroughly, then the furniture covered with dust cloths and my linens packed away in lavender so that they'll be fresh when I come back in the spring."

"Of course, I will!" Blythe replied over the lump in her throat.

For all the cheerful reassurances they had all made about Sara's return in the spring, Blythe felt sure none of them really believed it. She was so fragile, her health so precarious.

His mother's optimistic words seemed to grieve Malcolm. His expression underwent a change, then he spoke to Blythe briskly, "I'm sure you can take care of things, so we'd best be off." Again he seemed to hesitate as if there were something more he might say.

Blythe yearned to cling to Malcolm, beg him not to be gone too long. She had assured him that she would not be afraid to remain by herself for the days Malcolm would be away, and they had all taken her at her word. But now that the moment had come, Blythe felt somewhat shaken by the idea.

Malcolm did not linger but hurried down the veranda steps and into the waiting carriage. Blythe moved to the edge of the porch, waving and watching as the carriage finally disappeared around the bend of the drive.

At length, she turned and re-entered the house, her footsteps echoing hollowly on the bare floor. She stopped for a minute as the silence of the empty house dropped over her like a heavy cloak.

She stood quite still. Then, as if drawn by an unseen magnet, she turned and walked slowly down the hall to the downstairs suite known as the Master Wing, traditionally the rooms occupied by the Master of Montclair and his bride.

She had seen these rooms from outside and knew they were the ones Malcolm and Rose had shared. The windows were boarded up, and the inside doors never opened.

Her heart hammering, Blythe got out the ring of keys Malcolm had given her and, one by one, tried them in the lock. Finally, one gave a little, and she felt the knob turn under her clammy hand.

With a little shiver, she pushed the door open, inadvertently looking over her shoulder as if someone might see and try to stop her. The door creaked a little from long disuse as Blythe stepped into the darkened interior. A stale, acrid odor of smoke hung in the air. She moved into the center of the room, looking about her, half in awe, half in horror. It looked as if no one had touched a thing since the night of the disastrous fire that had taken Rose's life.

The bed curtains hung in charred strips from the blackened bedposts, the wallpaper's faded rose pattern was scorched and peeling, and no light at all seeped in through the boarded-up windows.

A slow sick feeling swept over Blythe, and her knees felt as if they wouldn't support her a moment longer. Cold perspiration beaded her forehead; a wave of nausea threatened to overtake her. She wiped her hands on her skirt, momentarily paralyzed, afraid she might faint.

The room was filled with frightening shadows, and an oppressive stillness shrouded the place. With a half-stifled scream, Blythe turned and stumbled out of the room.

chapter
20

THE NEXT MORNING, Blythe awoke to the sound of the soft voices of the Negro women under her open window as they arrived for work. She remembered with a start that she had asked them to come early to clean and straighten Sara's suite. As she got up and dressed, she felt stiff and unrested. She had not slept well. The house seemed full of strange noises and every time she drifted off, something would jolt her wide awake.

After starting the women on their task, Blythe went downstairs to make some coffee. They finished, then left at noon, and Blythe found herself alone again and dreading the oncoming night.

"How foolish!" she scolded herself and decided to turn her attention to a project she had been planning to undertake for some time, that of repairing some of the chair coverings in the small sitting room.

The beautiful crewel work was frayed and faded against the beige linen background. She had learned embroidery at the convent in Sacramento. In fact, Sister Helena had commended her needlework highly and had taught her the more intricate stitches. Blythe hoped she could remember enough to repair this lovely stitchery.

She recognized some of the symbols—pears, for divine love; the lily, for virtue; cherries, sweetness of character; the tulip, for the resurrection; and the carnation, for pure love.

Concentrating on her needlework, her mind wandered freely. She missed Malcolm's presence although he took little notice of her. She even missed Sara and the routine of seeing to an invalid's needs. At least, she had felt needed then. And, most of all, she realized she missed the easy companionship of her rides with Rod Cameron.

What she enjoyed about being with Rod was he reminded her of Malcolm—the "old Malcolm" she had known at the ranch. His voice held the same gentle, teasing quality Malcolm's used to have, and he treated her with the same quiet courtesy. Rod possessed all the qualities she had loved in Malcolm—the sensitivity, awareness of life, the sense of humor that had seemed to vanish since they left California.

The sound of hoofbeats on the drive broke into her thoughts. She dropped her needlework and ran to the window, surprised to see Rod, as if summoned by her thoughts, cantering up to the front of the house. He had another horse on a lead.

She hurried out onto the porch to greet him as he dismounted.

He gave her a challenging grin. "Think you're ready for a new mount?"

"Well—" She walked slowly down the steps, admiring the sleek thoroughbred. "She's a beauty, but—"

"The students this year are all inexperienced riders and need the slow practice in the ring before taking on a horse like Treasure. She's a little too lively for a beginner, but she needs exercise. I think you can handle her."

Blythe offered her hand to the animal, who shied nervously before stepping nearer to nuzzle the outstretched palm, searching it for a tidbit of sugar. Still, Treasure's ears twitched, and her tail swung like a metronome.

"Lively, you say? A little nervous?"

"Just needs a pair of firm, gentle hands." Rod smiled.

"If you say so." Blythe sounded a bit doubtful.

"I do say so."

"Well, then, I'll only be a minute." Blythe smiled, feeling a warm surge of anticipation. What fun to have Rod come today just when she was feeling low, and the prospect of riding through the autumn woods was far too tempting to resist.

She raced to her room, shed her workdress, put on a riding skirt, tied back her hair, and pulled on a pair of boots.

Rod helped Blythe into the sidesaddle, then handed her the reins. With a quick pat of the mare's neck, he mounted his own horse.

They started off toward the far meadow into the shadowy woods.

It was a glorious day for riding. The sun sparkled from a cloudless sky, and the air held the tangy scent of cedars and late blackberries. Treasure strained forward until Blythe gave the mare her head. Rod looked back laughing as they gained on him. At the crest of the hill, they reined their panting horses, dismounted, leaving them to rest, and walked over and sat on the rocks overlooking the river below.

Blythe lifted her face to the sun, sighing contentedly. "This must be as close to bliss as one can get."

"Yes—" Rod gazed into the distance. "I never knew how to appreciate all this, never knew how much I loved it . . . until the War . . . when I was away. Saw other woods just like this, blown to bits with musket fire. Heard the screams of dying men and horses—" He broke off abruptly. "Sorry. I didn't mean to spoil this lovely day with brutal memories." He turned an inquiring glance on Blythe. "Where were you then?"

"During the War? Well, of course, I was just a little girl. I don't think I even knew it was going on. You see, Pa had come out west in '49, as a very young man. He was from Kentucky, a poor boy from a big family. He went, like so many, to seek his fortune in the gold fields. After my mother died—"

"Tell me about her."

"I don't remember very much about her. All I really know is what Pa told me. She was Spanish . . . a dancer with a traveling troupe. She originally came from a gypsy family who lived in the Sierra Nevada hills near Granada in Spain. She told Pa her stepfather sold her for a lot of money to the musical troupe. That's not unusual among gypsies, I suppose. Anyway, they taught her to dance. Then they came to America to tour the West.

"I know she was a popular performer. I have her trunk with some old playbills. She was called 'The Gypsy.' Wore red satin dancing slippers with real silver buckles and a lace mantilla—" Embarrassed, Blythe broke off. "My, but I'm running on! I guess that must seem a strange kind of background—a gypsy dancer and a Kentucky farm boy—for a Montrose bride, doesn't it?"

"Not at all! I think it's fascinating," Rod said. "Rather like a fairy tale."

"Except fairy tales always end 'And they lived happily ever after'—" Blythe's voice trailed away. "Of course, Mama and Pa *were* happy together. Maybe their story was like a fairy tale . . . but not mine."

Blythe clapped her hand over her mouth. She had not meant to say that.

"Aren't you happy, Blythe?" Rod asked. She looked stricken. "You *aren't* happy, are you? Why not, Blythe?"

"The truth is—" Blythe began, then hesitated. Dare she confess her deepest secret . . . even to Rod?

He reached out his hand, turned her face, and raised it so she had to look at him. His eyes searched hers. "What is the truth, Blythe?"

"Malcolm is still grieving . . . mourning Rose!" she burst out.

A shadow crossed Rod's face.

"And what's more . . . he blames himself," she added breathlessly.

Rod frowned. "Blames himself? But why? It was an accident. And he was away fighting at the time."

"I know! I know! But that doesn't seem to matter. He is consumed with guilt."

Rod shook his head. "That's tragedy on top of tragedy! No one was to blame for Rose's death. To grieve a loved one is enough to bear without adding senseless guilt."

Blythe stood up suddenly, walked over to the edge of the cliff, her back to Rod so he wouldn't see her eyes brimming with tears.

He followed her. "Is that what's making you so unhappy, Blythe? That Malcolm is miserable over misplaced guilt? Is that it? Or is there something more?"

"He still loves her." Blythe breathed the words.

"Of course, he does," Rod said quietly. "He'll always cherish her memory . . . but you're his wife now. He loves *you*—" But his statement lost momentum as she protested.

"No, there's no room in his heart for me," she said firmly, sadly. "I mean . . . nothing to him. I'm not enough. I'm not Rose."

"You are *you*," Rod replied, his voice rough with emotion. "You're a beautiful, generous, caring woman. Any man would be a fool not to see that . . . not to love you."

Blythe turned to face him, lower lip trembling.

He gazed at the lovely upturned face—not only beautiful but interesting. The strong jaw was softened by the sweet curve of her cheek, the innocent mouth. Her dark eyes, so troubled now, stared back at him. The last of the sunlight burnished Blythe's auburn hair with gold, and it took all Rod's willpower not to reach out and touch it.

"Blythe, I hate to see you so unhappy. I wish there were something I could do. If you—if there is ever—*anything* at all—"

The sympathy in Rod's eyes, the compassion in his voice moved

Blythe deeply. But she knew she must not give way to the emotions colliding within her. It would be disloyal to Malcolm to take advantage of Rod's obvious desire to comfort her.

"Oh, Rod, there's nothing you can do. I mean, I spoke recklessly—shouldn't have—I didn't mean to imply . . . that is—"

"When will Malcolm be back?" Rod interrupted her determined attempt to remedy her impulsive words.

"By the end of the week . . . at least, I think he will." Blythe moved to loosen Treasure's reins. "It's getting late."

"Yes," Rod agreed and untied his horse, also.

They rode back to Montclair in silence. In front of the house, Rod reached over and took her reins.

"I won't be over tomorrow. Garnet and her husband are back from Europe for a short visit before going on to New York. But I'm leaving Treasure with you. I'll take her down to the barn and have one of the boys rub her down and give her a bucket of oats. I thought you might enjoy having her for the next few days."

Blythe slid out of her saddle, came around to Treasure's head, stood there stroking the mare's soft nose for a few moments. "You don't have to do that, Rod."

"I want to. You need to get out, away from here." A muscle in his jaw flexed. He glanced in the direction of the old stables, now neglected and run-down. "Montclair used to be known for its fine horses. Owners came from miles to buy foals in the spring. . . . If Malcolm would only take an interest, maybe—" He stopped mid-sentence, his lips tightened. "I apologize. It's not for me to say." He turned his horse. "Well, goodbye for a few days, Blythe. Do remember what I said, won't you? If ever you should need me . . . anytime . . . for anything—"

"Thank you. I'll remember."

Watching Rod ride away, Blythe knew she had come dangerously close to confiding everything in him. His warmth and sympathy had almost persuaded her to yield to that sweet temptation.

She entered the house, and its emptiness hit her forcibly, like a blow. The loneliness of the past months engulfed her—a loneliness that seemed to have no end, a longing that promised to go unsatisfied for a long time to come.

Blythe thought of Rod, of that moment that had trembled between them. Her blood tingled, raced through her young body, awakening the yearning to touch and be touched, to hold and be held.

Dear God! she pleaded, drawing in a ragged breath. She should not be thinking of Rod Cameron like this. She shivered, suddenly cold.

Maybe when Malcolm came home, things would be different, better. *Please, dear God, make them better. Make him love me.*

chapter
21

ALTHOUGH Malcolm had been indefinite about the exact date or time of his return, Blythe became anxious when she had still heard nothing from him by the end of the week. She told herself he had probably remained in Richmond, visiting old friends longer than planned after seeing his parents off to Savannah.

But by the afternoon of the fifth day, Blythe was much too restless to remain at the house and went down to the stables. Treasure whinnied at her approach, just as eager as she to be off and galloping along the woodland paths.

The horse's hooves clattered over the rustic bridge, then thudded on to the pine-needled trail leading to the little house in the clearing.

Ever since discovering Eden Cottage, Blythe had been mysteriously drawn to it. What if she and Malcolm had come here immediately after their marriage instead of to the big house? Could they have had a chance to get to know each other better? Would he have learned to love her here? Probably not, Blythe sighed. This is where Malcolm had brought Rose, and surely this place held even more sad memories for him than Montclair.

She passed the cottage and rode on, her mind full of troubling thoughts that not even the cool autumn wind on her face could dispel. Suddenly she realized she had come to the property line dividing Montrose and Cameron property, marked by a low, stone fence. Treasure took it easily and, before she knew it, Blythe was close enough to see Cameron Hall. She reined in and looked across the meadow to the sweeping front lawn.

It looked so serene, the rosy stone mellow in the October sunlight.

Late roses were blooming in the well-tended gardens and, on the far side, a group of students in their school smocks were playing croquet on the smooth green grass. It was such a pretty scene that Blythe moved even closer, hidden from view by an oak tree. House and gardens exhibited the care, pride, and hope that was sadly missing at Montclair.

Blythe started to turn Treasure around, but something held her. She slipped down from her saddle, tethered her horse, and crept forward, keeping well out of sight. She drew so near that she could hear the girls' voices, their laughter, the clonk of the mallet as it hit the ball.

As she watched, the front door opened, and Kate, Dove, Rod, and an elegantly dressed couple walked out onto the veranda. The newly-wed Devlins!

Garnet looked like a Paris fashion-plate! The new silhouette coming into vogue was perfect for her figure—the molded bodice and skirt drawn back to cascade in full tiers. Her costume was smoke-blue, kilt-pleated in front, trimmed with braid and tassels. On her elaborate coiffure perched a blue bonnet adorned with a blue-feathered bird.

Something made them all laugh just as an open carriage, driven by a uniformed coachman, rounded the side of the house and came to a stop in front. After good-byes and embraces, the couple descended the steps and got into the splendid victoria drawn by two high-stepping chestnut horses, and with more waves and calls, started down the drive.

Blythe stood looking after them until the spell was broken by the sound of girlish voices. "Mr. Cameron! Mr. Cameron!" She turned to see a cluster of girls gathered around Rod, then burst into giggles as he strode off toward the stables.

Obviously, the young ladies at Cameron Hall admired their riding instructor extravagantly. *Not that it would be hard to do*, Blythe thought, smiling to herself.

Riding back to Montclair, Blythe kept seeing Garnet in her elegant Parisian outfit, worn with such an air of assurance. Garnet, like Kate and Dove, possessed this inborn grace Blythe envied.

But perhaps she could learn it, Blythe encouraged herself. Perhaps she could yet make Malcolm proud of her, make him glad that he had married her. Maybe she had not been "to the manor born," but she had the courage to think she could change, learn to do and say the right things, to dress properly. It would take time, of course, but she could try.

Even though remembrances of past failures clouded that hope, Blythe clung to it. What else could she do if not at least pretend to believe a better, brighter day was about to dawn for her?

When Malcolm had been gone a full week—allowing ample time for the journey to Richmond and back and a few days' visit with friends— Blythe was certain he would return on the seventh day.

She rose early to ready the house for his homecoming, cleaning and polishing everything in sight before going out to gather flowers. She had spent hours weeding the overgrown beds and, little by little, some of the flowers were blooming there again. Mixing these with some wild Queen Anne's lace, she placed the bright bouquets in vases about the house.

In an alcove at the end of the dining room, she set a table for two, realizing, with a kind of rising excitement, that this would be the first time she had prepared a meal for Malcolm alone, the first time they would spend time together at Montclair without anyone else.

Blythe had found herbs growing in the kitchen garden. Delighted with her discovery, she had picked and dried some she recognized. Now she roasted a chicken with basil and oregano, prepared sweet potatoes, and made biscuits ready to pop in the oven when Malcolm arrived.

As she hurried upstairs to bathe and dress, fresh hope stirred. Maybe Malcolm's homecoming would be a new beginning for them. Maybe he had missed her, too.

She took extra pains with her hair, brushing it to a gleaming russet, then fixing it with the high-backed tortoise-shell Spanish comb that had belonged to her mother. She fastened a lace collar Sara had given her to her brightest flowered dress and tucked one yellow rose into her waistband.

She went downstairs and stationed herself at the parlor window to watch for him. It was just dusk, soft lavender shadows cast a lovely haze on the gardens. The crushed shell driveway was a winding white ribbon in the growing darkness as Blythe looked down, hoping to see a hack from the train station coming up to the house.

But when it was fully dark and still Malcolm had not arrived, a knot of fear lodged in Blythe's throat. What could have happened? Could Sara have fallen ill, and Malcolm remained in Richmond to assist his father? Flashing through her mind were all the possible mishaps that her husband might have encountered.

With a growing dread, she lit the lamp, put some wood in the kitchen stove, and set a kettle of water on to boil for tea. She had lost all appetite for food. The biscuits baked too early had dried up. She threw them out, but removed the chicken from the oven and put it aside to be warmed up later, should Malcolm still come.

Shivering, she put on a shawl. The grandfather clock in the hallway counted out the waiting hours, each one a knell of foreboding.

At last, convinced that Malcolm would not be home this night, she locked up and slowly climbed the stairs to her bedroom.

Numb with fatigue, she undressed. Before getting into bed, Blythe went to the window and peered out into the relentless darkness. Wordless prayers filled her mind, but hope ebbed away. Malcolm would not come.

She lay in bed rigid, sleepless. The small fire in her hearth sent grotesque shadows against the wall.

Unconsciously, she waited.

It began to rain, and she could hear the rustle of leaves as the heavy drops pelted the tree outside and slashed against her windowpane. *Malcolm, Malcolm, where are you?*

The clock downstairs struck a mournful midnight. The rain pattered against the windows. The fire sputtered as it burned low.

At dawn, Blythe awoke with a start. She lay there for a moment, listening. The house was soundless, empty.

She rose stiffly, poured water from the pitcher into the washbowl, and splashed her face. The pale light filtering through the bedroom windows did little to lift the heaviness from her heart. Drawing a long breath, she went downstairs.

Trance-like, she moved through the motions of the morning— putting the kettle on the stove, throwing a few sticks of kindling into the fire. She should eat something, but her stomach was in knots.

Instead, she took the shawl from the hook beside the door and went outside, thinking the fresh air might clear her head. From the porch, she could see that the ground was wet after the heavy rains of the night before. She sank down on the top step, hunching her shoulders against the chill, staring down the long drive.

A kind of numbness gripped her. She exhausted all the probable causes of Malcolm's late return, each one only bringing the panic closer. Although she could not articulate them, her prayers bordered on desperation. She sat there, keeping her vigil, until she was stiff with cold and anxiety. Then, awkwardly getting to her feet, she went back into the house.

In the kitchen annex the kettle was hissing. Blythe removed it from the burner, measured out tea into the brown earthen pot, poured in the boiling water. She got down a cup and filled it with some of the hot liquid.

Blythe did not know how long she had been sitting at the kitchen table when she heard carriage wheels on the driveway, then heavy steps on the porch. The front door opened and, as she rushed into the hall, she saw Malcolm.

He stood in the doorway, supporting himself with one hand braced against the frame. He was hatless, his shirt open at the neck, no cravat. His clothes looked as though he had slept in them; his eyes were dark hollows in his gaunt face.

"Malcolm!" Blythe gasped. "What's wrong!"

He gave a hoarse laugh. "Wrong? What's *wrong? Everything!* That's what's wrong."

He started forward, but stumbled and almost fell. Blythe ran to his side, and he leaned against her heavily.

"You look dreadful! Come, let me help you."

Malcolm made a choking sound that was half laugh, half moan. But, Blythe put her arm around his waist and led him toward the library. There, he slumped onto the sofa, letting his head fall back against the upholstery.

Blythe knelt and pulled off his boots, one by one. Then she tugged off his jacket. By now, she was breathing hard, for Malcolm was a dead weight. Lastly, she lifted his legs onto the sofa, where he slid into a prone position. Quickly she slipped a pillow under his head and, reaching for the afghan, covered him with it.

Malcolm's eyes were already closed. Blythe stood looking down at him, relieved that he was safely home, bewildered by the condition in which he had arrived.

All through the long day, Blythe asked herself the unanswerable questions—questions to which only Malcolm held the key. She wept, paced, and prayed. But there was no peace for her in prayer, no solace in tears.

Outside, the sky darkened. By late afternoon, it began to rain again.

She positioned herself at the kitchen table, drinking cup after cup of strong coffee to fortify herself against the unknown. Every few minutes, she tiptoed out into the hall, put her ear to the library door, and listened for some sound.

When she heard Malcolm stirring, she hurried back to the kitchen, reheated the coffee and, carrying a steaming mugful, knocked gently at the closed door. Finally, she heard the sound of the key grating in the lock, and Malcolm threw open the door.

It took all the self-control Blythe could muster to remain silent. Malcolm was shockingly pale and, when he took the cup from her, his hands were shaking. This man, who had always maintained an impeccable appearance—even at the ranch—was now unkempt, his two-day beard a dark stubble on his chin, his eyes red-rimmed and haunted.

He glanced at Blythe, then dropped his gaze, a shamed expression on his face. "I owe you an explanation, an apology," he mumbled.

"You don't owe me anything!" protested Blythe. "I'm just glad you weren't in an accident or—"

Malcolm shook his head and his lip curled. "No accident. It was deliberate . . . if inexcusable."

Then he launched into a long, rambling story. "After I put my parents on the train to Savannah, I ran into some old friends. Friends? Maybe not . . . rather, acquaintances, I should say." He gave a short, harsh laugh. "Very prosperous ones, too, from the look of them. Would you believe even some *Southerners* profited from the War?"

It seemed one thing had led to another. The friends had asked Malcolm to stay over, wining and dining him much too generously. And there had been card games. He had lost all track of time.

Malcolm shrugged. "As I said, there is no excuse . . . no excuse."

"I was worried—" she said quietly.

"Sorry." He took another sip of coffee. "It won't happen again."

But it did.

Within a fortnight, Malcolm left for Richmond, telling Blythe that he must follow up on some business opportunities to restore the plantation to its former productivity. But when he returned four days later, it was with evidence that not only Montclair but Malcolm himself was sinking deeper and deeper into despair and ruin.

chapter
22

THE NEXT TRIP took Malcolm only as far as Mayfield. This time he drove the farm wagon for the purpose of getting supplies for themselves and the sharecroppers, the freed Negroes who worked on the land.

When Malcolm had not returned by nightfall, Blythe was frantic at first. In retrospect, as the hours passed and she sorted out the fragments of their life together, she could begin to see the pattern Malcolm had established, beginning on shipboard en route from California. Drinking and gambling "friends" could be found anywhere. Indeed, she recalled hearing Malcolm tell Pa that, in the Yankee prison, there had been nothing to while away the tedious hours, and so the prisoners had gambled even their rations on the turn of a card. It seemed a strange addiction for a gentleman, but Blythe could no longer deny the truth.

All she knew about drink was summed up in vivid memories of the poor wretches who staggered out of saloons in Lucas Valley or slumped in a drunken stupor against the walls of buildings or stumbled along the wooden sidewalks, as "decent folk" stepped aside in disdain. Young as she had been, she had felt pity rather than condemnation.

Now, she felt an even greater pity, mixed with love and dread. Was Malcolm destined to come to such an end? And if so, what would become of her . . . of their marriage?

Even when he was at home, Blythe now began to look for signs of his drinking—the unfocused, glazed look in his eyes, the slow response, his keen mind fumbling to grasp even the simplest question. He seemed to be growing old before her eyes, his skin sallow, his dark hair slashed with iron gray. She was appalled and frightened. Nothing in her experience had prepared her for this. Malcolm seemed bent on destroying himself, and, unless she did something to stop him, he would succeed.

In desperation, Blythe decided to go to Kate Cameron for advice. After all, Kate had known Malcolm since boyhood. If anyone could help them, it would be this gracious woman. But Blythe chose a time when she knew Rod would be giving riding lessons. She did not want to encounter him in her distraught state.

She found Kate in her little parlor off the music room, and, against the backdrop of little girls practicing scales, Blythe poured out her heart.

Mrs. Cameron's thoughtful gray eyes fastened upon her as Blythe confided her darkest fears. From time to time, she nodded, and Blythe had the distinct feeling that here was one who could give her complete attention and understanding to another. It was a sensation of profound relief after all the weeks of lonely silence.

At length Kate spoke. "My dear child, how you have suffered. I only wish I had known—" Her gaze drifted to the tranquil scene through the window and Blythe's eyes followed hers—the slumbering meadows under a light icing of frost, the undisturbed peace of the countryside while, within Blythe's heart, there was turmoil and confusion. "The Bible tells us that 'love suffereth long, and is kind. . . . Love beareth all things, believeth all things, hopeth all things, endureth all things.' Occasionally, we find ourselves in circumstances not of our own making. Through no fault of yours, my dear, you are in just such a dilemma—one that will challenge you far beyond your years or experience." She paused. "If you love Malcolm . . . and I believe you do sincerely . . . there is something you must know, though it pains me to tell you—"

The lovely eyes brimmed with tears of sympathy. She reached out and put her hand over Blythe's tightly clenched ones. "The Montrose men are known for a certain streak of recklessness. Malcolm was his mother's favorite, though all the Montrose sons were adored and pampered. They got by on their looks and charm . . . that is, until the War—" Once again, she broke off, remembering.

"Bryce, Garnet's first husband, seemed to understand that was not enough and matured splendidly before the end. Lee, Dove's husband, died too young for us to know what he would have become, though we heard he died bravely, leading a cavalry charge. That, too, may have been sheer recklessness, however." Kate sighed.

"At first, when we heard Malcolm had gone West, we all hoped . . . expected, really . . . that he would take over Montclair when he returned. We all had to start over, you know. There wasn't much left for any of us after the War. Why that didn't happen . . . well, only Malcolm knows.

"Perhaps he has lost hope. And when hope is gone, life is ended. Hope is necessary if we are to go on living constructively. It is the core of man's spirit, for it is closely linked to that other essential . . . faith."

"Faith?" Blythe echoed. "Faith in God? I think Malcolm believes in God."

"Yes, but there is a difference between *belief* in God and *faith* in God. As Paul says 'Faith is the substance of things hoped for, the evidence of things not seen.' We Southerners had to believe that God would help us put things right . . . had to have a vision of the future, even though we could not see it. Malcolm seems to have forgotten that."

When Blythe rose to go, she embraced Kate, dreading the moment of departure. "You are always so serene. What is your secret?"

"God has been very good, and I have learned to trust that his purposes are being fulfilled . . . even when it appears most unlikely. You know, we must look for the good in every adversity, learn to expect God's miracles, for He delights in surprising us. Pray to be strong, child. Trust that God is working in your life *and* in Malcolm's—"

Blythe bade Kate a tearful farewell.

Mounting Treasure at the side of the front porch, where she had left her, Blythe started down the drive toward the gate. Before she reached it, she heard her name. Turning, she saw Rod cantering up from the riding ring.

"Blythe!" he greeted her as he came alongside. "I didn't know you were coming over today!"

"It was an impulse," she told him. "I came to see your mother."

"If I'd known you were here, I'd have hurried my riders through their paces faster. I'm sorry I haven't been over to ride with you these last few weeks. We have more students this year, and all of them, it seems, are realizing a lifelong dream to become expert equestriennes!" He sounded amused.

Then his smile faded, and his expression grew serious. "You've been crying, haven't you?" he demanded in a gentle voice. "What's the matter, Blythe? Is something wrong at Montclair?"

At the sympathy in his voice, Blythe blinked back tears. "I didn't mean for you to see me this way," she murmured.

He leaned over, placed his large hand over hers where it rested on the pommel. "But I want to know why you're unhappy. Tell me."

Blythe shook her head. "I can't. I mean . . . I shouldn't."

"Is it . . . Malcolm?"

Startled, she looked at him. "Yes, but—"

"Never mind. I know. I've seen him several times in Mayfield. He has—" Rod's eyes narrowed. "He hasn't done anything to hurt you, has he?"

"Oh, no! It's just that—" Her voice broke. "I don't know what to do."

"Let me ride home with you."

"That isn't necessary," she protested.

"I insist." Taking the lead, Rod suggested, "Let's cut through the woods."

At the clearing, where a low rock fence divided the Cameron land from the beginning of Montrose property, Blythe halted her horse. "You don't have to come any farther, Rod. I'll be fine now."

"I'll see you home." Rod was adamant. "Then, if Malcolm's there . . . if you need help . . . you won't be alone."

She put a restraining hand on his arm. "No, Rod."

"But I want to help you."

"Malcolm is never violent. It's just . . . sad." The tears started to flow again. "Things might be different . . . if he wouldn't drink."

"If it were only that," Rod replied grimly. "Malcolm's drinking is only a symptom of something much deeper, I'm afraid. It's his escape from life. It's not your fault, Blythe," he said hastily, seeing her stricken look, "but Malcolm feels he has nothing left to live for—"

"You mean since Rose—"

"That, of course, and the War and his venture out West—all failures."

"You make it sound as if he had more reason for dying than living," she said, feeling a certain dread grip her, almost holding her breath for Rod's reply.

"It's clear that he's wretchedly unhappy—" Rod let the words hang between them.

Before they parted at the edge of the woods, Rod took Blythe's hand. "I don't like the idea of your being alone over there. It's neither right nor fair that you should be lonely . . . I know what it's like. Until you came—" he began. "What I mean to say is that since my twin brother . . . was killed, there's been an emptiness . . . one I can't explain—"

At once Blythe's own loneliness, her soul's need, her heart's seeking rushed out to meet his. She closed her eyes, feeling a momentary wave of dizziness.

"Since you came, since I've known you—" Rod's voice deepened.

Suddenly, Blythe felt she should hear no more. She tried to withdraw her hand, but Rod held it more firmly.

Then, very carefully, as if trying to choose only the most precise words and phrases, Rod said, "Blythe, if ever you should need me . . . at any time . . . for any reason . . . I want you to promise me you'll send one of the farm people to Cameron Hall. I'll come night or day. You have only to ask."

Blythe lowered her eyes so as not to read a clear message in Rod's intent gaze—a message that conveyed more than sympathy for a hurting friend.

"Thank you," she replied simply. "I have to go now. Malcolm may be home . . . may need me. Thank you, Rod." With that, she gave Treasure a little slap with her reins and started toward Montclair, already dreading what might await her there.

It was the War, Rod had said. And Kate had said it, too. The War was responsible for everything—the death, destruction, disease, the madness, the senseless suffering, the devastation of the land. The War she had been too young to know about was slowly, inexorably, destroying her life.

chapter

23

DURING the last week in October, a violent windstorm blew the trees bare of their glory, and a hard rain began to fall steadily, blotting out the remembrance of Indian summer with a veil of daily drizzle.

After his return from the disastrous trip to Richmond and the subsequent one into Mayfield, Malcolm barricaded himself behind the closed library doors.

A succession of dreary days increased Blythe's feelings of isolation and loneliness. Prevented by the weather from riding, she was confined to the house, where a dreadful personal drama was playing itself out.

In these days her thoughts turned more and more to Rod Cameron. She knew she had seen in his eyes the same strong attraction she felt. She remembered the sudden quickening of her heart. Deprived as she was of the fulfillment she had expected to find in her marriage, Blythe's vulnerable heart cried out for love. Although she knew it was wrong to feel this way about a man who was not her husband, she questioned whether or not she had a husband in the truest sense of the word.

Blythe spent hours on her knees, praying for some solution to her problem. She must find some way to help Malcolm, to excite him about the possibilities of restoring Montclair . . . anything.

If proof were needed of the deteriorating state of the house, Blythe had it after the storms of the week. The roof was leaking in virtually every room, and although she had set out as many pots and pails as she could find, there was already extensive damage to floors and walls. Something had to be done.

She broached the subject to Malcolm when he finally emerged from the library for supper. "I spoke to Lonnie," Blythe told him as she set a dish of chicken dumplings on the kitchen table where they ate now instead of in the dining room, "and she said Will and some of the other men would be willing to repair the roof if you'd get the shingles. You know, they still feel this house belongs to them, too, somehow."

Malcolm's response was a harsh laugh. "Do you realize how many shingles it would take to roof a house this size? I know *they* don't . . . but I can't afford to buy them, anyway—"

"Oh, but we ought to be getting the money from the sale of Pa's ranch soon, shouldn't we?" Blythe asked.

Malcolm's face blanched. He stared down at his plate, then shoved it away and stood up with such haste that he knocked his chair over backward with a resounding crash.

Blythe jumped, dropping her fork, and stared at Malcolm.

"There . . . isn't any money," he said grimly. "There's not going to be any money . . . any *more* money, that is. It came weeks ago . . . and it's gone . . . all of it. How do you think I was able to take Mama and Father to Richmond, put them up at the best hotel, buy them tickets on the train to Savannah? And as long as the truth's coming out . . . I lost the rest of it in a card game!"

With that declaration, Malcolm picked up the chair, pushed it aside, and strode out of the kitchen. A moment later Blythe heard the library doors slam shut.

Alone at the table, Blythe buried her head in her hands. The utter hopelessness of it all washed over her. Without money or any way to earn it, nothing could be done. In spite of Malcolm's disclosure, however, she felt no anger, only a soul-deep despair.

She wished they had never come to Virginia. Maybe if they had stayed out West, Malcolm would still be the gentle, soft-spoken man she had grown to love. Now, he was a stranger—the mood swings, the flashes of anger, the quick harsh words, the bitterness. It was a frightening change.

Later, as she lay across her bed in the room where she had slept alone since coming to Montclair, she heard Malcolm moving about below. He was pacing restlessly. It was then she wept, for both of them. But the tears that flowed were comfortless and unhealing.

In the morning Malcolm was gone—where, she did not know. Ironically, the rain had stopped, and a bright sun shone, making everything look fresh and glowing and all the more heartbreaking.

By early afternoon, the sun had dried the ground. Unable to stand the gloom of the empty house, Blythe went out to the barn, saddled Treasure, and rode out. Lost in her own thoughts, she gave the horse her head and soon found they were on the familiar path bordering Cameron land.

She had not consciously planned it, but she was not surprised to see Rod astride Sultan, coming toward her along the path. Nor was the joyful lifting of her heart at the sight of him completely unexpected. Blythe felt her pulse race, a sudden inner trembling as he reined his horse alongside hers.

"Beautiful day!" he greeted her, his eyes shining as they swept over her.

"Yes. It's wonderful . . . after all the rain," she murmured, turning to look at the river, afraid her expression might betray her happiness at coming upon him.

She knew her words sounded stiff, but her heart was thudding so loudly she could hardly speak. What was different about today from any of the other days she and Rod had been together? She knew only that something tangible, yet unspoken, sparked the very air around them.

In silent agreement, they walked their horses down the little hill that led over the curved, rustic bridge and into the clearing where, just beyond, they could see the small house.

At the bridge, Rod swung out of his saddle and tied Sultan to one of the posts before walking over to Blythe and holding up his hands to lift her down. His hands circling her waist remained a minute longer, then he quickly released her and went to loop Treasure's reins around the other post.

Together, they walked to the middle of the bridge, leaning on the railing and looked down into the water flowing over the rocks with a rushing sound. The woods behind them were still. Not even a bird song or the stirring of a leaf disturbed the utter quiet.

Then Rod spoke softly, "Do you remember the day we sat in the arbor at Eden Cottage and ate grapes . . . and you asked me if I knew the Scriptures well?"

Blythe nodded. That sun-splashed day of happiness wrenched her memory. It had been perfection—without shadow of any kind. Then, she had gone home to find Malcolm had returned from Massachusetts without Jonathan, and her world had begun to change.

"Yes, I remember."

"Well, look up Deuteronomy 28:30." Rod was looking at her with a peculiar intensity.

As their eyes met, there was the stunned realization of what was possible. For an instant, the rush of the water below was deafening; the sunlight, dazzling; the bridge beneath her feet, unsteady. Rod's gaze held hers as if his eyes could plumb the very deepest part of her soul.

It was a moment of recognition, knowing that what she saw in Rod's eyes mirrored her feelings. With that knowledge came the awareness of danger.

"Blythe—" On Rod's lips, her name had never sounded so beautiful. As he leaned toward her, Blythe drew back, one hand to her throat.

"Oh, Rod!" she cried in a choked voice. "We can't!"

Spinning around, she ran to Treasure, untied the reins, and swung herself up into the saddle. Without a backward look, she started in a gallop for Montclair.

By the time she reached the barn, the mare was in a lather. Taking off the saddle, Blythe rubbed her down, gave her water, then slipped a feedbag of oats over her head. With weighted steps, she walked toward the house, feeling so exhausted that when she reached the porch, she clung to one of the columns.

She closed her eyes, swaying dizzily. She knew she would have to forget that moment on the bridge, what she had seen in Rod's eyes, what she had felt. There could never be anything but friendship between them. If either one of them acknowledged there was more, it would end forever that companionship she had found so sweet, so comforting—the only joy she had known since coming to Montclair.

They must not let that happen. Even if what they felt for each other were real, there could be no happy ending for them.

Blythe went in the house. There was no sign that Malcolm had returned. It could be hours or even days before she saw him again. She mounted the steps, one foot dragging behind the other.

In her bedroom, she took off her boots and was beginning to unfasten her riding skirt when she remembered the Scripture Rod had suggested she look up.

Curious, she got out the Bible the minister's wife in Lucas Valley had given her after the wedding. "Every couple startin' out should have a family Bible," she had said. Pointing to a glossy page in the center, she had explained, "There's places to set down all the important events of your marriage—the names and birthdates of your children—"

Children! Blythe thought, as she thumbed through the index. That hope had long since vanished.

Then she found the verse Rod had given her and read it over and over, trying to comprehend what he was saying to her.

"Thou shalt betroth a wife, and another man shall lie with her: thou shalt build an house, and thou shalt not dwell therein: thou shalt plant a vineyard, and shalt not gather the grapes thereof."

In searching honesty, Blythe probed her conscience. Had she, in her loneliness and disillusionment, sought the solace of Rod's love, encouraged it?

"God, help me!" she moaned, slipping to her knees. "I never meant for this to happen. Tell me what to do."

The words came into her mind, but she tried not to hear them, for they were too hard for her to bear. Yet they repeated themselves gently, insistently, irrevocably. *You must be ruthlessly honest with yourself and with Rod. Give up even the thought of him, what might have been between you.*

She knew in her heart of hearts that if she and Rod yielded to their feelings, it would be sin. Stripping away all illusion, all romantic fantasy, the truth was it would be wrong.

It didn't matter that Malcolm did not love her. She was still his wife and, now and forever, not free to love anyone else.

Blythe felt a tearing hurt, knowing that emptiness inside her would remain unfilled, that she might never know the keenest joy a human being can know on earth. The pain was real as she surrendered her will, but she begged to be free of a love that was not hers to enjoy.

When she got to her feet, the breaking had begun.

chapter
24

MALCOLM did not come home that night or the next.

Blythe had resigned herself to the tragic reality of what she was helpless to change. Indeed, she had come to the conclusion that the only person she could change was herself, and this she resolved to do. It was clear that she must not see Rod again, and, in order to avoid a chance encounter with him, she kept to the paths on Montrose land, no longer riding into the woods or to the clearing near Eden Cottage.

She went about her duties in the house with dogged determination and, since the weather remained unseasonably warm, worked in the gardens, too. Choosing those tasks that required the most physical exertion, she wore herself out until, exhausted, she fell into bed each night to sleep deeply and dreamlessly. Though she was suffering, she felt renewed courage and strength.

On the third day of Malcolm's absence, Lonnie spoke up as they folded linens together. "I's gwine to hab to leave early dis evenin', Miss Blythe," the black woman said. "Tonight's de first night of de revival, and I doan want to miss it."

"Revival?"

"Yes'm. The circuit-rider is here, and dey's a tent meetin' tonight in de grove 'tween here and Cameron Hall. Old Mr. Montrose always gib permission to the preacher to hold dem on de grounds in de old days and, since Freedom, we jes' do lak always."

"Is it like church?" Blythe asked curiously.

"Yes'm. Some say it even better than reg'lar church. Lots of folks gets saved. Then they's a baptism in the river on Sunday."

Blythe was curious. "Is it just for . . . you know . . . your people?"

"Oh, no ma'm! Mr. Neville, he preach to black and white folks jes' the same. He say befo' God, all men alike. No diff'rence 'long as our souls are washed clean by the Blood."

Blythe looked at Lonnie in amazement. "How do you know all this?" She knew the nearest church was in Mayfield, and the former slaves rarely got into town.

"Oh, I's been knowin' 'bout Jesus since I was jes' a li'l gal. My Aunt Tilda, she teach me from the Bible. She was Miss Rose's maid and Miss Rose taught her to read. Tilda gone up No'th now, but she done sent me a Bible after she left, and I'm teachin' my own chillen." Lonnie nodded in satisfaction.

"Would it be all right, do you think, if I went to the revival tonight, Lonnie?"

"Oh, yes'm. You's welcome. All white folks is," Lonnie replied. "De tent's real easy to find. You can see it in the clearin' from the top o' the hill."

Something stirred within Blythe. She missed going to church as they had on a few occasions in Lucas Valley. Those church suppers and socials were warm memories, but somehow she sensed that, tonight, she would find something quite different from the usual fellowship.

Lonnie told her the service began at six o'clock, but that the singing and "praying up" began earlier. So Blythe saddled Treasure and left just at dusk. Sure enough, she spotted the tent in the little clearing, just as Lonnie had described.

Inside, the tent was close and hot, the smell of canvas and sawdust mingling with the peculiar odor of warm bodies, the starch of freshly laundered clothes, the leathery one of Bibles.

Blythe slipped into a seat in one of the back rows where a handful of white people, mostly women, had already gathered. She did not recognize any of them, but quickly spotted several of the Montrose servants and tenant-farmers.

Her heart was pounding, and every nerve was taut with a kind of excited anticipation. Blythe had not a clue as to what awaited her.

After awhile, the murmured conversations hushed and a ripple of movement flowed through the assembly. Blythe stretched her neck a little to see what was happening at the front.

A large man with a wild thatch of graying hair had mounted the improvised platform. He was gaunt, rather stooped of shoulder, yet with a commanding demeanor. He wore a shabby, swallow-tailed coat, and he was clutching a Bible, so worn it looked as if it might fall apart.

A lectern had been placed in the center of the platform. Beside it on a small table was a pitcher of water and a tumbler. But Mr. Neville did not go directly there. Instead, he paced back and forth, head down, mumbling in an audible voice.

All around her, Blythe heard expressions new to her: "Lord! Lord!" and "He prayin' hissef up," and, from the front row, a high-pitched voice saying, "Merciful Jesus! Preacher gittin' ready!" She felt herself growing tense. What in the world would happen now?

At length, Brother Neville strode over to the makeshift pulpit. His voice was resonant, piercing.

"I aim to speak about the Commandments of God, how Moses brung them down from the mountaintop to the people. The Lord has spoke to my heart. Hear this! Many here tonight are not keepin' God's Laws."

There was a rumble of "Amens" from the crowd.

"If they wasn't meant for us to obey, why did God give 'em?" the preacher demanded in a loud voice.

Spellbound, Blythe listened as Brother Neville exhorted his listeners, repeatedly punctuating his thoughts with two or three gestures that appeared to be characteristic. Occasionally, he would pound the lectern, raising the Bible in one hand. At those times a few pages would inevitably escape and come drifting to the stage. As his preaching grew more and more fervent, he loosened his cravat, wiping perspiration from his brow with a large handkerchief.

"I tell you, brethren and sisters, that the Lord meant what He said when He told the Israelites: Don't steal! Don't lie! Don't envy! And Jesus said the same thing . . . different method, mebbe . . . but the same message, for He said He had come, not to do away with the laws of Moses, but to fulfill 'em! And Jesus Christ is the same yesterday, today, and forever!"

The crowd was following every word, every gesture. As he wound into his sermon, he was accompanied by an ongoing chorus of voices, crying out for mercy or encouraging the preacher with their "Amens."

"But even though the Law was give first to the Israelites," Brother Neville continued, "it was meant for all. The Laws of Moses sometimes seem downright hard, but Jesus came to show God's love, came to show us he understands our struggles. God don't see our failures. He sees us as covered by the blood of Jesus . . . *if* we open up our hearts and take Him in as Lord and Savior. If not—" And here Blythe held her breath. What dire prediction would he make for those who had not done so? "You need to decide *tonight* where you want to spend eternity. Will it be heaven . . . or hell?"

There was not a sound throughout the tent. As one body, the congregation leaned forward, intent on hearing every word. Blythe found herself praying for those lost souls who might be present, for herself! And what about Malcolm? Had he really come to a place of faith in Jesus Christ? His present actions made it questionable.

Brother Neville's next words jolted her to awareness again. "And should you be excusin' yourself from this sermon, think on your own life. If you are a Christian, are you actin' like it? Have you trusted the Lord to take you through the wilderness? Are you countin' on Him to take care of you, or are you eat up with cares and worries? Have you turned it all over to Him? He's waitin.'"

Blythe gasped. He must be reading her thoughts!

Then, very abruptly, Brother Neville stopped his pacing and stood with closed eyes, obviously in deep prayer. As if on some unspoken cue, the singing began, softly at first, then rising to a glorious crescendo as, one by one, the people joined in a hymn of praise and commitment.

"Counted with the few, the loyal, brave and true, I want to be counted with the few. . . ."

Blythe found herself singing along with the rest, clapping her hands instinctively to the rhythm of the music.

The singing went on and on, moving from one hymn to another without a break. Then, unlike anything Blythe had ever heard before, a song broke out—a plaintive, throbbing, soul-stirring blend of voices that brought her to unexpected tears.

Above the wondrous music, Brother Neville's voice could be heard. "Don't any of you think you came here tonight on your own. You are here by divine appointment, drawn here by Jesus Himself. There was somethin' He wanted to say to you, somethin' He wanted to give you. Don't leave this place without it!"

All around her Blythe felt people moving, then she saw them spilling into the aisles, making their way to the front of the tent, falling to their knees there. The singing continued, high, sweet, and with a sort of unearthly melody.

To her amazement she felt herself get up, propelled by something she could not fathom, drawn by an unseen force. The next thing she knew, she was on her knees on the sawdust floor. Mr. Neville was coming down the row, laying hands on the bowed heads of the other seekers. Blythe closed her eyes tight, thinking wildly, *What am I doing?*

Then she felt the pressure of hands on her head, heard the preacher's deep rumbling voice above her head. "Just give up. Let Him take all your heavy burdens. And, if you've never asked Jesus to save you from eternal damnation, just open up your heart right now and repeat these words after me: O God, I confess with my lips that Jesus died for my sins and that God raised Him from the dead in glory. I ask Him now into my heart to be Lord of my life, and thank Him mightily for His salvation."

Blythe repeated the words, adding her own prayer for guidance and direction. As she did so, her heart stopped pounding, and a warm sensation flooded her.

Somehow she found her way back to her seat. The congregation was singing again, this time a rousing hymn, "There is power, power, wonder-working power in the precious blood of the Lamb."

Choked with emotion, Blythe slipped out of the tent into the night, gulping the fresh, frosty air. She felt wonderfully clear-headed, but also dazed by the amazing thing she had done.

She found Treasure with no trouble, for it was almost as bright as day. A full moon, high in the dark sky, lighted their way back to Montclair. Nearing the house, Blythe did not feel her usual depression. Tonight she had been touched by a loving Presence, and she was no longer afraid.

chapter

25

BLYTHE CAME awake as the first gray fingers of dawn crept through her bedroom windows. She had not slept soundly. She never did anymore. But now, instead of letting fear overtake her, Blythe lay awake and prayed—prayed that no harm would come to him, wherever he was, whatever he was doing.

Since the night of the tent meeting, Blythe had felt a new strength, a new resolve to live each day as the Lord would have her live it. She and Lonnie sometimes read the Bible together after the chores, before Lonnie left. It was a precious time, for Blythe needed support, and Lonnie was a rock of faith.

Blythe lay there a few minutes longer, listening hopefully for some sound. But the echoing silence of the empty house gave her the answer to her question. She whispered the prayer she had begun to use each morning: "Dear Lord, I give you this day. Be with me and guide me. Give me courage to face whatever lies ahead. In Jesus' name, I ask. Amen." Then she rose and dressed.

She moved down the stairway in the tomblike stillness, along the downstairs hall with its gloomy shadows, out to the kitchen. When she pushed open the door, she started back with a frightened gasp. Malcolm was seated at the table, his arms crossed, his head down, his shoulders shaking.

At the sound of the door opening, his head jerked up, and Blythe saw that he had been weeping. His eyes were bloodshot, red-rimmed. When he looked at her, he winced and wiped away the tears with the back of his hand.

Experience had taught her what to look for now. It was obvious that

Malcolm had been drinking. But he was sober—cold sober, Blythe realized. She stood there, unable to move or speak.

It was Malcolm who broke the tense moment. Shaking his head sorrowfully, he said, "Poor Blythe. You've picked the wrong man to idealize."

Blythe longed to go to him, throw her arms around him, cradle his dark head against her breast, comfort him, but something in his expression stopped her.

He got to his feet shakily, pulled out one of the kitchen chairs, and motioned her to sit down opposite him.

She sat. Malcolm looked dreadful—drawn and tired, but sober. He was at least sober.

"Blythe, I've done you a terrible injustice," he began, "and I've vowed to rectify it. Your father trusted me with your inheritance. . . . *You* trusted me . . . and I've betrayed you both."

When she started to protest, he held up his hand, halting the words that died, unformed, on her tongue. "Just listen to me. Whatever drove me to the gambling tables . . . pride, greed . . . it was wrong. Once I began to lose, I became obsessed with the notion of winning it back. Of course, it was the devil's own lie. A gambler never wins." He stood, turned, gripping the back of the chair with both hands for balance. "I have lost everything . . . not only money, *your* money . . . but my self-respect. I've dishonored my family name. I've brought Montclair to the point of ruin."

His voice broke. Instinctively, Blythe reached out her hand as Malcolm sat down again, clasping his hands together.

"I was desperate. I didn't know what to do! I tried to blot out all that I'd done in drink. That didn't work, either. Finally, I've come face to face with myself. The havoc I've caused. The hurt to innocent people. You, Blythe. You deserve better than . . . this, what I have come to."

She started to speak, but again he silenced her with a gesture. "No, don't sympathize . . . and don't pity me. Let me finish. There are things I have to say—things that are important if I'm to go on living . . . with any kind of honor."

He swallowed and took a long breath, then looked directly at her. His blue eyes blazed with a frightening intensity. "I promise you, Blythe, that I'm going to make all this up to you. A day of happiness for every day of unhappiness you've suffered by my irresponsible behavior. I'll get back the money I've lost . . . by honest means. No more drinking, no more cards! I promise you that things will be different. I will find a way to bring Montclair back, too. It may take the rest of my life . . . but I *will*."

Blythe gazed into his eyes. It seemed as if she were looking into his very soul. Could she read genuine repentance there . . . or just regret that he had brought shame to himself, disgraced his family? Suddenly, she knew. This was the real Malcolm—before the War, before Rose died, before his life became a wasteland. She saw the Malcolm who remained uncorrupted—gentle, intelligent, gallant—before tragedy and loss took their bitter toll.

Could she help reclaim that man—whole, healthy, with renewed vigor and pride in himself and his heritage? Hope stirred in Blythe's heart. Yes! Yes, with God's help, she could!

That day marked the beginning of a special time at Montclair, and that night Blythe fell on her knees with a thankful heart, praising God for answering all her prayers for Malcolm.

True to his promise, Malcolm began his struggle to regain some semblance of a normal life. He got up early each morning, attempted to eat the hearty breakfast Blythe prepared, and rode out to the fields. There, he talked to the workers and returned to his desk, full of plans and figures for recouping the financial losses Montclair had suffered in the years of neglect.

"I'll take out a loan," Malcolm told Blythe with determination. "Our family has been well known here in Mayfield for several generations. I don't know the bank manager personally—he's new in these parts, came here after the War—but that won't matter. The name Montrose still means something," he said with confidence. "We'll plant more fields, bring in some cattle, some sheep . . . like in the old days." His voice rang with enthusiasm and Blythe felt a lift of hope.

The Malcolm she remembered from the days at the ranch returned. He sought out her companionship in the evening hours rather than secreting himself in the library. They would build a cozy fire in the fireplace of the small parlor, and Malcolm would read aloud while Blythe knitted. He read from one of his favorite books, *The Idylls of the King* by Alfred, Lord Tennyson. He showed her what was written on the flyleaf: "To my dear son, Malcolm—a real Knight in Shining Armor, From his loving mother, Sara Leighton Montrose."

There were precious moments for Blythe—times when Malcolm

would lay down his book and open his heart to her, sharing things from his childhood that she had never known until now.

"When Mama was so ill, I used to read to her," he told her. "Now, I realize she chose books a child would enjoy more than an adult—tales of derring-do and adventure. We read *Robinson Crusoe* and *Robin Hood* and then the book that I think was my favorite of all—a translation of *Morte D'Arthur* by Geoffery of Monmouth, the best-known account of the legend of King Arthur.

"That book made quite an impression on me. As a boy, I persuaded my brothers, Bryce and Leighton, and of course the Camerons, Rod with his twin, Stewart, to play at being knights. We created our own Round Table, drew up a code of honor, strict rules of behavior, and a proscribed requirement to attain knighthood." Malcolm laughed a little. "Of course, we older fellows put the younger ones through their paces—"

Whenever Malcolm spoke of his friendship with the Camerons, Blythe felt a thrust of guilty pain. She had tried to crush any thoughts of Rod, telling herself that her feelings for him were fueled by loneliness and longing. He had supplied kindness and understanding when she most needed it. But she could not help wondering if he, too, waged a private battle against their unspoken love.

Malcolm went on, "We all took it very seriously, actually. In fact, we carried it too far into real life later on. I know we went to war with the same lofty cause, the same idealism and standards of honor, gallantry, and courage, we had 'played at' as boys.

"There was a rude awakening when we learned that war was really — carnage. Oh, there were acts of heroic bravery. I saw them myself. But I also saw the brutality, the ghastly waste—

"Well, for all my striving, I never reached the Holy Grail." Malcolm gave a wry smile.

"But, Malcolm, there's the future to think about," Blythe reminded him. "There's so much joy still to be found in life. At least, that's what Kate Cameron says, and what I, too, believe."

Malcolm smiled at her, amusement as well as tenderness in that smile. But Blythe's optimism remained strong, especially when Malcolm announced he had an appointment with the Mayfield bank manager.

"There should be no problem," he told her. "Mayfield is growing, the Northerners are flooding in here because of the milder climate. The community is beginning to prosper. If Montclair prospers, too, it will help everyone. We can hire more people to work the land." He rubbed his hands together with an air of satisfaction.

"I'm sure things will go well, Malcolm," Blythe agreed.

That night Blythe went to bed and right to sleep without the usual tossing and turning. In the night, however, something disturbed her deep slumber. Half-awake, half-asleep, she thought she heard someone calling her name.

"Blythe!" A tap at the bedroom door.

She sat up.

"Blythe." It was Malcolm's voice. The door opened, and a slanted arc of light shone on the bare floor. The tall dark silhouette of Malcolm's figure holding a lamp in one hand was framed in the rectangle of the door.

"What is it? Is something wrong?" she asked, her voice husky with sleep.

"May I come in? I need . . . to talk to you. I couldn't sleep. I need—" He paused.

Wide awake now, Blythe asked, "Would you like me to go downstairs with you, make some hot milk?"

He shook his head and approached her. Sitting down on the edge of the bed, he placed the oil lamp on the table beside it. She saw the weary slump of his broad shoulders under the dressing gown.

"Oh, Blythe, I've made such a wreck of things," he confessed, pressing his temple with his fingers. "I've hurt so many people, disappointed them, failed them. I can't stand my own thoughts—" The words ended in a moan.

Blythe sat up, pushed back her hair. Impulsively, she held out her arms to comfort him. He leaned his head against her shoulder, and she stroked the thick, silky hair. She felt a shudder go through him, then his arms went around her, pulling her closer.

"Oh, Blythe, poor Blythe. It was wrong of me to bring you here, wrong of me to marry you!" he groaned.

"Don't say that, Malcolm!" she begged, her arms tightening around him. "I'm *glad* I came, *glad* you married me! I love you, Malcolm."

He raised his head then, staring at her with wild eyes. "But you don't even know me. How can you love me?" He shook his head sorrowfully. The light from the lamp sharpened his features, illuminating the angular planes, making his eyes dark pools of pain.

Blythe brought her hands from his shoulders, placed them on either side of his face, then kissed him full on the mouth. She felt him stiffen, then a second later his arms tightened around her. As he began to respond, Blythe felt her heart swell with surprise and joy. This is what she had longed for, dreamed of, hoped would happen.

"Oh, Malcolm, everything will be better soon. I know it will," she whispered. Then she threw back the covers. "Come, Malcolm. Stay with me—"

He hesitated only a moment, then he stood, untied the cord of his dressing gown and, as she moved over, got in beside her and gathered her into his embrace.

Blythe lifted herself on her elbow and looked down at Malcolm's sleeping face. Relaxed, the harsh planes of his face were softened and the mouth so often twisted in a mocking smile rested in a sweet curve. The dark lashes of his closed eyelids shadowed the cheeks and hid the hopelessness that haunted his eyes. Asleep, Malcolm looked young, defenseless, gentle—as if all the horrors, all the disappointments of his existence had been erased.

She longed to touch him, to trace the outline of his lips that had kissed hers so passionately, to run her fingers through the dark hair with its scattering of silver, but she dared not. She could not risk waking him and perhaps see him regard her as if he didn't know her, as if this wondrous thing had never happened.

She slipped out of bed so as not to disturb him and went over to the window where a rising moon was transforming Montclair with its shimmering beauty. Was this the harvest moon people spoke of? She watched the pale orb move behind the bare branches of the tall trees outside. Oh, if only harvest could come to this run-down plantation, a new harvest of hope.

Tomorrow, Blythe prayed, would begin a new time of sowing, a new time of reaping. Whatever Malcolm thought or felt or would remember when he awoke, Blythe knew he had placed his stamp upon her—body, mind and soul—and that now she belonged to him forever.

chapter
26

IN SPITE OF his pallor and the wracking cough that persisted, Malcolm looked splendid as he was preparing to keep his appointment with the bank manager in Mayfield.

Blythe had steamed and brushed his gray, broadcloth coat, polished his boots, ironed his best white shirt. As she handed him his broad-brimmed black felt hat, she surveyed him proudly. Malcolm had the unmistakable air of a gentleman.

"How do I look?" he asked, staightening his cravat and touching the jade stickpin in the shape of a four-leaf clover Garnet had given him years ago.

"Very handsome!"

"And prosperous?" he quipped. "You know you have to look as if you don't need the money when you transact a bank loan."

"You look like the Master of Montclair ought to look!" she declared, laughing.

Suddenly Malcolm was serious. He pulled Blythe into his arms, hugged her tight, pressing her cheek into the bosom of his ruffled shirt.

"Thank God for you, Blythe! I do need you so."

Need you! the little hungry part of Blythe's heart taunted. He had said, *need,* not *love!* How long she had yearned to hear him speak those words. But it didn't matter anymore. She understood why he couldn't say them to her . . . yet. They still belonged to Rose.

He held her against him a moment longer. "Well, I'm off to slay the dragon like a good knight!" he said heartily.

Blythe had insisted Malcolm take Treasure into town. The mare was a

177

younger, finer-looking animal than the old workhorses Malcolm had sometimes ridden on his rounds of the plantation.

Curried and combed, her mane and tail shiny, Treasure was stamping her feet impatiently in front of the house where one of the Negro boys had brought her. A group of grinning black children stood watching as Malcolm went down the veranda steps.

At the bottom he turned and made a sweeping bow to Blythe, who was standing in the doorway. His jaunty air touched her heart and she smiled and waved back. Then he mounted, and Blythe moved to the top of the steps to watch as he rode down the drive. To her surprise, at the bend, he reined, turned, and took off his hat, waving it high in the air.

Her heart caught. Malcolm was like a cavalier, riding off to do battle. And that's what it was for him, she knew. A Montrose begging for a loan! Unthinkable! It must have taken all the fortitude he could muster to suppress his pride enough to do this thing . . . for the sake of honor.

Dear God, Blythe prayed. *Be with him . . . help him today!*

All day long, Blythe kept busy. She turned the collar on some of Malcolm's old shirts, darned socks, rearranged kitchen drawers. Blythe knew it was a half-day's ride to Mayfield and back, and mentally calculated the time Malcolm would be at the bank, signing papers and doing whatever one must do to arrange for a loan.

The victor should return to a festive meal, she decided, and planned a menu of Brunswick stew concocted of chicken, corn, peas, carrots, and potatoes in a thick, creamy sauce, and an apple cobbler. Preparing the vegetables and fruit and making the crust took most of the early afternoon.

By mid-afternoon, the sun, which had shone brightly for a while, was blocked by scurrying dark clouds. Thus far into the month of November, they had been blessed with good weather, but now it began to rain—at first a fine drizzle, turning rapidly into a steady downpour.

As it grew later and darker, Blythe lighted the lamps and took up a post at one of the parlor windows, peering into the darkness for some sign of Malcolm.

As on countless other evenings, she heard the grandfather clock striking the hours—six, seven, eight. . . . She clenched her teeth to still their chattering. "Oh no, dear God! Please don't let him have stopped somewhere! Don't let him be drinking again!" she pleaded through tight lips.

The old house moaned as the wind rattled the windowpanes and sudden bursts of rain splintered, staccato-like, against them. A log in the fireplace crackled, fell apart with a sharpness that caused Blythe to start.

She never knew how long she stood there at the window. There was no consciousness of aching muscles strained with tension, or stomach knotted with anxiety. She was frozen like stone, knowing with dreadful certainty that something terrible had happened to Malcolm.

Then, wavering in the dark, blurred by the sheets of rain that misted her view, she saw lights coming toward the house—lanterns swaying and bobbing as they came closer.

She broke and ran out into the hall, flung open the door. The wind tore it from her hand and dashed it against the wall as she pushed out onto the veranda, her skirts whipped by the force of the wind-driven rain. Soaked instantly, she clung to one of the columns.

Three men were approaching on horseback. Straining to see through the rain-veiled darkness, she recognized the figure slumped in the saddle. It was Malcolm! Another man walked alongside, supporting him. A third followed, holding the lantern aloft.

When they reached the foot of the step, she saw Rod in the flickering lamplight, assisted by his Negro groom, Ambrose, from Cameron Hall. Heedless of the rain, Blythe rushed down the steps. To her horror, Malcolm fell forward out of the saddle. Seeing that his face was bruised and bloodied, she stifled a scream.

"What happened?" she asked Rod.

"Later. Let's just get him inside, get these wet clothes off him, put him to bed." Rod's voice was calm, but urgent.

The black man and Rod carried Malcolm into the house. Blythe, still in shock, followed blindly.

In the front hall, the three men halted.

Rod turned to Blythe. "We'll put him to bed," he said, then hesitated, waiting for her instructions.

Blythe felt a hot flame of embarrassment burn her face. Now, there would be no more secrets. Rod would know how it was between her and Malcolm.

"In the library," she said quickly. "He sleeps in the little room off the library."

When they disappeared down the hall, she stood absolutely still for a long moment, wringing her hands. She had heard it said that people did such things under stress, and she was doing it now. Then, instinctively, she rushed upstairs for extra quilts. Then, she hurried into the kitchen to fill the kettle with water and put it on to boil. The men would be needing something hot to drink.

When Rod, followed by Ambrose, stepped into the kitchen, Blythe handed them mugs of the freshly brewed coffee. The black man discreetly retreated to a corner, leaving Rod to talk with Blythe alone.

"Is he all right?" she asked numbly.

"For now. He'll sleep, but—" Rod paused— "I'd send for Dr. Lynn in the morning."

It took effort to force the next question past her lips. "Is he . . . drunk?"

Rod shook his head. "He may have been drinking, but I'm afraid it's worse than that. When we found him, his pulse was very weak."

"Found him? How? Where?"

"Actually, it was Treasure who alerted us to trouble. She came galloping, riderless, into our stable yard, and Ambrose rushed to the house to report to me. At first, I was terrified that something might have happened to *you*. But when I saw the man's saddle . . . well, I knew Malcolm must have been riding and that he was in some kind of trouble. Ambrose and I went out to look for him—"

"Oh, Rod!"

"He was lying, face down, in a ditch by the side of the road, not far from Cameron Hall. He was on his way home, Blythe."

Rod went over to the stove, refilled his mug from the blue enameled coffeepot, then took a seat at the kitchen table.

Her knees trembling, Blythe sank into a chair across from him.

"The rain must have blinded him," Rod began. "It was very dark and windy. A tree branch had fallen across the road in front of him. We assume Treasure shied, reared, and threw Malcolm into a ditch. That's where we found him. He was unconscious, bleeding from the head. . . . He's very ill, Blythe." Rod measured her reaction. "He's never fully recovered from his prison experience, you know. Pneumonia weakened his lungs."

"Yes, I know. He was quite ill when he came to our ranch." She bit her lip, recalling that day when the old miner had brought Malcolm to them—feverish, weak, "dying," Pa had said.

"Well, the doctor will know more," Rod said, staring down into his mug. Then he lifted it and drained it in a single gulp. "I'll send one of our boys to Mayfield first thing in the morning with a message for Dr. Lynn to come out," he said, rising and donning his heavy coat.

"Thank you, Rod," Blythe replied quietly, "for . . . everything." The words seemed inadequate, but she did not trust herself to say more.

At the front door, Rod paused. "I'll bring Treasure back tomorrow."

"No, Rod. Don't."

"Why not?"

"I won't be riding her anymore," Blythe said firmly. "Malcolm will be needing me now."

A look passed between them that needed no words. It spoke of a love that strengthened, comforted, endured, and, in the end, relinquished.

"Good night then, Blythe," Rod said finally, "and God bless." Then he disappeared into the rainy night.

All that long night, Blythe sat at Malcolm's bedside, wringing out cloths with cool water to press against his face and brow as he tossed restlessly on the pillow. At times, he mumbled incoherently, and she soothed him as she might a fretful child.

Toward morning, he opened his eyes. They were glazed and bright with fever, and his skin was hot to the touch.

He recognized her immediately, then a kind of anguished memory seemed to come over him. "Blythe! Blythe, I'm sorry . . . so sorry."

"Hush, Malcolm, hush."

"I've failed you again, Blythe."

"You haven't failed me, dear. Hush now and rest."

He began to cough, a hoarse, rasping cough that seemed to wrack his whole body. It left him weak, gasping for breath. She watched him fearfully, then pressed the folded damp cloth again on his forehead.

He closed his eyes wearily. "They turned me down, Blythe. Can you believe that? 'No collateral,' the man said. Montclair . . . not acceptable as collateral."

"Don't exert yourself. It will only make you worse. Please, Malcolm, it doesn't matter. We'll manage."

He struggled up, his eyes flashing. "But it does matter!" he protested. "To be turned down—like that! *Me,* a *Montrose!* Is the word of a gentleman no longer enough?"

"Please, dear, lie back. You must rest. The doctor is coming in the morning. You must get well first. Then we can talk about . . . other things."

Exhausted, Malcolm fell back against the pillows. "Don't worry, Blythe. I told him I didn't need his money! I still have another card to

play. . . . Card? Ha! My luck hasn't entirely run out. I told him—"
Malcolm started to laugh, but the laughing caused a fit of coughing.

This time the paroxysm lasted so long that Blythe was terrified. By
the time it was over, Malcolm was too weak to utter another word. She
held his hand, continuing to stroke his forehead until he drifted off to
sleep.

But Blythe's heart was stone cold within her. Malcolm's mention of
cards had pierced her heart like a knife. Had he been gambling to raise
the money needed to restore Montclair? And if so, what had he used for
stakes?

When the doctor emerged from Malcolm's room the next morning, the
expression on his face sent slivers of fear through Blythe's body. She
wiped her clammy hands on her skirt.

"He has a slight concussion," Dr. Lynn began, studying her as if to
decide whether or not she was prepared to hear the worst. "He may
seem confused, not make much sense when he tries to talk." Then,
averting his eyes from Blythe's anxious face, he spoke with deliberation.
"Your husband, Mrs. Montrose, is a very sick man. I have to tell you the
truth. His lungs are filling with fluid." The doctor shook his head as he
repacked his valise. "All you can do is watch and pray. I don't want to
give you any false hope. His condition had deteriorated even before this
accident—"

Blythe felt a sickening terror—Malcolm was going to die!

When Doc Sanderson had told her Pa hadn't long to live, Malcolm
had been there to support her, along with an entire community of
caring people. But this time was different. This time, she would have to
walk through the valley alone.

chapter
27

THE ONE PERSON Blythe knew she could trust—the one to whom she most wanted to cling for support and strength was forbidden to her. The two hearts who could best comfort each other were bound by that unspoken code of honor they had silently pledged to live by. Blythe knew she could depend on no one except God, and she thanked Him daily for her new faith in His power to sustain and uphold her.

Lonnie became her steadfast help in nursing Malcolm, spelling Blythe for times of necessary rest, staying longer than her other chores required to assist Blythe with the new tasks the sick man's needs demanded. Blythe often saw Lonnie's lips moving in prayer as they lifted or moved Malcolm, and at times she came upon the black woman singing hymns in a high, clear voice—a voice that had risen above the others the night of the tent revival. There was one hymn that Malcolm had come to favor, and Lonnie taught it to Blythe.

When he was lucid, Malcolm told her fragments of his story until she had at last pieced it all together. "When the bank refused to give me a loan, I felt humiliated . . . angry . . . determined to show them I didn't need their money. . . . I threw aside everything, my caution, my promises to you and myself. I went to the Mayfield Hotel. . . . Always a card game going on in the Gentlemen's Lounge. . . . Stakes were high . . . more than I could afford." Here Malcolm's voice trailed off in self-contempt and loathing. "Sorry, Blythe. Should have known better."

"Don't worry about it now, Malcolm. There are other ways we can get money. We can sell some of the land . . . the far fields that aren't being planted now . . . cultivate smaller acreage, raise a quick cash crop like alfalfa or corn—"

Malcolm closed his eyes. "Too late . . . too late."

"Don't tire yourself, Malcolm. We can talk about this when you're well," Blythe said, her cheerful attitude masking her anxiety.

But Malcolm was already slipping away, not listening. He was back in that semi-conscious state from which he awakened less and less often as the weeks dragged on.

The day-to-day routine seemed a lonely struggle. Lonnie helped Blythe turn and bathe Malcolm, change his linens. But it was she who kept the night vigil, coaxed him to take a little nourishment, and when he was wakeful and restless, read to him by the hour.

His most frequent request was *Idylls of the King,* and Blythe soon became as familiar with the adventures of Sir Gawain and Galahad as Malcolm. But when he awakened during the night, he would ask for a verse or psalm from the Bible that was always kept in the drawer of his bedside table.

The first time she had lifted the Bible from the drawer, she had been startled to see that its covers were blistered, blackened and curled around the edges. When she opened it, she knew the reason. Inside, in a delicate script, was inscribed the name, ROSE MEREDITH MONTROSE. This had been Rose's Bible, somehow salvaged from the devastating fire in which she had died. Malcolm must have kept it all these years. Had he read it? Wept over it? It didn't matter. Blythe did not feel embittered nor resentful anymore. Rose seemed so much a part of Malcolm, so much a part of Montclair, but it was a benign presence. Blythe did not fear nor was she jealous of Malcolm's first love.

The Camerons sent over fruit and preserves, Dove's blanc mange custard, and calf jelly to tempt the sick man's failing appetite. Blythe assumed Rod brought them, though she was not sure, for Lonnie always answered the door. Once, she saw him ride away as she watched from behind the curtain of the sick room. But she looked at him as if she were seeing someone she had known long ago in another world.

Blythe now slept on a cot at the foot of Malcolm's bed, alert to his slightest movement or call.

One such night, she awakened and, rousing herself, saw him struggle to sit up. Instantly, she was at his side. It was almost more than she could bear to see those sunken eyes, the dark hollows of his wasted face.

"What is it, Malcolm?" she whispered. "What do you want?" She took one limp hand, stroked it.

"Sing to me. . . . Sing Lonnie's hymn."

Blythe cleared her throat, wishing she had the other woman's lovely soprano voice, but even though she quavered on the high notes, she tried. "Softly and tenderly, Jesus is calling," she sang, "calling for you and for me . . . calling, 'Oh, sinner, come home.'"

"Home," Malcolm murmured, closing his eyes again.

Blythe's throat tightened but gamely she went on singing, wondering how soon Jesus would call Malcolm home.

On an unusually warm, sunny day for December, Lonnie insisted, "Miss Blythe, honey, you gwine to break iffen you doan git away some. I's gwine to be right here if Marse Malcolm need anything. Jes' you put on your bonnet and shawl and get out in de fresh air and sunshine. Take a little walk. It'll do you good and he'p you, too."

Persuaded, Blythe went downstairs, took the knitted shawl off the hook by the back door, tied her bonnet under her chin, and stepped outside. She walked along the garden path down to the meadow. The air was clear and sharp. Taking several long breaths, she quickened her pace.

Her thoughts still on Malcolm, she walked without any particular direction. Before long, to her surprise, she found herself approaching the rustic bridge.

At once, visions of Rod standing here beside her, stopping just short of telling her he loved her, assaulted her memory. She had turned and fled, hurrying back to Montclair, back to safety. It all seemed so long ago now, as if it had happened to two other people.

She halted, not wanting to go any further, knowing this path led to that clearing in the woods where the little honeymoon house nestled. She did not want to revive any errant desires or regrets. Today was all she could handle. She turned back toward the house as the Scripture verse flashed through her mind, "Sufficient unto the day is the evil thereof."

A few yards from the house, she felt a sudden inner compulsion to get back to Malcolm. She picked up her skirts and began to run. Inside the door, she dropped her bonnet and shawl and rushed down the hall.

Lonnie looked up as Blythe burst into Malcolm's room, and put her finger to her lips, indicating by a nod of her head that Malcolm was sleeping. Then she got up from her place beside the bed and tiptoed toward Blythe.

"I'll bring you a cup of tea 'fo I leave fo' the day," she whispered.

All at once, Blythe felt a leaden weariness, so heavy she wanted to weep. She fell to her knees beside the bed. Dwindling afternoon light lingered in the room and touched Malcolm's face. It was gray, drawn beyond recognition. Gone was the high color, the healthy glow of the days on the ranch.

Lonnie stole into the room, left the cup by Blythe's chair, and went out again noiselessly.

Blythe continued to kneel by the bedside. Malcolm stirred, opened his eyes, and gazed at her. There was a look of tenderness on the emaciated face, and when he slowly opened his eyes, for a moment they looked young, eager, alive.

His lips formed a name, and Blythe bent closer . . . only to hear— "Rose! Rose . . . forgive me, Rose?" he mumbled brokenly.

"Of course, my darling," Blythe whispered, touching his face gently, the source of this present anguish unknown to her.

Then he said, "Sing to me—"

With the greatest effort, Blythe began, "Softly and tenderly, Jesus is calling—"

She sang it over and over until her voice tired and she could force no sound. She leaned against the mattress, feeling overcome with fatigue. Her eyes grew heavy, and she laid her head on the pillow beside Malcolm's and fell asleep.

She dreamed of Lucas Valley, of that sunny December day when she had stood with him in the little wooden church and vowed to love, honor and cherish "for better or worse, for richer or poorer, in sickness or in health." She had been so happy that day, so pleased with her mail-order dress and the straw bonnet with its blue ribbons and roses, proud that the tall, handsome man at her side was soon to be her husband.

The happiness of the dream was still upon her as she came slowly awake. She blinked her eyes as the misty memory of the hope and promise of that day lingered.

She lifted her head from the pillow and saw that the room was full of shadows. Suddenly she realized the hand she held was cold. While she had been dreaming of the joys of beginning a life with Malcolm, she had awakened to find it ended.

chapter

28

ON THE DAY of Malcolm's funeral, the December air shimmered with a kind of sharp brilliance. Malcolm's casket, draped with a Confederate flag, was carried up the hill to the Montrose family cemetery.

Blythe, slim and erect, in black dress and bonnet swathed in crepe, her face hidden by the thick veil that shadowed it, stood a little apart from the small group gathered around the gravesite. She remained unmoving as the minister read:

> As for man, his days are as grass;
> As a flower of the field, so he flourisheth.
> For the wind passeth over it, and it is gone;
> And the place thereof shall know it no more."

Blythe did not know the minister. Kate Cameron had made the arrangements, but somehow his words seemed chilling and abstract. So Blythe was especially glad she had asked Lonnie to sing. As the clear, true voice rang out in the crystal winter air, Blythe rejoiced, knowing Malcolm would have wanted it so.

"Just a closer walk with Thee; Grant it, Jesus, if You please—" The beautiful plea of the believer soothed Blythe's sore heart.

After the casket was lowered and the shovelful of symbolic earth placed on top, the people began to leave, stopping to offer condolences to Blythe as they filed by.

The mourners were mostly old friends of the Montrose family, obligated by ancient ties and tradition to pay their respects. Still, she accepted their sympathy gratefully.

The Camerons were the last to speak to her.

Kate kissed her cheek. "Won't you come home with us, Blythe, dear? I hate to think of your being alone in that empty house."

Blythe shook her head. "Thank you, Mrs. Cameron, but I *need* to be alone for a while."

"Well, my dear, remember, if there's anything . . . anything at all we can do . . . you have only to send word."

"I know," Blythe nodded solemnly.

Kate passed by, and Dove took her place. The two Montrose widows embraced silently.

And then Rod was standing in front of her. His face showed nothing but concern, his emotions in check. Only his eyes revealed how much he cared, how much he longed to comfort her. He took her cold hands in both of his, brought them to his lips, and pressed a kiss on them.

"Whenever you want me to come . . . I shall be here."

Blythe was grateful for the veil, glad he could not read the longing in her eyes. She did not trust herself to answer, merely bowed her head, and Rod stepped aside to join the Cameron ladies.

No one lingered. They all hurried down from the windy hilltop to their carriages and horses, eager to be away from this place of sorrow, this reminder of their own mortality in the week before Christmas.

Lonnie wanted to stay overnight with her, but Blythe refused. "You have a husband and children who need you at home. I'll be fine . . . really."

"I lef' some soup simmerin' on the stove. Now, Miss Blythe, you try to eat, you heah? We can't hab you gittin' sick and po'ly yo'se'f," Lonnie cautioned, and with one or two anxious backward glances, she finally left.

Blythe walked out onto the front porch, feeling suddenly stifled in the house. As a purple dusk crept along the edges of the fields, a flock of birds triangled against the darkening sky. Somewhere in the woods an owl hooted.

Blythe shivered, drew her shawl more closely around her, and went inside. The minute she closed the door, a wave of dizziness swept over her. Everything swam before her eyes, the floor tilted, and she leaned back against the door to steady herself.

After a few minutes, she drew a long breath and straightened. She had a sour taste in her mouth and her stomach felt queasy. Then she remembered she had not been able to eat breakfast that morning, nor had she had anything to eat this whole, long, stressful day. In fact, despite Lonnie's scoldings, she had not eaten properly for weeks.

She would make herself some tea, she decided, starting for the kitchen. As she went down the hall, she glanced into the dining room. The long table was laden with covered dishes, cakes, pies that people had brought in the Virginia tradition—gifts of food for the bereaved family. Family? But there was no family at Montclair anymore.

She had sent a telegram to Mr. Montrose in Savannah of Malcolm's death, and he had wired back saying Sara was prostrate with grief, unable to travel, and he must stay with her. They would come home in the spring. In the spring? Spring seemed a thousand years away.

Blythe felt infinitely weary as she sat sipping tea at the kitchen table. The reality of what had happened was just beginning to penetrate her stunned consciousness. That Malcolm was really gone, that she was now really alone in the world seemed impossible.

Her head throbbed dully, and she rose. She had had almost no sleep for days now. She would go to bed. In the morning, when she was more rested, she would be able to think more clearly, plan what to do next.

So many thoughts tumbled about as she walked through the empty house. She was only seventeen, but she felt old—as old as this house. The portraits lining the wall of the stairway reminded her of the other women who had come here as brides. The sense of responsibility weighed heavily. Was it all to end here? For once, she felt a rising sense of relief. At least, her father had not survived to see the sorry state she had come to. He had died, believing she would find a better life in Virginia.

There was still much to do, Blythe thought as she laid her aching head on the pillow. Malcolm must have a proper headstone, some appropriate epitaph—perhaps something from his beloved *Idylls of the King*. She must look up a passage from Tennyson's book tomorrow. Tomorrow, she would feel stronger. Tomorrow—

But in the morning, when Blythe tried to get out of bed, a terrible nausea swept over her. She clung to the bedpost, hoping it would pass. But it didn't, and she was horribly sick.

Spent, she climbed back into bed and curled up under the covers. Her mind went racing back . . . counting. Slowly, a possibility dawned. Could it be? Was it possible?

It was awhile before she attempted to get up again. She dragged on her flannel dressing gown and groped her way downstairs to the kitchen. Tea would soothe her jumpy stomach, stop the pounding of her head.

She was sitting at the kitchen table, her cold hands warming themselves around the hot cup when she heard Lonnie's voice, her footsteps on the back porch. In another minute, she and Cora came into the kitchen.

"Yo' feelin' po'ly, Miss Blythe?" Lonnie asked as she hung up her shawl.

"I'm better today, Lonnie."

"Had anything to eat yet?" Lonnie inspected her pale face with a frown.

"Not yet."

"Now what did I say yestiddy?" scolded Lonnie, getting down the cast iron frying pan. "I'll jes' scramble up some nice eggs—"

Blythe's stomach lurched at the thought. "No, no, Lonnie, thank you. Nothing."

"Yo' jes' gwine to wither away, Miss Blythe, if you doan eat!"

"Later, Lonnie, I promise. But now I want you to do something about all that food folks brought. There's way more than I can ever use. So, you and Cora pack it all in one of the big wicker hampers and take it down back to share with the other families."

"Oh, ma'm!" squealed Cora, delighted.

"Yo' shure?" Lonnie was doubtful.

"Yes. Now you two go on. I'm going back upstairs to dress. There are things I must attend to."

Blythe hoped they would hurry. She needed to be alone to sort out this startling new fact of her life, decide what she must do.

If she really were carrying Malcolm's child— Oh, if only Malcolm had lived to know it! A child would have made up for so much he had lost!

Suddenly the thought overwhelmed her. Their child—if it were a son, and somehow she believed it would be a boy—was heir to Montclair! The future came into focus. Somehow, she must hold on to all this . . . for the child.

How to do so was not immediately clear. Perhaps she could sell off some of the land, reinvest it in the farm. She would have to consult with someone who could advise her.

Already, Blythe felt a renewed vigor. She was young and strong. She had observed her father's skillful management of the ranch, had helped him keep books. There was no reason why she could not restore Montclair to its former splendor, save her son's inheritance! With God's help, she would do it! With God, nothing was impossible!

chapter
29

IN THE NEXT few days, Blythe gave herself to a thorough evaluation of Montclair, the house and property. There was much to be done, and she made countless lists, wrote down endless questions that must be answered. Preoccupied, she was distracted from the sense of sorrow that might otherwise have overwhelmed her.

Three days before Christmas, on her way downstairs just a little past eight in the morning, the front door knocker clanged, echoing through the house. Wondering who might be visiting at this early hour, Blythe hurried to answer it and opened the door to a man she had never seen before.

Dressed in a cheap, ill-fitting coat and a stovepipe hat that he did not bother to remove, he thrust a sheaf of papers at her. "You Mrs. Malcolm Montrose?"

"Yes," she replied, puzzled as to who the rude stranger might be.

He rattled the papers under her nose and, startled by his gauche behavior, she took them.

"This is a sheriff's eviction notice!" he bellowed. "You have three days to remove yourself from the premises, taking with you only your personal belongings. This house and all its contents, including furnishings, silverware, dishes, cooking utensils, is in the possession of the creditor of the deceased Malcolm Montrose and will be sold to reimburse the rest of his creditors at Sheriff's Auction. Good day to you, ma'am."

With that, he spun on his heel, clattered down the porch steps, hopped into a shabby buggy, flicked the reins over a sway-backed nag, and set off in a slow jog down the drive.

Shocked, Blythe's eyes raced down the pages. On the last page, in Malcolm's familiar handwriting, was his signature, signing over Montclair and all its possessions to someone named RANDALL BONDURANT.

Blythe stared down at the paper she held in her shaking hands. She read the words again. Even as they registered in her brain, her heart rejected their meaning. No, it couldn't be! Malcolm had lost Montclair? To a stranger . . . in a card game?

Slowly, the enormity of it pierced her frozen mind. Her first thought was of Malcolm.

"Thank God, he will never know!" How guilt-ridden he would have been to suffer a sheriff's eviction. Then she thought of Sara and Mr. Montrose. What disgrace to their family name!

Blythe never knew how long she stood there, locked in disbelief. Stiffly, she turned back into the house. The man had said three days! She looked wildly about at the gold-framed family portraits on the walls. The brides of Montclair stared back at her from the stairwell. Her gaze sought out the lovely furniture, the priceless vases, the Chinese rugs . . . all to be left here for strangers.

In the parlor across the hall, the furniture was covered with dustcloths, like gray ghosts. This room had not been in use since the War, Mr. Montrose had told her. Once, this place had been the scene of delightful parties, the kind Montclair had been famous for. The walls had rung with laughter and the gay tap of dancing feet, the rustling of fans and the swish of taffeta skirts, the voices of flirtatious young ladies and handsome young men.

This room represented the world Malcolm had known—before the War, before Rose's death, before the Yankee prison and California—before he had returned to the shell of his home, his shattered dreams.

In panic, she thought of seeking advice from Kate or Rod at Cameron Hall, but quickly rejected the idea. They would be getting ready for their annual Christmas party, a tradition of long standing. Kate had told her about the event, regretting the fact that Blythe, in mourning, could not attend.

"By that time, I'll be gone," Blythe said aloud, her voice resounding in the emptiness.

She would have to hurry through Malcolm's things, a task she had put off as too painful. Now she must make all those decisions—what to take, what to leave behind. Where she would go, she did not know.

She'd think about that later. For now, she would simply do what had to be done.

Blythe let herself into Malcolm's room. She had not entered it since she and Lonnie had tenderly washed and dressed his body for its final placement in the box made for him out of native white oak, felled by one of the Negro workers and lovingly crafted by the plantation carpenter.

As she went in, Blythe felt a pang of sadness. In this room, in the weeks of his last illness, Malcolm had given her some of the love she had longed for so long.

At the foot of the bed was a trunk. Blythe knelt and opened it. To her surprise, there was little there—a few books, his War medals, some faded photographs. It seemed an invasion of Malcolm's privacy to go through his things like this. But, she reminded herself, at least she would not be leaving them for indifferent strangers. Anything she found that she did not want to keep for his son, she would burn.

She took up the photographs. One was a group picture of his classmates at Harvard, and there were pictures of his two handsome brothers in Confederate uniform. The baby picture she gazed at longest. This must be Jonathan. He had Malcolm's hair, but Rose's marvelous dark eyes. She wondered, fleetingly, if the child to be born would resemble his half-brother.

Then, to her surprise, she found a well-worn New Testament. She hadn't known Malcolm used anything but Rose's Bible, the one she had buried with him.

When she lifted it from its resting place, she opened it carefully and read an inscription: *Beloved Husband, I hope you will find in this book the love, comfort, and guidance you will need in the days ahead.* It was signed, *Always, Your Rose* and dated, June, 1861.

Rose must have given this to Malcolm before he left for the War. As she held it, a slip of paper fell out and Blythe picked it up. The edges were rough, as though it had been ripped from some kind of notebook; the print, faint, but still legible.

> I asked God for strength, that I
> might achieve,
>
> I was made weak, that I might
> learn humbly to obey.

I asked for health, that I might
do greater things,

I was given infirmity, that I might
do better things.

I asked for riches, that I might be happy,

I was given poverty, that I might be wise.

I asked for power, that I might
have the praise of men,

I was given weakness, that I
might feel the need of God.

I asked for all things, that I
might enjoy life,

I was given life, that I might
enjoy all things.

I got nothing that I asked for—
but everything I had hoped for.

Almost despite myself, my
unspoken prayers were answered.

I am, among all men,
most richly blessed.

                    —Anonymous Confederate soldier

Tears blurred the last few lines. Had Malcolm written this himself? Or copied it from someone else? No matter—Blythe's heart leaped with the joyous conviction that Malcolm had, indeed, known the Lord and, in the end, was reconciled to his tragedy.

Blythe stayed up all that night, packing and burning papers and letters. She kept his favorite books—*The Idylls of the King* and a book of Emerson's essays, a gift of Rose's to him on their first Christmas, thinking perhaps when she was settled somewhere, she would send it to Jonathan Montrose. The boy would likely cherish something belonging to his father with his mother's handwriting.

At dawn, Blythe sat down to her last and most difficult task, that of writing Malcolm's parents. In carefully chosen words, she presented the situation without blame or bitterness. She wrote tenderly of Malcolm's last days, of his faith and brave resignation. She felt Mr. Montrose, at least, would read between the lines and soften the blow for Sara.

Lastly, she wrote a letter to Kate Cameron, which she would post in Richmond, thinking it best to be gone when it was received. In it, she explained why she was leaving and thanked Kate for her friendship and many kindnesses. She started to add that she hoped someday they would meet again, but decided against it. It was better to make Mayfield and the Camerons, along with Montclair, a closed chapter. She did not write a separate note to Rod, but included him, along with Dove, in her closing.

"I will never forget your gracious warmth, the way you opened your home and hearts to me. God Bless and Keep You All."

There was more to do, and time was flying. Blythe put the worn leather New Testament and the poem inside in the pile of things she would pack with her own.

Searching to be sure she had removed anything of value from Malcolm's trunk, her eyes fell on a legal folder. She took it out, opened it, and was startled to see her father's handwriting on the first document.

Her eyes widened as she read: "I, Jedediah Dorman, do assign the sum of $2500 in gold pieces to Malcolm Montrose when he marries my daughter Blythe, as well as the profit from the sale of my property, including the house, barn, 60 acres of grazing land and all livestock."

Below that simple statement were two signatures—her father's and Malcolm's.

Blythe's blood ran cold. How clear everything was now. She understood Malcolm's long indifference now, his reluctance to make her truly his wife. It was not his faithfulness to Rose's memory alone that had kept him from her side, but the bitter fact that Pa and Malcolm had struck a bargain . . . and that she was it—a "bargain bride."

Attached to this statement was an envelope on which was written: IN THE CASE OF THE DEATH OF MALCOLM MONTROSE, THIS IS TO BE OPENED BY HIS WIDOW, BLYTHE DORMAN MONTROSE.

With trembling hands, she broke the seal of the heavy parchment envelope and drew out the enclosed letter written in her father's hand.

"My dear daughter,

When you read these words, sorrow will have come upon you. You will know by now the arrangement I have made with Malcolm Montrose. I hope it was a wise one and that you have been happy and well cared for. If for any reason, you find yourself without funds, this will sustain you until you can reach New York City and contact the firm of Cargill, Hoskins and Sedgewick—lawyers who have my Will and instructions.

> Your loving father,
> Jedediah Dorman."

Inside was a small suede pouch. Blythe pulled the leather strings and drew in her breath sharply at the contents—three $100 gold pieces.

Blythe let the pieces slither through her fingers, making a ringing sound as they tumbled one on top of each other into her skirt. They felt cold and hard, and she shivered, pulling the knitted shawl closer around her shoulders.

Was it possible her father could have foreseen disaster? No! Surely not. He had trusted Malcolm completely—Blythe was certain of that. But Jed Dorman was a prudent man. He had known misfortune as well as fortune. Above all, he had wanted his daughter safe and would not leave anything to chance.

When Lonnie came up to see if she was all right, Blythe told her the news. "I'm going away, Lonnie, but I'm sure the new owner will need workers. I think you and your families will be safe."

Lonnie threw her apron over her face and let out a low, keening wail. "Oh, Miss Blythe! Miss Blythe!"

"You mustn't cry, Lonnie. You believe the Lord will take care of you, don't you?"

"Ain't yo' nevah comin' back, Miss Blythe?"

"I can't say, Lonnie. Nobody knows the future," she replied.

The black woman finally left with two baskets full of food and other household items Blythe thought she and some of the other plantation families could use.

That night Blythe packed her own things. Along with her "treasures" that had belonged to her mother, Blythe carefully wrapped the Montrose betrothal ring Sara had given her. She had never felt right about wearing it herself. It should be given and received in abiding love, and this had never truly been hers with Malcolm. Perhaps, one day—

her son would give it to someone who would become a beloved bride of Montclair.

That day dawned bleak and gray. A misty rain fell when Blythe set out to make a last pilgrimage around Montclair. She walked through the garden and paused at the stone pedestal on which the bronze sun-dial rested. Its inscription seemed to belie the tragedy and turmoil, the terrible events that had marked the last few days at Montclair. I COUNT ONLY THE SUNNY HOURS.

Once upon a time it may have been true. Not now.

She walked up the hill to the family cemetery. Malcolm's grave was yet unmarked, but Blythe had left instructions for Kate Cameron to see that a headstone was erected with the inscription:

> God's finger touched him and he slept.
> Brief is life, but love is long.

The iron gate opened grudgingly, creaking on its rusted hinges. Blythe stood near the newly mounded grave and said good-bye to the husband she had loved so long and who only lately, she believed, had come to love her. Her glance wandered to the grave next to his, the granite marker over which hovered a brooding stone angel.

ROSE MEREDITH MONTROSE,
BELOVED WIFE OF MALCOLM,
MOTHER OF JONATHAN

Eyes brimming with tears, Blythe turned and left, regretting anew the fact that Malcolm had not learned he was to be a father for a second time. She had to go away, bear his child alone somewhere, but not on this land, for he had gambled it away. Yet, it was sorrow Blythe felt, not bitterness.

That night she made a slow tour of the whole house, committing to memory the things she could not take with her—things she would one day tell her son about his ancestral home. She fingered the table, inlaid with delicate-hued marble forming a bird design and thought of the jeweled eyes that had been plucked out and carried away by maurauding Union soldiers. She let her hand trail across the wide banister of the circular stairway and felt the saber scars marring the smooth surface. Pausing before a framed watercolor of Montclair as it looked in 1812, she read the name, Avril Dumont, and wondered if this bride of Montclair had fared well in this house.

She entered the nursery from the master bedroom, up the tiny narrow stairs. Here, close to their parents, generations of Montrose babies had been nursed by their Negro mammies. Here, all the Montrose children had played, the rocking horse and dollhouse still waiting. But Blythe's children would never know this room.

Finally, she closed each door and went into the room that had been hers since coming to Montclair less than a year ago. A mysterious silence had fallen over the house—a sadness that had no name.

Of one thing Blythe felt sure, however. This house had once known grandeur and would know it again. A Montrose had built it, and a Montrose would live here again. How this would come to be, Blythe did not know, but she was convinced of it.

Then, at last, there was nothing left to do but wait for the hack Lonnie's son had been sent to Mayfield to hire. It would arrive the next day to take her to the train station. There, she would board the one morning train to Richmond. Mentally, she calculated the days just passed. Tomorrow would be Christmas Eve.

chapter
30

"ALL ABOARD! All aboard for Richmond and points north!" shouted the conductor, swinging down from one of the cars on the train which had arrived at the station with a great shriek, a clanging of brakes on the steel rails, and billows of hissing steam.

Lifting her skirts, Blythe stepped onto the small, square stool giving access to the higher steps of the train and made her way through the narrow passage into one of the coaches. It appeared to be empty. Was no one traveling on Christmas Eve except herself? *Yet why should anyone choose to leave the warm hospitality of Tidewater Virginia at this season?* she thought miserably.

Blythe found a seat by a window, her nose wrinkling slightly at the acrid smell of soot, coal dust, and stale air. Looking out through the grime-streaked window, she saw a splendid carriage pulling up to the station.

The door opened and an elegantly dressed man alighted. His driver carried handsome leather bags, and the porter quickly tagged them. The conductor seemed to know him, for he tipped his hat and bowed obsequiously as he came aboard.

"Yes, sir, right this way, Mr. Bondurant," she heard the conductor say.

Blythe froze. *Bondurant!* Malcolm's creditor! The man who had won Montclair on the turn of a card!

Instinctively, Blythe shrank back against the scratchy, green covering of the seat and averted her head as the two men passed along the aisle beside her.

Her face concealed by her heavy black veiling, she risked a quick look and caught the fleeting impression of a tall man wearing a tweed cape and trailing the scent of spicy and expensive tobacco.

Blythe's heart sank. How incredible that he, the winner, and she, the loser, should be on the same train!

With a jerking start, a jolt, then the chug of the engine, the train lurched forward, gathering speed as it rolled down the track. Her face pressed against the glass, Blythe watched as the little yellow station grew smaller and smaller, the sign MAYFIELD shrinking until she could no longer read the letters.

The familiar countryside began to rush past and, as each mile took her farther away, propelling her into the unknown, Blythe felt a kind of exhilaration. In spite of her uncertain future, Blythe's innate optimism buoyed her spirits, and her newly tried faith assured her that all would be well.

When they arrived in Richmond, Blythe saw Bondurant again. With so few passengers, the encounter was inevitable. He was met by a man in a dark uniform, a servant, she assumed. She watched him as he strode through the station with the confident air of one who enjoyed the best that wealth and prestige could buy.

Blythe had a long wait in Richmond, and then again in Washington for the train to New York. The empty terminals spoke visibly of the festive season when families gather to celebrate the birth of the Christ child. *Only the unfortunate, the homeless, the bereaved would be alone on such a day,* she mused, *and now I am all three.*

Blythe was unaware of curious stares from the train and station workers required to work on this holiday. Obviously in mourning in her black cloak and crepe-ribboned bonnet, she made a poignantly charming picture, young and beautiful.

Not knowing how to buy a sleeping car ticket to New York, she sat up all night in the sparsely filled coach. It did not matter, for she could not have slept anyway, she knew. There were too many troublesome problems to solve—what to do when she arrived in New York, where to stay, how to assume the care of herself and her coming child.

She would go immediately to the law firm, she decided. There, she could learn the sum of her inheritance and where she could afford to stay until she knew what next step to take. She fought the intermittent panic.

Her heart thumped treacherously as the train slid into the New York station on December 26 with a great puffing of steamy smoke, a grinding of gears.

The conductor, making his way through the car, stopped at her seat. "Could I find you a porter, miss?"

"Yes, please. And then, perhaps, a hack to take me into the city?" He touched the bill of his cap. "Of course. Follow me."

Once outside the huge terminal, she was assailed by strange sights, sounds, smells. She had known only the solitude of a convent, the vast stillness of Pa's ranch in the Sierra foothills, the quiet seclusion of Montclair. This cacophony of milling people, neighing horses, noxious fumes assaulted her senses, and she reeled under the impact.

The porter hailed one of the cabs from the row parked along the curbing, and it came rolling up, drawn by one of the saddest-looking horses Blythe had ever seen. The poor creature was badly in need of currying, its ribs showed through its shaggy sides, and even the harness seemed too heavy for its scrawny back.

When the porter hoisted Blythe's trunk atop, she tipped him, hoping it was an appropriate amount.

"Where to, miss?" the cabbie asked.

Blythe glanced at the card she held in her hand and read off the address of the law firm.

The brownstone building housing the offices of Cargill, Hoskins, and Sedgewick was impressive. The inner suite boasted dark oak paneling, leather furnishings, and plush carpet. Behind the desk in the reception area, a haughty-looking man in a stiff bat-wing collar peered over his glasses at Blythe.

"I would like to see either Mr. Cargill, Mr. Hoskins, or Mr. Sedgewick," she said quietly, struggling to present a composed appearance.

"And whom shall I say wishes to speak with—" Here the man paused, his voice edged with sarcasm— "Mr. Cargill or Mr. Hoskins or Mr. Sedgewick?" he mimicked.

Blythe drew herself up and replied coolly, "Mrs. Malcolm Montrose of Montclair in Mayfield, Virginia. I am the daughter of his client, Jedediah Dorman."

His eyes skimmed her, taking her measure. Then he said, "One moment, madam, and I shall see if one of the gentlemen is free." With this, the man disappeared down a corridor of closed doors.

Only minutes later, one of them burst open and a portly, gray-haired gentleman came marching toward Blythe, all smiles, hands outstretched in greeting.

"My dear Miss Dorman!" he said heartily.

"Mrs. Montrose," Blythe corrected.

"Yes, of course . . . Mrs. Montrose. Come in, come in," he said, offering her his arm. "I am George Cargill, one of the senior partners." Blythe could not resist a glance at the obviously astounded clerk.

Seating her in a comfortable leather chair, Mr. Cargill went behind his massive desk and sat down, folded his plump, pink hands in front of him, and smiled ingratiatingly. "Now what can we do for you?"

"I came directly here after arriving by train from Richmond," she explained. "I am recently widowed, Mr. Cargill, and among my late husband's belongings, I found a letter from my father, instructing me to seek you out if . . . if I should ever find myself alone."

"I see. Go on."

"I also understand my father made a will, drawn by your firm. I should like to know the status of my finances in order to make some plans for the future."

"Well, naturally. But I'm afraid Mr. Sedgewick handled your father's account and investments. It is he who has the full particulars regarding your inheritance. Unfortunately, he is out of town, a family holiday, you know—"

With a start, Blythe realized it was the twenty-sixth of December. Christmas had come and gone without her notice. "Oh, yes, of course."

"We expect him back in the city tonight, so we shall set up an appointment for tomorrow. I'm sure he'll be very happy to meet you and assist you in any way possible."

"But you can, I hope, recommend a proper place for me to stay. A reasonably priced one?" Blythe suggested, feeling the strain of recent past events.

"Better than that. I will have our own driver and carriage brought 'round to drive you."

"Thank you. I *am* very tired. I have had no sleep since I left Virginia—three days now."

Mr. Cargill looked aghast. "You did not engage a sleeping car?"

"No."

Mr. Cargill shook his head in disbelief. "My dear lady, with what I know of your father's holdings and investments, if the railroad company had been aware of your presence on their conveyance, you would have been granted a private compartment!"

In the plushly upholstered carriage on the way to the hotel, Blythe wondered what she would learn about her financial condition in the morning. Mr. Cargill had seemed very sure of himself when he handed the driver a card with the address of the hotel, and they arrived after what seemed a long ride in front of a large building with a lavish façade.

The driver deposited Blythe, with her trunk and reticules, on the curbing, where she was greeted by a doorman who escorted her into an ornately decorated lobby. Even if the cost for a night's lodging seemed exorbitant to Blythe, she knew the establishment was respectable and a safe place for a woman traveling alone.

She placed a gold piece on the counter, and the desk clerk's eyebrows shot up. He gave the metal bell an authoritative tap, motioning the bell-cap front and center.

"Take madam's bag," he ordered, then with a deferential bow, handed Blythe the key. "Room 210, and we hope you have a pleasant stay. If you require anything further, just ring for room service. There is a steward on each floor."

She followed the red-uniformed attendant down carpeted halls with her head held high, determined to maintain an air of dignity despite her pounding heart. Only once before had she stayed in a hotel—with Malcolm in New Orleans, on their way to Montclair.

It was not until the maid had left and she was alone in the unfamiliar room, however, that the full weight of her plight struck her.

Blythe walked over and looked out the window. Holding back the heavy draperies, she saw it was beginning to grow dark. The streets below were crowded with carriages, people all hurrying somewhere . . . home? The fact that she was now completely homeless came down upon her with intensity.

She was alone in the world. Absolutely alone . . . and with no prospect of anything more . . . except for the baby that was coming. She squared her shoulders. Whatever lay ahead, she trusted God would be with her, to guide and protect her.

Tomorrow when she knew what her father had left her, she could make plans. Tomorrow.

She slept very little. The unfamiliar surroundings—this room with its high ceilings, heavy draperies, and muffled sounds of the city streets below—kept her tense and restless much of the night. She awoke in starts and, when the first, steely-gray light of dawn crept through the slits between the drawn curtains, she was fully awake.

At the front desk, she asked for a cab to be called. Clutching the card bearing the address of the attorneys, Blythe stepped out onto the steps of the hotel, while the uniformed doorman whistled for one of the high-wheeled, black vehicles. The wind was mercilessly cold, sweeping soot in its gusty drafts. Blythe was grateful for the protective covering of the veil on her bonnet, if not overly warm in her lightweight coat.

When she arrived in the law offices, she found Mr. Sedgewick to be entirely different from the jovial Mr. Cargill. He regarded Blythe impassively as he recited a long list of her father's investments and what her annual income from the interest on the capital of her inheritance would be. Blythe drew in her breath incredulously.

Her father had left her valuable stocks in thriving enterprises, among them a silver mine in Colorado, railroads and shipping lines.

It seemed impossible. She and Pa had lived simply, much like the other ranch families in Lucas Valley. Why, she had had no idea! If she had only known this before . . . she could have saved Montclair . . . saved Malcolm!

Mr. Sedgewick's voice intruded. "You are a very wealthy young woman, Mrs. Montrose," he said finally as he closed the folder marked DORMAN.

The enormity of his announcement sank slowly into Blythe's stunned consciousness. The world that only last night had seemed a frightening place was suddenly transformed. Before her lay endless possibilities.

Even at this very moment, she thought of Rod. Although she had promised herself not to look back, not a day had passed since leaving Virginia that he had not slipped into her mind. What if she returned to Montclair, used her father's inheritance to pay off the debts, and reclaimed her child's heritage? What if she and Rod—? She shook her head. It was useless to speculate. Her first duty was to the child she was carrying, Malcolm's child. She shouldn't even be thinking of another man just now.

No, it was best to go away. Happiness for herself and Rod, under these circumstances, was impossible. If things had been different—

"So then, Mrs. Montrose, what are your plans?" Mr. Sedgewick asked, leaning back in his leather chair, steepling his fingers and tapping them meditatively.

Blythe could not tell what made her say it, but as soon as the words were spoken, she knew she had made the right decision. "I'm going to England."

Mr. Sedgewick's wispy eyebrows rose alarmingly. "To England? But my dear young lady—an Atlantic crossing in December? That could be very treacherous." His eyebrows rose another inch. "Do you have relatives . . . friends there?"

"No."

"Then why—?" Mr. Sedgewick frowned. Then, seeing Blythe's mouth set stubbornly, he changed his tactic. "Would it not be better to choose a milder climate at this time of year? I have friends, an English couple, the Ainsleys, who winter in Bermuda. I could give you a letter of introduction. I'm sure they would be happy to find you a cottage to spend the next months. Then in the spring, when they return to their home in England, you would have congenial traveling companions. England is lovely in April—"

Blythe considered his suggestion for a long minute. Perhaps he was right. Her father had intended her to follow his lawyer's advice.

"Very well, Mr. Sedgewick, I would be most grateful if you would arrange it for me."

CHAPTER
31

THE OIL LAMP burned low, sputtering and sending elongated shadows against the rough plaster walls of the room above the barn that had once housed the Camerons' magnificent carriages. Now it served as Rod Cameron's plantation office and apartments.

Rod sat at his desk, open ledger books before him, tallying the figures for the year's costs. For the third time, he added a row of numbers, a frown etched deeply in his brow. Then he twisted the pen he held in his fingers and, with a groan, tossed it aside and ran his hand through his thick russet hair.

"Where is she? Where could she have gone without a word to anyone?" His voice, echoing in the cavernous room, mocked him.

Unable to bear the thought of Blythe's being alone, Rod had ridden over to Montclair Christmas afternoon only to find the place deserted, Blythe gone. Later, her letter came.

How desperate she must have been! But why, after all they had shared, hadn't she reached out to him?

Everyone in Mayfield knew Montclair had been lost to a stranger who had taken over the property and was even now restoring the house and gardens to its antebellum glory. Why couldn't it have been Malcolm?

But if it had been Malcolm, Blythe would still be married to him. Impatiently, he rose and paced the bare-planked floor, the heels of his riding boots cracking like the lash of a whip.

Thou shalt not covet thy neighbor's wife, the Scripture commanded. Rod knew that full well. Who would have ever imagined he would fall in love with the wife his friend had brought home from California?

But his heart had betrayed him. How long those feelings had existed, he couldn't be sure. He only knew he loved Blythe deeply, devotedly, completely . . . and forever.

The setter, who had been asleep at his feet, watched his master hopefully. But Rod did not have a moonlight stroll in mind. He strode over to the bookcase, pulled out a worn book from the shelf, then carried it back to the desk, where it fell open to a marked page. The marker, fragile with age, was a rose.

Immediately, that fall day came vividly to his memory. He had taken a bouquet of his mother's roses to Blythe. He could still see the golden lights in her auburn hair as she bent over the flowers, the image of her face as she breathed in their dewy fragrance.

Carefully, he picked up the bud he had pressed in his favorite book of poetry later that same day. As he touched it, it crumbled, its powdery substance dusting the page, and his eyes fell on two lines he had marked:

Such a one do I remember, whom to look at was to love.
O love, what hours were thine and mine.

Rod slammed the book shut and clenched his fist, pounding the table. "She couldn't have simply disappeared! There must be some way to trace her whereabouts."

Would she have gone back West, to that little mountain town she had spoken of with such affection? But she had told him there were no relatives there. She was alone in the world.

"Dear God, I must find her!" he prayed aloud. Just then, a thought crossed his mind. "Lonnie!" Surely the black woman knew where her mistress had gone. He would ride over first thing in the morning, question her about Blythe.

"Why didn't I think of that before?" he groaned. "If I had only said something to her, declared my love. But I thought it wouldn't be right . . . proper . . . to say anything so soon after Malcolm's death. I thought if I waited. . . . I thought she *knew!*"

His heart contorted with a sharp physical pain. *Blythe! My beautiful Blythe!*

He saw again her tall, slender figure, the fine features, the smooth, peach-blushed complexion, the dark red sheen of her hair . . . and his longing to see her, hold her in his arms, kiss the soft sweetness of her mouth overcame him.

"I will find her!" he vowed, striking his palm with a balled fist. "If I have to go to the ends of the earth . . . if it takes me the rest of my life . . . I will find her!"

Four days past her eighteenth birthday, Blythe awoke from an exhausted sleep and opened her eyes. For a full moment, she lay there, unable to will herself into full consciousness.

Then she remembered the Scotch midwife announcing to her through her fogged state, "You have a boy, Mrs. Montrose, a brawny lad with hair as fair as goldenrod, but with a promise to be as red as your own!"

She smiled sleepily and looked out the window at the rolling green countryside. The house she had leased was in Kent. The cottage, of timber, stucco and stone, nestled in a lovely little walled garden at the end of a lane just off the winding cobblestone street that ran through the village.

The village itself was little more than a hamlet, with a few stores and houses, an inn, and a small stone church of Norman architecture. Dominating the town from the hillside was an imposing turreted structure, once a monastery. Since the days of Henry VIII, however, it had been the property of a noble family named Marsh, although it still retained the original name of Monksmoor Priory.

To Blythe, seeing it now, it looked like something out of one of the illustrations in Malcolm's book *The Idylls of the King*. Every day as she had walked by on her daily "constitutional" as recommended by her English doctor, Blythe was drawn by a curious bond she could not explain. She must learn more about it.

As she heard her child cry out from the cradle in the adjoining room, then hush as the old nurse rocked him, Blythe's thoughts turned to this new life she had brought into the world. What was to be his name? Malcolm? No, somehow Blythe did not want to give him his father's name. Rather, he should have a name that would stand for all the ideals to which his father had aspired—strength, courage, honor. It should be a noble name, one their son would bear with pride.

And then it came to her.

During the long months of waiting, she had read and reread Malcolm's favorite books, especially the various versions of the Arthurian legend and the Bible. Following the Apostle Paul's admonition, she had meditated on only those things that were "true . . . honest

211

. . . just . . . pure . . . lovely," casting out of her mind the pain and anguish of her past.

Arthur. Why not call the boy Arthur? She would think on that.

On an English summer morning, misted with rain and scented with flowers, Blythe, with the couple with whom she had become close friends in Bermuda, Lydia and Edward Ainsley, along with Nanny Bartlett, carried the baby to the village church to be baptized.

Blythe had been attending services here for several months and found them, while much more formal than any she was accustomed to, quiet and lovely and somehow very meaningful.

The church was of gray stone, a small Gothic structure, built six hundred years ago. Coming from the raw mining town where the buildings were hastily constructed of green wood, Blythe was awed by the patina of the years that cast everything here in a mellow glow.

Once, when Lydia and Edward had come down from London to see the baby, Blythe had discussed with them the matter of his name.

"Most English boys receive several names at their christening. Edward did, didn't you, dear?" Lydia said, gazing at her husband fondly. "His full name is Edward Albert John. So you have quite a choice, you see. And, in the Church of England, babies have godparents, you know, to look after the spiritual welfare of the child should anything, heaven forbid, happen to the parents."

This was a new idea to Blythe, but a pleasant one. Edward beamed happily and Lydia seemed delighted when Blythe asked them if they would do the honors.

Entering the church now, Blythe handed the baby to Lydia and entered the hushed atmosphere reverently. The light, filtering in through stained-glass windows, bore the heraldic symbols of some of the families of the surrounding countryside, along with biblical characters. There was the scent of beeswax candles, of oiled oak, the mingled fragrance of flowers.

The ancient baptistry stood to the side of the center altar, underneath an arched window depicting John baptizing Christ in the River Jordan.

There were kneelers with red velvet cushions circling the raised dais where the vicar stood, in starched surplice. Blythe took her place there while Lydia Ainsley, carrying the baby, stepped up toward Reverend Thompson, with Nanny Bartlett close behind.

As the vicar began the service, Blythe could not help thinking how strange it was that she had come from California to this place, to bring this child conceived another three thousand miles away, to be christened here in this historic chapel.

Then her attention returned to the present moment, for the vicar was speaking of her.

"Lord, we give thee humble thanks that thou hast been graciously pleased to preserve through the great pain and peril of childbirth, this woman, thy servant, who desireth now to present this child to be received into the Christian community.

"Merciful Father, grant that this child may reject all sin and that all things belonging to thy Spirit may live and grow in him. Grant him the power and strength to have victory and triumph over the world, the flesh, and the devil.

"So, then, dearly beloved, we have come hither to baptize this child." The vicar turned to Edward Ainsley. "Dost thou, in the name of this child, renounce the devil and all his works, the pomp and vainglory of this world, the sinful desires of the flesh, and follow the Lord our God in the Person of Jesus Christ?"

"I do renounce them and promise to abide in the faith of the Lord Jesus," replied Edward in a deep voice. "With God's help."

"What is to be the child's name?"

"Arthur Geoffrey Paul."

Blythe glowed. Malcolm would approve of her choice. Arthur, for his legendary hero, King Arthur. Geoffrey, for Geoffrey de Monmouth, who had first translated the legend into English, and Paul, for the "great lion of God."

Of the three names, Blythe had decided to call him "Jeff," the nickname for Geoffrey. It seemed right for a little boy born in England.

And one day Blythe would take Geoffrey Montrose back to Virginia to reclaim his inheritance, Montclair. Yes. Malcolm would have wanted it this way.

Family Tree

In Scotland

Brothers GAVIN and ROWAN MONTROSE, descendants of the chieftan of the Clan Graham, came to Virginia to build on an original King's Grant of two thousand acres along the James River. They began to clear, plant, and build upon it.

In 1722, GAVIN's son, KENNETH MONTROSE, brought his bride, CLAIR FRASER, from Scotland, and they settled in Williamsburg while their plantation house—"Montclair"—was being planned and built. They had three children: sons KENNETH and DUNCAN, and daughter JANET.

In England

The Barnwell Family.

GEORGE BARNWELL first married WINIFRED AINSELY, and they had two sons: GEORGE and WILLIAM. BARNWELL later married a widow, ALICE CARY, who had a daughter, ELEANORA.

ELEANORA married NORBERT MARSH (widower with son, SIMON), and they had a daughter, NORAMARY.

In Virginia

Since the oldest son inherits, GEORGE BARNWELL's younger son, WILLIAM, came to Virginia, settled in Williamsburg, and started a shipping and importing business.

WILLIAM married ELIZABETH DEAN, and they had four daughters: WINNIE, LAURA, KATE, and SALLY. WILLIAM and ELIZABETH adopted NORAMARY when she was sent to Virginia at twelve years of age.

KENNETH MONTROSE married CLAIR FRASER. They had three children: KENNETH, JANET, and DUNCAN.

DUNCAN married NORAMARY MARSH, and they had three children: CAMERON, ROWAN, and ALAN.

CAMERON MONTROSE married LORABETH WHITAKER, and they had one son, GRAHAM. Later CAMERON married ARDEN SHERWOOD, and they remained childless.

After the death of his first wife, LUELLE HAYES, GRAHAM MONTROSE married AVRIL DUMONT. Although they had no children of their own, they adopted his nephew, CLAYBORN MONTROSE.

The Montrose Family

CLAYBORN MONTROSE married SARA LEIGHTON, and they had three sons: MALCOLM, who married ROSE MEREDITH; BRYSON (BRYCE), who married GARNET CAMERON; and LEIGHTON (LEE), who married DOVE ARUNDELL. BRYCE and LEE were killed in the War-Between-the-States. CLAYBORN and SARA's daughters-in-law were ROSE MEREDITH (widow of MALCOLM, deceased), who left one son, JONATHAN; DOVE ARUNDEL (widowed, with one daughter, DRUSCILLA); and GARNET CAMERON (widow of BRYCE MONTROSE, who remarried (JEREMY DEVLIN).

The Cameron Family

DOUGLAS CAMERON married KATHERINE MAITLAND. They had twin sons, RODERICK and STEWART, and one daughter, GARNET. STEWART was killed in the war.

The Saga Continues!
Be sure to read all of the "Brides of Montclair" books, available from your local bookstore:

1. *Valiant Bride*

To prevent social embarrassment after their daughter's elopement, a wealthy Virginia couple forces their ward, Noramary Marsh, to marry Duncan Montrose. Already in love with another, Noramary anguishes over submitting to an arranged marriage.

2. *Ransomed Bride*

After fleeing an arranged marriage in England, Lorabeth Whitaker met Cameron Montrose, a Virginia planter. His impending marriage to someone else is already taken for granted. A story of love, conscience, and conflict.

3. *Fortune's Bride*

The story of Avril Dumont, a wealthy young heiress and orphan, who gradually comes to terms with her lonely adolescence. Romance and heartbreak ensue from her seemingly unreturned but undiscourageable love for her widowed guardian, Graham Montrose.

4. *Folly's Bride*

Spoiled and willful Sara Leighton, born with high expectations, encounters personal conflicts with those closest to her. Set in the decades before the War Between the States, the story follows Sara as she comes under the influence of Clayborn Montrose, scion of the Montrose family and Master of Montclair.

5. *Yankee Bride/Rebel Bride: Montclair Divided*

In this stunning epic Civil War novel, Rose Meredith and Garnet Cameron mirror the raging conflict of a hopelessly divided nation. Their lives become forever entwined in the challenges they face, characterized by the drama of the men they marry and the sides they choose.

6. *Gallant Bride*

In 1870, Blythe Dorman falls in love with a mysterious stranger, Malcolm Montrose, who has come to the California gold fields in the hope of recouping his family fortune. As part of a secret agreement with her dying father, Malcolm takes Blythe back to his ancestral Virginia home and to searing tests of her faith and loyalty.

More books in this series due soon! Look for Lost Bride *and* Destiny's Bride *in 1991.*